ALL THAT WE HIDE

KAREN BUSCEMI

ISBN: 9780578595740

Cover design/book design by Karen Buscemi

For Darryl (and his parents)

"It is not length of life, but depth of life that matters."

Ralph Waldo Emerson

PART 1

CHAPTER 1
HOME SWEET HOME

I'd been a prisoner at Trudeau Sanitorium for just over a month. It was my penance for contracting tuberculosis and disrupting Mildred VanHoosen's self-absorbed life with my needs. I'd spent the last thirty-two days wondering what her penance would be for denying me the vaccine that every single one of my friends had received. Friends who were currently on milkshake-sweet dates that were guaranteed to result in - at the bare minimum - a trip to first base, while I was wrapped in a paper-thin scratchy blanket, set out on the porch of the main building, along with a dozen other unfortunate souls, for another round of "cold cure" treatment. Did I mention it was early January and fourteen degrees?

But Mildred VanHoosen didn't like any funny business. She actually used the phrase "funny business" while refusing her only child the vaccine offered by our family physician, the hairy-eared, decrepit Dr. Arthur Burge, who apparently was more up on modern times than Mildred VanHoosen. Dr. Burge assured her that the vaccine was not only perfectly safe, it worked. It was practically miraculous. He said that by 1960, tuberculosis would be the least of anyone's concerns. One would think that would be enough evidence to give the go ahead. Even UNICEF was traveling the world to administer the vaccine to the needy. But Mildred VanHoosen just crossed her legs, reached into her fire-engine red purse for a mint, and shook her head.

I don't want you to get the wrong idea about me. I didn't turn all crazy and angry after being awarded my tuberculosis diagnosis - a mere ten months after Mildred VanHoosen no-noed the vaccine. That would be far too predictable, don't you think? No, I had been crazy and angry since the day I discovered my parents were complete frauds.

"Marilyn, wake up. It's time for your pill."

I startled awake, wondering how I had managed to fall asleep while simultaneously shivering. My chest felt like a boulder was lying on it. I looked up and instantly relaxed. It was Betty, my favorite nurse. Strike that. It was Betty, the only nurse I could stomach in this God-forsaken place. Damn, I was almost nice when I was groggy. No wonder I didn't like that feeling.

Betty was kind because, in addition to bringing me extra water because she knew I was terrible at swallowing pills, she also didn't try to act like my mother. All the other nurses assumed their most important duty was to mother the patients. But not that tender type of mothering one may desire when confined to a massive sanitary compound far from home. No, quite the opposite. It's the type of mothering that would give a teenager cause to run away from home, filled with unsolicited advice, non-stop criticism and a particular affinity with preparing themselves for martyrdom in the afterlife.

And still, they were angels compared to Mildred VanHoosen.

"Come on, now." I opened my mouth at Nurse Betty's command and she placed a pill on the middle of my tongue then handed me a cup of water filled to the rim. I drank as fast as I could, grimacing on the initial swallow that swept the pill down the lubricated slope of my throat. I coughed a few times, mostly for dramatic purposes, and put the cup back in Nurse Betty's hand.

"Isoniazid?" I asked, already knowing the answer, as I subconsciously scratched at the welt on the inside of my forearm.

She nodded. "Sorry kid. I know it doesn't like you on the outside, but it's doing a lot of good on the inside."

Isoniazid was one of a combination of drugs used to treat different types of tuberculosis. It has a number of potential side effects, as I learned all medications do, including a nasty rash. And, yes sir, I appeared to be the only Lucky One at dear old Trudeau covered in bright-as-day, scaly red patches.

"I'll bring you some salve for your arm," Nurse Betty said. She placed a hand on top of my head, just for a moment, and then walked away, the stiff cotton of her snow-white dress rustling in her wake. I don't know why she did that, the hand on the head thing, but I secretly liked it. I also secretly liked even more that I'd never seen her do it to any of the other patients.

I don't know what possessed Mildred VanHoosen to marry my father, Pierre VanHoosen, who, I discovered just one year ago, isn't really named Pierre. It's Paul. Paul Harold Sledge. I innocently stumbled across his birth certificate in the attic while collecting some items for a home ec project on, I kid you not, house-cleaning styles. Because this was worth researching.

I guess my stumbling wasn't exactly innocent as it was in a boxed marked PRIVATE! in all capital letters with an exclamation point to really drive it home. But, damn, if you're going to have such a private box sitting up in the attic, wouldn't you at least tape it closed? I know I would. But no, this box just had the flaps folded into each other, so I just went WHOOPS! (with exclamation point), and flipped that box open. There were a lot of private papers in that box. Seriously. Heavy-duty packing tape should have been keeping the contents of that treasure trove from curious eyes, let me tell you. But they didn't, so I did, and that right there was where it all began.

My crazy, angry attitude, that is, although my attitude was just at the beginning stages of being crazy and angry. It was more like a little batty and kind of miffed. Because it really was only the start of it all. How was I to know the fraudulent behaviors would get worse and worse the deeper and deeper I dug? You would be at least a little batty and kind of miffed, too, if you found out your father, Pierre, was really your father, Paul Harold.

The woosh-woosh-wooshing of Nurse Betty's cottons signaled her return. I couldn't wait to get that salve on my damn arm, but she arrived empty handed.

"You've been sprung from the chairs, kid," she said while unwrapping me from my mummy-like state of scratchy blankets.

"Thank God." I sat up too fast, earning a whopper of a dizzy spell. Nurse Betty put an arm around my shoulders to steady me. Hard to believe I was once the fastest runner in my class.

"I think you sometimes forget how sick you are," Nurse Betty said, still clutching me like a prized possession.

"Hard to forget when I can't walk twenty feet without resting." I shrugged off her embrace and kicked off the last of the blankets, hating how exhausting it was just to do that. With the blankets gone, my frail body - embarrassingly visible through the flimsy white nightgown - showed yet another consequence of tuberculosis. In just over a month's time, I had lost ten pounds, a huge amount, considering my normal weight hovered around ninety-eight. I was rail-thin to begin with. Now I was so skinny, my pancake-like breasts were flatter than crepes. Minus any fruit filling. At this rate, I would never get asked to prom.

Nurse Betty handed me my robe that had been hanging off the back of the chair and I wrapped it around me, tying it tight, grateful for a softer form of warmth. I held her arm, slid my bare feet into the slippers positioned next to the chair and slowly, slowly stood. Everything rocked back and forth, as if this long row of deck chairs really were on a massive ship, and this whole time I'd been on a fantastical journey to an exotic locale. But almost as soon as it started, my world ceased rocking, and my focus returned, assuring me that all the horizontal people wrapped up like papooses were in fact extraordinarily sick, and possibly dying, and not at all the pretty ladies in floral frocks and men in smart striped shirts that I so wanted them to be.

We did a super-slow shuffle into a waiting wheelchair, and she pushed me back to the infirmary that I currently called home, both sides of the big white room lined with small white beds covered in thin white sheets. There was absolutely no privacy here. And what was worse, I was the youngest person here by a good twenty years, with a handful of patients wrinkled enough to be of great-grandparent age. Maybe great-great-grandparent age. I had hoped to be placed in one of the many cottages spread around the grounds, where smaller groups of similar age and sex were typically assigned, but my doctor, Dr. Whitlaw, said I was too sick to be anywhere but the infirmary. Can you guess why? That's right, because Mildred VanHoosen didn't bother to get me medical treatment until I was coughing up blood on her new yellow sofa. Apparently, that got her attention. I'm grateful I had enough energy to get from my bed to the pale-hued couch in time for the full-on coughing fit to crescendo.

After helping me out of my robe, Nurse Betty tucked me rather cozily in my bed, which sorely needed a thicker mattress. She reached into her skirt pocket and pulled out a tube of salve. If my arm could rejoice, it would have. As she carefully applied the thick concoction to my lobster-colored patches, I spotted a rather cute boy I had never seen before sitting up in a bed across the room. He was positively beaming at me. It may have been the most mortifying moment of my life.

"Betts," I said to Nurse Betty with the familiarity of a much older, sophisticated friend after a couple of whiskey sours, "who's the kid across the way?"

Nurse Betty straightened up and whirled around, locking eyes on the cute boy and ensuring that, oh yes indeed, he knew without a doubt that I had been talking about him. Know what he did? He waved at her, that same goofy smile spread wide across his pale yet very-nice-to-look-at face. I had to take back what I had said before: *this* was now the most mortifying moment of my life.

She turned back to me and went about applying the salve all matter-of-fact, as if she hadn't just embarrassed me. "That's Henry," she said. "Just arrived today from Detroit."

Something in my chest twanged like a beat-up guitar. "He's a long way from home in this strange place with even stranger people." Nurse Betty clicked her tongue at me. "Present company excluded, of course."

"Of course." She capped the salve, slid it back into her pocket, and reached under my bed for my old brown suitcase.

"So, what the hell is he so giddy about?"

Springing the locks, Nurse Betty opened the suitcase, revealing the meager belongings I had been allowed to bring. She waved two books at me: National Velvet and Brideshead Revisited. I quickly pointed at Brideshead and she tossed it on the foot of the bed. It was a great escape to read a book with characters even more screwed up than the ones in my own life. Made me feel the slightest bit more normal. "Maybe he's just figured out what it feels like to fall in love," she said, shutting the suitcase and sliding it back into place.

I stuck my tongue out at her like a bratty toddler. "If this is his idea of love," I chided, motioning at my body, "then his heart is more messed up than his lungs."

"Get some rest," Nurse Betty ordered, pulling the string on the little lamp above my bed to illuminate my immediate area. "Dinner is in a couple of hours and then it's Bridge Night in the Community Room."

"Can't you just kill me and get this over with?"

She placed her hand on my head for that magical moment. "I could, but then who would annoy me?"

"Odds are good that our pal Henry over there could take over without a hitch."

As Nurse Betty swished away, I lifted my head for a quick peek across the way. He was still smiling at me.

❖

I sprang awake covered in sweat. Isoniazid gave me crazy dreams. This time it was a giant man with a bald head, claw-like hands and small but piercing red eyes. He was making his way down my street, moving away from the flying saucer that had crashed on top of Mary Ann Tapeo's house (not a real big deal; she was bossy and in love with her enormous pointy breasts), crushing the concrete under the house into jagged blocks.

All my neighbors had escaped to their bomb shelters, but not me. I stood alone on the front lawn, careful not to trample Mildred VanHoosen's beloved irises. Even in my nightmares, that woman got under my skin. Which reminded me, where were my parents? Not that I would expect them to be there to protect me. But I had clearly conjured The Thing From Another World (my favorite movie character ever). A teenage girl needed protecting from an alien creature who survived on human blood. The memorable quote from the movie was, "Keep watching the skies." Let me tell you, I'd been keeping a close eye on my overhead surroundings ever since. Even in my nightmare, with The Thing coming toward me, I was looking up, more concerned that other like creatures would be joining him.

Suddenly, a taxi appeared behind me and my father hopped out, looking handsome with his close-cropped hair and pressed Navy uniform. I was surprised to see another man get out behind him. He was of similar height and build, maybe even more handsome than my father, with bright blue eyes, high cheekbones and a boyish smile. He was very toothy, but in a good way. I was instantly smitten, but the spell broke when I saw the man and my father turn and head for our house. They either didn't see me or didn't care. I cried out for my father. This was my first time seeing him since he had left to fight in World War II, and I was desperate for him to run to me and throw me in the air like he used to. He didn't look in my direction. But the very handsome man did, and all I saw in his blue eyes now was hate. He put a hand on my father's back and guided him into the house.

By the time I remembered about The Thing, it was too late. He was already upon me, ripping me apart. That's when I woke up.

I pulled myself into a seated position, knocking Brideshead off the bed, and glanced at the clock on the opposite wall: seven-thirty. I had slept through dinner and the boy across the way was gone. I heard a long grunt from a couple of beds over. Grumpy Nurse Doris was on duty, and from the look of it, the old man she was tending to had soiled the bed, which would put her in an even worse mood since it was up to her to clean it.

This was going to be a long night.

❖

The next day was Sunday, the day I had been waiting for since being admitted to Trudeau: Maggie Ryder was coming for a visit.

Maggie Ryder was the coolest girl I knew. She was seventeen, graduated high school a year early, and had an exciting job as a salesgirl at Macy's in Philadelphia, wearing fresh-pressed cotton dresses, stockings, and grown-up pumps. She wore her blonde hair short and pin curled, making her look far more sophisticated than I ever could with my girlish brunette ponytail. She was even allowed to drive her dad's Buick when he wasn't using it. I had never sat in the driver's seat of a car, and sometimes wondered if I ever would.

All of this said, I had absolutely no idea why Maggie chose me for her best friend. Or why she had agreed to a six-hour train ride to visit me in this place when my parents hadn't yet made the trip, which Mildred VanHoosen had labeled "dreadful". Never let it be said that Maggie Ryder was not an adventurous girl. Or that she didn't have a heart.

Mildred VanHoosen could learn a thing or two from that girl.

I ate a big breakfast of scrambled eggs, toast with jelly, and a fruit cup from the comfort of my uncomfortable bed, and asked Nurse Betty to brush my hair and pull it back tidy. I wanted both energy and a nice appearance for Maggie. Too bad my fingernails were bitten down to nothing. It was a disgusting habit, I knew, but what else was one supposed to do to pass time in this place? My choices were as follows: read, work a crossword puzzle, play cards (or some other lame non-strenuous group activity) with old people I didn't know, sleep, eat. Nail biting was as good an option as anything else. Luckily, Maggie loved me for my biting wit, not my standards of grooming. Or lack thereof.

I looked at the clock. Almost ten-thirty. Maggie's train arrived at two o'clock. What the hell was I going to do between now and then?

"You sure look pretty today."

I knew without turning my head it was Henry. Mainly because no one outside of the nurses spoke to me here. And Dr. Whitlaw only spoke to the nurses about me – as if I wasn't laying right there, fully capable of speech.

"As opposed to how horrifying I looked yesterday?" I have no idea why I chose to be mean. Except that I often do choose to be mean.

"Yeah, you really looked like hell yesterday."

My jaw dropped. His eyes were focused on mine, his forehead crinkled as if he were deeply pondering the details of my appearance from the day before. My insides felt hot – enraged, really – and I did some pondering myself, mostly what they would do to me here if I slugged this kid square in the face.

And then he started laughing. An all-out boisterous guffaw that started deep in his belly and shook his entire body. I couldn't help but smile. Until all that laughing turned into one hell of a coughing fit, doubling him over. He grabbed for my metal headboard to hold himself up while his other hand held fast to his forehead. People with tuberculosis can easily cough themselves into a whopper of a headache. Which is why people with tuberculosis shouldn't try to be so damn funny.

"Do you want to sit down?" I offered, scooting over. See, I could be nice when necessary.

He nodded, the coughing still violent, and landed his bottom with a thud beside me.

I felt stupid. There was a cute boy on my bed – a total first – and he was possibly dying. Or at least passing a lung through his throat. I would have called for a nurse, but I was pretty sure he was making way more noise than I ever could. I wanted to help. After all, this was happening because he came to talk to me. So, I gave him a few pats on his heaving back. Because, that was helpful, right?

In between coughs came the woosh of Nurse Betty and I instantly relaxed. She'd know what to do. She was doing this slide-run sort of movement, and when she got close enough, I understood why. She was carrying a bowl filled with hot water. She set it on the little table beside my bed, positioned Henry's head over it, and then threw a towel over the top of him.

"Steam helps to quiet the cough," she explained while rubbing gentle circles on his back. Sure enough, in just a couple of minutes, the coughing slowed then completely subsided. Nurse Betty lifted the towel and Henry sat upright. He looked positively drained. "Let's get you back to bed." Nodding weakly, Henry allowed Nurse Betty to pull him to a standing position. She slid her arm around his back and ushered him, at a snail's pace, across the room, his slippers sliding along as they went. She turned and gave me a quick look. I wasn't sure what I was supposed to take from it.

Feeling worn out myself from Henry's ordeal, mentally anyway, I decided it would be best to pass the remaining time until Maggie's arrival with a nap. Hopefully for three good hours. And hopefully without ruining my neat hair.

I must have some strong will, because I stayed asleep until two-fifteen. My hair, however, not so much with the will. I could feel the rat's nest on my right side where it had been pressed against the pillow. But I'd trade good hair for making time fly any day of the week. I propped myself on my elbow to get a peek at Henry. He was still out cold. Poor kid. He sure looked sweet when he slept. His pale skin was soft and smooth, and his dark blonde hair, which I'm guessing he combed up and back with hair cream pre-tuberculosis, was loose about his face. It was pretty angelic, really. It was his lips, though, that made the greatest impression. They were big, but not freakish big. I guess it was fair to say they were full. I'd always heard that term applied to the mouth of a woman, but I assure you, this boy had full lips. If I knew what it was like to kiss a boy, I bet I'd say kissing a boy with full lips was the best.

Nurse Betty appeared, smiling brightly. "You have a visitor," she announced.

I kicked off the blankets and reached for my robe. "Hooray!" I cried, simultaneously patting down my hair and leaping from bed.

"Whoa there," Nurse Betty cautioned. "That's more movement than one sick girl can handle. Let's go slow so you've got enough left over in the tank to enjoy the entire visit."

"Yes ma'am." I could not stop smiling. I could not wait to get to Maggie.

To get to the Visiting Room we had to wheel through the infirmary, down a long hallway flanked with little offices and storage rooms, and past the dining room, where I had yet to take a meal. It looked kind of depressing in there, with meager wood furnishings and hideous oil paintings. But I supposed it was better than trying to enjoy my chicken pot pie while some guy a few beds over defecated himself.

I was worn out and breathing heavy – mind you, I was riding in a wheelchair – by the time we reached the Visiting Room, but one look at Maggie and I completely forgot I was sick.

CHAPTER 2
MADE IN THE SHADE

"Mari-boo, I fear I'm crushing you!" Maggie said in her usual sing-song voice. She was responsible for the only nickname I ever had, and she was also the only one who used it.

"Even a skinny bird like you can crush my new frame." I posed as best as I could in my wheelchair like the Macy's models did when showing the new spring styles. My father, of all people, once drove me into downtown Philadelphia to see a fashion show there. Maggie was already working at the store and was able to reserve us two seats in the front row. I'm pretty sure she told the floor manager my father had a lot of money – which he didn't. I mean, he had money, Mildred VanHoosen's father had more, but still he preferred to buy on sale. Said that's how people with money kept their money.

I'm not sure who enjoyed the special treatment more, my father or me, as we both relished the prime view and fizzy clear sodas served in tall, thin glasses with paper straws that only the front-row guests appeared to have been granted. I remember being aware of how similar all the models looked. Tall and thin with perfect hourglass figures, shiny long, brown hair, and small, straight noses. One girl's hair could have passed for dark blonde, but that was as outlandish as it got. Not that I was complaining. They were a combined vision of loveliness. A far cry from my ragtag self. Maggie could have been one of those girls, if only she were a few inches taller. While she wasn't as petite as me, she didn't possess those ever-so-long legs all the models seemed to have. All my length – the little that I had – wound up in my torso, so I understood. No boy goes wild for a long torso, let me tell you.

Nurse Betty left Maggie to take over as my driver, and she pushed me to a little round table in the far back corner of the room. We had much to discuss and couldn't risk eavesdroppers.

"Love your robe," Maggie said, rolling her eyes.

"Hardy har har. Can we cut the small talk and get to the good stuff?"

Maggie flashed me a fake look of shock. "The nerve! Don't you have the decency to ask me about my trip? I've been on a train for six hours for you, you know."

I sighed dramatically. (Everyone should possess a good dramatic sigh.) "Fine. How was your trip?"

"A total bore."

I raised my eyebrows. "That's it?"

She uncrossed her legs and leaned forward, placing a sharp elbow on the rickety table. "Come on now, Mari-boo, haven't we got more important things to discuss?"

"Fine. Tell me what you've got."

"You were right about Mildred never locking the door. I waited until she left for the market in the morning and let myself in."

She painstakingly fluffed the skirt of her gingham dress and placed her hands neatly in her lap, pacing her story for the ultimate suspense. I loved that girl, but damn, she was predictable. And sometimes, very annoying.

"You didn't tell me Mildred got a new dinette," she went on, now with an accusatory tone. "It's a dream. Really, all that chrome and turquoise-and-white striping? An absolute dream."

I rolled my eyes. "Enough stalling. Did you find the papers?"

She dismissed my antsiness and kept to her sluggish storytelling tempo. "Did you not think it was a dream?"

"To be perfectly honest, I didn't know about the new dinette. The same old scratched-up brown one was sitting in the kitchen when they shipped me off to this place."

She knitted her brows, as if disappointed in my lack of decorating knowledge. "Well, just wait until you see it. You'll be mad for it. I promise you."

"Maggie!" I shouted. A few heads turned in our direction, causing me to lower both my head and my voice. "Did you find anything or not?"

Really, Mari-boo, it wasn't so much about what I found as what I didn't find."

"Lord." I slumped back, crossing my arms tight. "And what, exactly, didn't you find?"

"Your father, Mari-boo. There wasn't a trace of Pierre anywhere."

Where was my father? It was the question I asked myself while hugging Maggie goodbye for the fifth time, if you could call what I could muster a hug, clinging to her and begging her to promise a return trip. It was the question I asked myself while Nurse Doris begrudgingly gave me my sponge bath, rubbing at my painfully rashy skin a bit too enthusiastically, in my non-medical but most logical opinion. My shame, as Mildred VanHoosen preferred to call my privates, would have been on display if it were not for my quick thinking to yank up the bed sheet vertically like a partition. Nurse Doris scolded me for exerting too much energy. I scolded her for practically taking away my virginity, from an optical sense, that is, which neither of us, it turned out, found too funny.

Where was my father? I asked myself later that evening while staring at Henry as he slept again, wondering if that boy would ever get enough energy to stay awake until Trudeau's official nine-thirty lights out routine, which was pretty uneventful (a few hasty good-nights, the echoing clicking sound of overhead lights being extinguished) and *never* changed. I guessed he wasn't missing out on much. But it sure would be nice to pass those final hours of the evening with him. That is, if he were so inclined to do the same with me. Maybe Henry could help me figure out the mystery of my father's whereabouts. Or maybe there was something else in that box of private papers carelessly stashed in the attic that would provide me a clue.

The following morning, I asked Nurse Betty to put me next to Henry on the chairs. I didn't care that it would be another day of sub-zero temperatures, including one heck of a whipping wind showing our measly scratchy blankets who's boss; I needed someone to talk to. Composing a letter to Maggie and then impatiently having to wait a whole week for a reply was more than I could bear. And for as cool as Nurse Betty was, I didn't want to drag her into my stuff. She was already doing more for me than the people who were supposed to be responsible for my life. But Henry. Henry, I was sure, could handle it. Even if it meant he didn't think too much of me for it. Even though he was the dreamiest boy I had ever set eyes on. At this point in my life, I needed a friend way more than a long-shot gamble for my first boyfriend.

Nurse Betty wrapped me in my blanket with an awful smug look on her face. I stuck out my tongue at her because she thought I was in love with Henry and longed to be close to him. She had zero idea just how messed up my life was. But she paid me no mind. She was content with her fantasy about being responsible for putting together two lovebirds. People were such fools.

A nurse I'd never seen before wheeled Henry to the chair beside me, putting a hand on his shoulder to keep him from trying to stand on his own while she set the brake with her foot. "Do you pay extra for all the additional coddling?" I figured it would be best to start our conversation with a joke before my truth turned it dark and stormy.

Henry grimaced as the nurse ran her arms under his armpits and lifted, her strong legs set wide and bent a little at the knees to make it easier on her body as she transferred him into the lounge chair. Her grunts gave away that she was handling the bulk of his weight. "Turns out my hearty laugh at your expense the other night awarded me 'no-exertion-whatsoever' orders." He half-smiled, but I could see the pain behind his expression. I wanted to reach for his arm, but my own was too mummy-wrapped under my blanket.

"Mr. Winters, this is no laughing matter," the nurse reprimanded with a sternness that made me look away. "You are a very sick boy. Your tuberculosis is in your central nervous system. If you aren't careful, it could affect your spinal cord and even your brain."

For a moment, I thought my heart had stopped. A strange surge of heat radiated up from my chest into my head, and in that moment, I was grateful to be lying down, perhaps for the first time since arriving at Trudeau – where a horizontal position was my normal point of view at the insistence of the nurses – as I am sure I would have toppled over had I been on my feet.

I barely knew this boy. Why would his health have such an impact on my own constitution?

Once the nurse left us, Henry turned to me with a sheepish look and proclaimed, "Awfully dramatic, eh?"

"If you say so." I pretended to turn my attention to the landscape in front of the side porch where we were positioned, the vast Adirondack Mountains serving as background to the expanse of hard, brown meadow dotted with tall red oak trees that looked as cold as I usually felt, stripped bare of their thick, pointed leaves.

"We haven't been properly introduced," he said, ignoring my attempt at an unaffected demeanor. "I'm Henry."

"I know," I said, keeping my eyes focused ahead.

"And you're Marilyn."

"I know that, too."

He chuckled. "I'd shake your hand, but I can't seem to find mine at the moment." He wriggled about in his blanket cocoon and I couldn't help but laugh. "That's better. So, tell me, Miss Know-It-All, is there anything you don't know?"

I turned to look at him, his bright eyes cutting through the crisp morning air like a blazing fire. There was no sense putting on airs with this boy. I didn't have the strength, mentally or physically. "I don't know where my father is. And I need you to help me figure it out."

Henry's jaw dropped. "Can't say I saw that coming." He cocked his head and furrowed his brow like a confused dog. I held my breath, expecting him to call out for a nurse to relocate him to the other side of the porch. I didn't want this kid to think me as weird as I had come to realize I was. But instead he exclaimed, "You've come to the right person." He forced an overdramatic British accent that put me at ease. "Consider Henry Winters at your service. Now start from the beginning, and don't leave out a single detail."

CHAPTER 3
RAZZ MY BERRIES

There was no place else to start except at the beginning. The first time I noticed something wrong I was eleven years old. World War II had ended almost a year before, and still, my father had not returned home from duty with the Navy. Just three months after the Germans surrendered, I watched with envy as Tommy Meyer, a crybaby kid from across the street, burst out his front door and down the walkway to get scooped up into his dad's bear-like embrace, bawling his eyes out like always, while long green snots connected his nose to Mr. Meyer's brown-green jacket. To show my disapproval, I waited until they'd all retreated back into the house – probably for a big celebratory dinner complete with chocolate pudding – then ran halfway into the street, throwing a rock as hard as I could at Mrs. Meyer's favorite rosebush, a deep red one set back in the yard under the picture window. I don't think I did any damage save for knocking a few petals off a single bud.

I stomped into my own house and demanded to know my father's whereabouts. "Where's my father!" I cried in the highest-pitch shriek I could muster to earn my mother's attention. The only answer was silence. Pouting and huffing, I barreled my way from one cramped room to the next in search of the only person who could solve this agonizing puzzle. I found her in the backyard hanging her bedsheets on the clothesline alongside Mrs. Sollars, her best friend and our next-door neighbor. They were bent over laughing as if they'd heard the funniest joke on earth. I was horrified by my mother's outfit: red, high-waisted shorts with a white bikini-style halter top. It was a style strictly worn by young girls, and even then, if it wasn't on the beach it was still shocking to see so much leg and midriff. My mother's legs were undeniably shapely, but that didn't make it right. Mrs. Sollars, on the other hand, was covered in a light cotton dress that fell to her knees. Much more appropriate for a mom – and she didn't even have kids yet. She and Mr. Sollars had been married a few years, but my mother said she "didn't have the baby angels on her side." It was the first time (of many) I wished I had been born to Mrs. Sollars instead of Mrs. VanHoosen.

On a little metal table placed off to the side of the clothesline sat their empty glasses with just a bit of melted ice withering away at the bottoms. Beside the glasses was my mother's preferred bottle of gin. I guessed that it, too, was empty or close to it.

Over the last year, that bottle had become more and more visible around the house until it was making its first appearance of the day at breakfast, my mother's new habit of dropping a generous pour into her morning coffee. I didn't know why she liked it so much, but I did know that when she ran out, she didn't like me so much.

It made me even angrier to see her having such a jolly time with Mrs. Sollars while I was missing my father so much. Therefore, I did what any overly dramatic girl would do. I screamed for my father as long and as loud as I could.

That got her attention. With eyes wild and nostrils flaring, she grabbed me by the arm and dragged me into the house where I understood without a doubt that a spanking was awaiting me. But I didn't care. All I wanted, if I wasn't going to get my father, was for her to be as miserable as me. She deserved that for not giving a damn about either of us. She sat in the stiff kitchen chair closest to the back door, and tried to yank me across her lap, but I was stronger than she realized, so she slapped me hard across the face instead. I cried, but it wasn't from the sting. I cried for what the war had done to us all.

❖

A month later, while getting ready for the first day of fourth grade, I got up the nerve to bring up my father again, although this time, I had the good sense to do it in a calm, hushed tone.

My mother was tying a yellow ribbon in my hair, which I hated and normally would have protested had I not needed to remain on her good side. She was humming a tune I knew, "Prisoner of Love" by Perry Como, which she had been playing a lot on the record player. I didn't particularly like it. It was slow and as dramatic as "The Guiding Light," my mother's favorite radio soap opera. The singer was distraught and not willing to do anything about his situation. He was weak. Why listen to something like that all day long?

I tried to be as nonchalant as possible. "Mommy, when is Daddy coming home?" She instantly stopped fussing with my bow and stared at me in the mirror.

"I don't know," she snapped. She stood, tightened the belt at the waist of her pale blue housecoat, and then walked out of my bedroom. Boy, that really burned me. I followed her into the kitchen, determined to get some kind of answer. Even if it was bad. Even if it meant she would hit me.

"Tell me!" My boldness both scared and enthralled me.

She turned, baring her teeth. "Who the hell do you think you are?" Her eyes were crazy and her hand was raised to slap me.

I cringed, terrified of the creature she was in that moment, but I wasn't giving up. "I want to know where he is. You have to tell me!"

She lowered her hand, sashayed over to the counter, picked up the gin bottle, and dumped such a generous portion into her coffee cup that it slopped over the sides of the fragile Bone china with hand-painted roses. After placing the cup to her lips and taking a long sip, she flashed me a smile that I could only describe as wicked. "Marilyn, my dear, I don't have to tell you a damn thing."

Six months later, my grandparents drove down from Scranton to stay with me while my mother disappeared for two weeks. It was a joyful time filled with bear hugs, sweet hard candies, and trips to the park bundled up in my pink winter coat with white furry collar. In addition to Mrs. Sollars, I knew I would be happy as a clam if Grandma and Grandpa Baker would take over as my parents. They were so fun and kind and...present. I couldn't comprehend how they could create another person who was so unlike them.

My mother returned fourteen-and-a-half days later, while I was sprawled out on the living room floor engrossed in a Pippi

Longstocking book. In that moment as she burst through the front door, a deep brown fox stole wrapped around her thin shoulders, my heart sunk. And then it began racing like it might shoot right out of my chest when my father followed her into the house.

CHAPTER 4
CRUISIN' FOR A BRUISIN'

"What happened next?" Henry's eyes were wide, the earlier pain I saw there now absent. They really were pretty, the color like a glassy lake in summer, with flecks of gold, the right eye possessing a few more flecks than the left. "Marilyn!"

I had really gotten lost in those eyes for a moment. "Yes?" I said as innocently as possible. My cheeks felt so warm I would swear it was July, but I knew a snowflake had just fallen on my forehead.

"Where had your father been all that time?"

I regained my composure, focusing on the fat snowflakes that were now making their way down from the heavens as opposed to staring at Henry's pleasant face. "They never said."

"Never said?"

"Nope." I wriggled, trying to loosen my flimsy blanket, desperate for the chilled air. How in the world was Nurse Betty so adept at wrapping humans into cocoons?

Henry looked positively dumbfounded. "This cannot be the end of the story. There is no way you shared all this drama just to leave me hanging."

"Oh, there's a lot more drama. Just not at this point in the story." I could see Nurse Betty step out onto the porch. She would be coming to retrieve us soon and then the story really would be over – at least for a while.

"I just want to know one thing," Henry said. "Did you not ask? Did you not ask your father where he had been?"

I narrowed my eyes at him. "Of course. You think after all that my curiously waned?" I shrugged. "He changed the subject every time I asked. But one time, maybe five or six months later, while I was sitting up high on a thick branch of the old oak tree that took up the bulk of our yard, I heard him talking to Mr. Sollars across the fence. Mr. Sollars had asked him about his time in San Francisco, which was strange, because my father had shipped out of New York and was stationed in the Philippines. And outside of wartime he had never been farther than New Jersey. Being in San Francisco for any length of time was an impossibility. Or so I thought."

Nurse Betty was at my side. Once she unwrapped me enough that I again had control of my hands, I placed a finger to my lips, my silent plea to Henry for his silence. I saw him nod as Nurse Betty led me away in a wheelchair.

❖

We ate lunch in our beds, Henry's 'no-exertion-whatsoever' rule being taken more seriously than I could have imagined, as Nurse

Betty sat beside his bed, feeding him the day's soup and a small bowl of something mushy. He was made to lay back almost flat, with a number of pillows propping him up so he could properly swallow. Apparently even sitting up on his own was too much for Henry's body to handle.

I slurped my own soup, wishing for another choice, as I was already so hot, my forehead was damp with perspiration. A single drop of sweat had escaped from my hairline and slid to the side of my nose, getting lodged in my right eye, which stung like the dickens. I tried not to flinch. God knew I didn't need the scalding broth to spill on my skin and burn my outside like it was burning my insides.

And then, realization setting in, I stopped eating, letting my spoon drop from my hand and clank hard into the bowl, causing hot drops of soup to splash up and sting my face. "Betty!" I cried, looking around frantically for her, now afraid I may pass out with hot soup in my lap. "Betty!"

❖

I awoke to the dim light over my bed. The quiet engulfed me. I wanted to look around, to see what was going on, but I was flat on my back and couldn't lift my head. My forehead felt damp and somewhat heavy. It must have been nighttime, but I couldn't be sure. I wasn't even certain if it was the same day that I had begun screaming. "Betty?" I whispered.

"Right here, pet." Her hand lifted the thing on my head, turned it over, and placed it carefully across my forehead. It felt cooler. It was a wet washcloth.

"What happened?"

"You have a fever, but we're not sure why yet. With tuberculosis, it could be a number of things."

I stared up at the plaster ceiling, trying to pretend my body wasn't trembling. "Am I going to die?"

"Heavens, no." Her face appeared over me as she tried to find a spot to sit on my narrow bed. "Fever is very common with tuberculosis. It's not life threatening, but it is important that we find out why you have a fever. It could simply be influenza, but it could also mean you have an allergy to one of your medications, among other things."

My body relaxed. "How long have I been asleep?"

"Most of the day." She folded down my blanket, exposing the top of my nightgown. Much cooler. "The doctor stopped by to see you once, but you'll have to be seen more formally in the exam room tomorrow morning."

"OK." My eyes did not want to stay open, but I wasn't yet ready to succumb to sleep. "Can I see Henry for a minute?"

"Absolutely not," Nurse Betty asserted. "Unlike you, Henry has tuberculosis of the central nervous system. It's very serious and he can't afford to get sicker. I'm sorry, but until you have been fever-free for two days, there will be no whispering with Henry Winters."

❖

After weeks of sitting alone, lying alone, eating alone, plotting Mildred's downfall alone, I *finally* had someone to talk to. Someone to share my secrets. Someone who – I thought – found me *and* my stories interesting. And now, who knew when we'd be able to sit together again? Or when I could tell him what I had found in that PRIVATE box in the attic? I felt lonelier than I did the day I arrived at Trudeau Sanitorium.

And I was so damn hot.

My exam with Dr. Whitlaw was pretty much what I expected. Too much poking and prodding and very little speaking directly to me. He concluded that my fever was indeed a symptom of influenza, as opposed to an allergic reaction or drug resistance, which I was assured, by way of him really just talking out loud to himself, would be more difficult to deal with. More difficult for them, maybe. But an allergy or drug resistance wouldn't keep me from Henry. And, if I was allergic to Isoniazid, then I wouldn't have this ridiculously annoying rash all over me. Which, now that I was thinking about it, was really getting itchy again.

"Do you have any salve?" I asked Dr. Whitlaw from my flat position on the examination table.

He looked at me as if I had asked for a dead dog. "What?"

"Salve," I repeated, holding out my arm for inspection.

He lowered his glasses, squinted at my arm (why did he lower his glasses if he had to squint to see?), and pushed the spectacles back up his nose. "No," he finally answered. "Ask your nurse."

Without another word he left the room, leaving me with a baby of a candy striper with delicate features and tiny hands. She could have been my age, maybe a year or two older at best, but she was even shorter. Her job was to first get me upright, and then assist me into the wheelchair for my three-hallway journey back to the infirmary. When she put my arm around her shoulder and let out an odd squeak-grunt that reminded me of a cartoon mouse lugging too much cheese, laboring to move me from the table to the chair, I laughed out loud. I couldn't help it. I didn't want her to feel bad, but it was like a butterfly trying to propel a horse.

As she rolled me down the antiseptic hallway, layered in apricot linoleum and flanked by dingy walls, we passed doctors and nurses, candy stripers and orderlies, and of course other random nameless staffers who came and went quietly, generally without notice. They walked with straight posture and casual gait. They breathed deeply and their eyes shone bright. They were not us. The sickly. The weak. The limited. The lonely. How I had taken wellness for granted. How I wished I could climb up to that thick branch in my backyard, regardless of who my parents were. Or who they wanted me to believe they were. Anything was better than this.

I spent the next four days sleeping in fits and starts. The brief moments I spent awake – to eat a little something, to begrudgingly be bathed with a rough yellow sponge – it was always Betty who was there. Betty mashing bananas with the back of a spoon and sliding them into my half-open mouth. Betty taking care to carefully dab the industrial sponge along my rashy arms. Betty keeping those arms slathered in more salve than usual. I'm sure Nurse Doris must have been there some of the time, after all, Betty had a work schedule and a life, I was sure, but I never saw Nurse Doris. Never felt her gnarly hands on my skin or felt the breath of her heavy sighs against my face. It was always Betty.

By the end of that week, I was allowed to sit up in bed. It was also the first time in a week that I was able to lay eyes on Henry. He, too, was sitting up, scribbling away intently on what looked to be stationary. Apparently, his 'no-exertion-whatsoever' rule had also been lifted, thank goodness. I could only hope he had felt my eyes on him, because he looked up from his work and met my stare, giving me that award-winning smile that made my stomach twist and tighten.

"One more day, pet." I looked to my right to see Nurse Betty hovering. Her hair was different. Shorter. Much shorter, actually.

"New look?" I teased.

She put a hand to her sheared locks and, I swear, she blushed. "I had some nervous energy and decided to take it out on my hair."

"I see." I gave her a once-over. She really looked good. "It's becoming," I finally said, earning me a sheepish smile. "Really shows off your cheek bones."

She pulled me forward to fluff my pillow, then propped me back into the softness. "Flattery will not speed up your next visit with Mr. Winters." She was trying to sound tough but I could hear the warmth in her voice.

"Yes ma'am." I put a hand to my own hair, wondering just how bad it really was. "Got any idea what Henry is writing over there?" I whispered.

"Actually, I do. A letter to his folks." She re-tucked my sheets, then reached under the bed to pull a book from my suitcase. I guess that meant I could read again.

"I wonder if he actually can stand his." I didn't really mean to say that out loud – the fewer people who knew my business the better – but it just slipped out.

"I understand he likes them very much. Misses them like crazy, too."

"Of course, he does," I said, hoping to sound two percent more compassionate than my last utterance.

"It's a shame really," Nurse Betty continued. "All they want is to get to Trudeau and spend time with their only child. But between his father having cerebral palsy and his mother being blind, it's an impossibility for them to travel so far."

"Oh." I felt like an absolute heel.

"The best they can do is write letters. They go back and forth almost daily. Henry often doesn't have the strength to sit up and pen his own letters, so then he dictates and I write."

Why did I suddenly feel so revoltingly jealous?

Once Betty got my morning dose of meds down my throat, she set her hand on my head while I coughed away the memory of the horrid horse pills, waiting until every last hack and bark had subsided before leaving me to my reading. I opened Brideshead Revisited – which page didn't matter as I wasn't planning on actually reading – held the hardcover in front of my face, and peered over the top at Henry.

He looked so happy, working on his letter, stopping occasionally to grab and scan what must have been a letter from his parents, written on thick vanilla paper. He had about the worst form of tuberculosis one could have, trapped in a sanitorium hundreds of miles away from his parents, who were plagued with their own unfortunate lots in life. So why in the hell was he always smiling?

In the time I have been residing at Trudeau, I have received exactly two letters from my parents. Both letters were written in Mildred VanHoosen's flowery hand, and she had signed them, "your mother and father," which was both unloving and a lie, as my father appeared to be missing – again. Her words were more sterile

36

than the infirmary, minimal in quantity, and without a hint of emotion. I didn't write back.

We were not a family that wanted for much. Mildred VanHoosen came from money, her father the owner of the air conditioned Starbright hotels, one in New York, one in Philadelphia, and one in Chicago. My parents could have afforded to travel here by airplane, assuming there was an airport nearby. At the least, they could have gone by train as Maggie did. But after nearly two months of imprisonment here, neither Mildred VanHoosen nor my father had come to see me. Their only child. Their flesh and blood.

For the life of me, I couldn't figure out why they ever decided to have a kid.

CHAPTER 5
DON'T HAVE A COW

Two days later, I awoke to an up-close view of a loose lock of Henry's dark blonde hair coiled against his smooth cheek, practically pointing the way to his soft, soft lips. I thought I had died and gone to heaven.

He was perched on the edge of my bed, sitting in profile, his focus fixed somewhere on the other end of the infirmary, his lungs huffing and puffing as usual. I was so overjoyed to have him close to me again, I did what any rational teenage girl would do: flung my arms around his waist and kissed his elbow.

I had no sex appeal whatsoever.

Henry put a finger to his lips and motioned for me to sit up. I did as instructed, taking care to keep my sheet high on my chest for fear he might see through my thin nightgown at such close distance. Once I got to his eye level, I could see what he was focused on: a bed surrounded by a handful of nurses, Dr. Whitlaw's deep-parted salt-and-pepper hair poking up above the herd.

"What happened?" I whispered, as if we might get busted for looking.

"Old guy died. Only been here three days."

I peered at Henry, who for the first time – with the exception of the Great Coughing Fit – wasn't smiling. How did he know anything at all about some old man?

"Three days?"

Henry ran a hand through his soft locks. I shivered, immediately feeling like a spaz for reacting to Henry's intoxicating movements rather than a poor old guy who just died of tuberculosis.

"Brought him in an ambulance," Henry continued. "His wife came in a separate car with her grown daughter. From what I could tell, the old couple was a bit on the senile side, and it took a visit from their daughter to figure out just how bad the old guy was." He brushed away a tear that had made its way to the top of his cheekbone.

A cool girl would have gently wiped that tear for him, appreciating his sensitivity while stroking his smooth cheek in the process, possibly even turning his chin in her direction so she could place her mouth against those impossibly full lips to bond them in this meaningful moment. Alas, I am not a cool girl.

"Where the hell was I when all this was going on?" I blurted, handling the moment like a champ.

"Fast asleep," Henry replied, turning his head in my direction. Our faces were so close. How I longed to rub my cheek against his. But I was frozen like a deer about to get plowed by a truck. He glanced back at the scene. "He didn't stand a chance," he continued, his voice cracking. That's when he reached for my hand and laced his fingers through mine, sending a shockwave from low in my belly to the top of my chest.

We watched in silence as they carefully moved the deceased man from his bed to a gurney, his distraught wife weeping in her daughter's arms. Once in position, they covered his body, including his face, with a white sheet. An orderly wheeled him away (I didn't want to know where) while Dr. Whitlaw and the others silently dispersed, their gazes uniformly cast downward.

The daughter led her mother out of the infirmary, keeping an arm tight about the old woman's shoulders. The only person left in the room who wasn't occupying a bed was Nurse Doris. She spotted Henry on my bed and made a beeline to us.

"Mr. Winters, what are you doing out of bed?" she demanded, her white shoe tapping at the floor.

"Why, comforting my good friend Marilyn, of course. She was distraught seeing the sad, old widow." He gave my hand a squeeze and I squeezed his back.

Nurse Doris snorted. "Nice try. Let's go. Right now." He released his grasp as she stuck her two fleshy hands under his armpits, lifting him to his feet.

"Ah, heck," Henry said, ducking his head and smiling. "I'm feeling great. Surely I can walk twenty feet on my own."

"No, you cannot," Nurse Doris replied. She tossed his arm over her shoulders and half-carried him back to his bed.

He turned his head back to me, making a goofy face as he was dragged away. "See ya soon, Marilyn. I haven't forgotten we still have a mystery to solve."

I gave him a wave and slid down under my covers. For once, I was glad for the solitude. There was way too much to think about.

If I had an actual list of things I wanted to happen to me before graduating high school, holding hands with a cute boy surely would have been high up on that list. But I never could have expected how it would feel. How the touch of a certain someone's hand could be so electric. How the moment would be all-encompassing. I was certain I'd never forget the instant Henry's skin met my own. The way my chest heaved and the hairs on my skin stood on end. It was downright magical. And I wanted more. Preferably without anyone croaking mere beds away.

When Nurse Doris passed my way again, I requested a pencil and paper, which was answered with a heavy sigh and a heavier shuffling of feet. I waited patiently, staring at the nothingness of the ceiling, and thinking how much better it would be if there were pretty pictures to look at, just like that famous artist did in the big church in Italy. The Sistine Chapel, I think it was called. Then none of us would mind having to lay around on our backs all day.

Nurse Doris finally reappeared with a small pad of paper and a brand-new pencil. I greedily snatched them from her grasp, thrilled to have such treasures. "Thank you," I remembered to say before rolling onto my stomach to write. I flipped over the top two pages of the notepad, not wanting any of my personal stuff to be easily read, and scribbled the headline, "Marilyn's List for 1952." I drew a thick line below and then started a numbered list:

1. Figure out where my father was after the war ended.
2. Figure out where my father is now.
3. Get better and get the hell out of Trudeau.
4. Kiss Henry Winters.
5. Maybe cut my hair like Maggie. Or Nurse Betty.

I reviewed my list. It was good. If I could accomplish everything on it, I would consider 1952 to be a great year, considering I would have spent the most of it in a sanitorium.

Flipping a couple more pages in the notebook, I wrote another headline, "What Happened To My Father After the War?" and made another numbered list:

1. No sign of him for over a year and a half.
2. Mildred VanHoosen wouldn't discuss his whereabouts.
3. Pierre/Paul wouldn't discuss his whereabouts.
4. The PRIVATE box in the attic.
5. The dream I had of my father returning home.

Now all I needed was a plan. And the help of two friends.

Later that afternoon, Henry and I were side by side again on the chairs. For the first time since arriving at Trudeau, it wasn't bitter cold. In fact, it was almost bearable. Nurse Doris said the temperature was forty degrees – practically a heat wave, in my book. The best part was it meant we didn't have to be wrapped like mummies during our time outside. I could actually move a bit and use my hands. A miracle!

I shared my list with Henry – the "What Happened To My Father After the War?" list, not "Marilyn's List for 1952", which had the entry about kissing Henry. No one was going to see that list.

"This is all very compelling, Marilyn," Henry said, turning on his side, because, for once, he could. "But we aren't going to get anywhere until you tell me what was in that box."

The box. The super-private PRIVATE box. The box containing the contents I was still trying to wrap my head around. "There was a lot of stuff in that box. I scanned a bunch of it, but I was afraid of getting caught, so I only went so far. Honestly, a lot of it I didn't understand. But I'm convinced it held all my parents' secrets."

Henry eyeballed me. "You're going to make me drag it out of you, aren't you?"

"Drag what out of me?" I turned on my side, too, so we could be face to face. Rather nice.

"The details, Dolly."

I don't know why, but Henry calling me Dolly, a term the boys reserved for the cutest of girls, almost shot me straight out of my chair and into the expansive meadow just beyond the porch.

"No, I'm sorry, it's just that everything is all confused in my head."

He reached over, laying his hand, palm side up, on the edge of my chair. I could see he had to exert to reach that far. He wiggled his fingers at me. I hesitated, although I knew exactly what he wanted me to do. He gave me an encouraging smile. One would think I was about to leap from a high diving board into a tiny pool, the way my heart was pounding. Finally, I pulled my arm out from under my blanket and set my hand in his. Our eyes were locked. If our chairs were a foot closer, I swear he would have kissed me, right then and there.

"Now do go on, Dolly," he said coolly.

How I wished I was that cool. I may not have been cool, but I knew I could be brave. After all, as a kid, I could climb trees higher than any of my friends. I grasped Henry's hand, and moved it onto his chair, never letting go. I could handle the exertion of the stretch. I could care for Henry just as well as Nurse Betty.

His expression made it clear that he approved, which made me

44

even braver. I released my grasp and began stroking the top of his hand and wrist. I had never touched a boy this way before. His skin was soft, and the pale hair on his arm bristled to my attention. His gaze went between my face and what I was doing to him. The strokes I made along his arm got longer, more purposeful. His smile grew with my touch. And his eyes were now focused only on my face, with an expression so intense, I knew I had to touch that face. I pulled back my arm so I could prop myself on my chair, now reaching out with my left arm, the top half of my body boldly moving toward him. I'm certain his chest tensed. Without a doubt, I knew that boy wanted my closeness as much as I wanted to be close to him. The very tips of my fingers had just made contact with his cheek, noting a hint of prickly stubble, when the bottom half of my chair kicked away from me, and I had to rip my hand away in order to keep my head from meeting the hard concrete below.

"What the hell?" I cried.

"No touching!" Nurse Doris boomed, loud enough for all the patients on the surrounding chairs to hear.

My cheeks flushed, my heart thudded, my stomach lurched. Every inch of my being wanted to simultaneously hide from the world and punch Nurse Doris' miserable face. To shroud my humiliation, I took the logical route and covered my head with the scratchy blanket, leaving my feet exposed.

"Ah shucks, Nurse Doris, Marilyn was only helping me get something out of my eye," Henry offered in his usually charming way. "She's a swell girl to be so kind to me."

Nurse Doris huffed. "Oh, I'm sure that's what she was doing." She pushed my chair farther away. Once the chair and I stopped moving, I peeked out from my blanket to see a fleshy woman with a puffy face staring down at me with an amused expression. Now *our* chairs were so close they were nearly touching. "If I catch you two at it again, I'll put you on opposite sides of the porch," Nurse Doris continued.

Somebody take me out of my misery, I silently prayed to no one in particular. *Please.*

"I don't blame you, honey, he's a catch," Puffy Face said, huffing stale breath up my nose.

I was certain there could be no worse a punishment for my act of boldness than such close proximity to this certain-to-be-overly-chatty twit.

CHAPTER 6
WHAT'S YOUR TALE, NIGHTENGALE?

Unlike Mildred VanHoosen, Maggie wrote me a letter every week without fail. My grandparents weren't far behind, with a stiff card embossed in blue with my grandmother's initials arriving for me at least twice a month. Her notes weren't very interesting, but they were kind, always filled with apologies for their inability to visit due to my grandfather's weak heart. He couldn't risk catching tuberculosis, she said. Apparently, no one on Mildred VanHoosen's side of the family was fond of the vaccine. My grandmother dutifully filled me in on the latest goings on with her bridge club, her book club and her gardening club. For all those clubs, the most exciting thing my grandmother had to report in all the time I had been away was Gwendolyn Shutney bringing in not one, but two, Crocus Sativus, which is pretty much just a really expensive plant. Between humdrum clubs to pass the time and bad hearts limiting any fun, old age sounded like a real drag.

I was thankful it was my turn to write to Maggie, as I had to tell her all about Henry, the chairs, the touching, and of course the wet rag, Nurse Doris. I also needed her to continue her role as my eyes and ears back home. At the very least, more snooping was necessary. At the very most, I wanted answers about San Francisco. And if anybody had the beauty and poise to get people talking, it was Maggie Ryder.

I burned through two pieces of stationery – Mildred VanHoosen didn't give me my own special stationery like most patients here used to send letters to loved ones, so I had to use the standard issue white, thin pages embossed with TRUDEAU SANITORIUM across the top of each page – just recounting my time with Henry. I tried to be honest, because liars stink, but I think I may have laid it on a little thick, the way I described how Henry had looked at me with such a butterflies-colliding-in-my-stomach intensity. I mean, it had happened, right? I wasn't imagining any of it. At least I hoped I hadn't imagined any of it. I'm sure he would have kissed me if he could have. Which made me wonder if I should take it upon myself to try to kiss him. I proved I could be bold today. With such newfound confidence, kissing Henry Winters wouldn't be so hard. Best to include these thoughts in Maggie's letter. She would know what I should do.

I went back to scribbling furiously in my ragged script, stopping only to scratch at my arms, which were extra itchy. I had hoped by now that my body would get used to the Isoniazid, and the rash – along with my deep embarrassment – would fade away, but luck does not favor me, therefore the rash had gotten worse. My arms looked like Rand McNally road maps, with uneven crimson blotches running every which way from my wrists to my elbows. I was actually grateful it was cold so I could wear long-sleeve nightgowns.

During a moment of a furious scratching fit, I looked across the room at Henry, who appeared lost in one of his books. It was weird that I could see Henry all day, every day from my bed. It would be easy to prop myself on a few pillows, lean back all comfy, and stare at him from morning until bedtime. But that would be even weirder. In fact, I spent more of my time while in bed conscientiously not looking at Henry than gazing upon him. I didn't want to come off like I was ape for him. Which of course I was.

If I wanted to, I could call out to him, as we were close enough to distinguish our raised voices over the daily sanitorium racket of sponge baths, meal service, pill distribution, and nurses talking too loudly to patients, as if our issue was with our ears instead of our lungs. Thankfully though, we were far enough away from each other that Henry couldn't hear when Nurse Betty would tease me about him. It was bad enough that the patients on either side of me must have known my business. Henry Winters did not need to overhear that I thought he was the most.

I guess everyone stuck in the infirmary, as opposed to the more private cottages that were spread out across the property, went about their days as if there weren't at least twenty pairs of eyes and ears able to see and hear what they were doing at any given time. That meant all butt scratches, nose picks, and unexpected belches were public knowledge. We were all better off pretending otherwise.

I had just reached the bottom of page three of my letter, my thoughts moving faster than my hand could write, when I felt his presence. My first reaction was to whip my letter to Maggie under the covers, to the farthest reaches of my bed, which of course, did not look suspicious at all.

"What's up?" I asked in the most non-nonchalant manner

possible. During my furious wrestling of the stationery, half my hair had fallen over my face in a beastly way, and this was the look I had maintained while trying to speak to Henry. Beastly non-nonchalant. So becoming.

Henry peered around then sat on the side of my bed. His breathing was heavy. "Bulk of the nurses went to lunch, so I figured I'd take my chances." He brushed a stray lock behind his ear, which made my jaw drop a little. Yeah, that's how I should have done it.

"Take your chances on what?"

"Getting a little time with my Dolly before one of the ol' gals catch me and raps my knuckles." He reached over and cleared the hair from my face like a gentle windshield wiper.

I gulped. Really, what else was there to do? Oh yes, the kiss. "Henry," I said, sitting up, suddenly very aware of the urgency of the moment, "I need you to do something for me."

He raised a thick eyebrow. "Oh yeah? Fill me in."

I checked the immediate area for eavesdroppers, then once fairly certain the coast was clear, I dipped my chin and gazed deep into Henry's pastel eyes. "I need a cover story for Maggie to use on an unsuspecting officer."

I was already situated in my lounge chair, half-asleep and half-watching two sandy-coated squirrels chase each other in dizzying, high-speed circles around the nearest of the red oaks, when Henry arrived later that afternoon, perking me right up. After the incident with Nurse Doris the day before, I was concerned we wouldn't be allowed to sit together, at least for a while. Instead, not only were we together, we also had been located to the far end of the porch, as opposed to being stuck somewhere in the middle as we generally were.

Theresa Bean, a portly candy striper with unruly orange hair, had control of Henry's wheelchair, turning it in the same direction as the lounge chair and securing the foot brake. We had to address Theresa Bean by both first and last name, as there were at least four Theresas working at Trudeau. The candy striper unloaded Henry from one chair to the other without any evidence of effort. As she went about draping him with the blanket, tucking the cover under his feet securely as he liked, I couldn't help but notice he looked thinner than usual.

The second Theresa Bean and the empty wheelchair were out of view, Henry blurted, "Marilyn, I've got it!"

"Shh, Henry!" I whisper-scolded. "Nurse Betty will hear you!"

"Nurse Betty already hears you."

I looked up and gulped, catching Betty and her cool new hair – and new red lipstick, it also appeared – coming up quick upon our chairs. The smirk plastered on her face assured me we weren't in trouble. Imagine my surprise when she responded by pushing my chair up against Henry's with the power of her white-soled shoe. Maybe I was hallucinating – I did have a life-threatening illness, after all – but I swear she winked at me before heading several chairs down to adjust the blanket of a weary-looking man of about seventy, who insisted on wearing a toupee so fake, it looked as if one of our resident squirrels was taking a rest atop his head. I had heard a couple of nurses refer to him as The Chronic Cougher, so I was grateful for the distance from his hacking. (And his unsettling hairpiece.)

The mild spell appeared to be sticking around, the sun feeling unusually strong for late March. With no clouds in sight and the sounds of birds calling in the distance, if I closed my eyes, I could believe it was spring. Between the weather and Henry situated so close I could feel his breath on my skin, porch time had officially become my favorite part of the day.

"So, what were you saying?" I asked, too distracted by Henry's proximity, and that he was stroking my arm with his forefinger, to focus. The fact that he didn't appear to be on the brink of vomiting from touching my rashy skin was nothing short of miraculous. "It's hideous," I blurted, stupidly drawing more attention to my unsightly arms.

'Nah," he answered, gently taking my arm in one hand, and reaching into the deep pocket of his robe with the other. He fished out one of those cool ball-point pens that were becoming popular. In fact, they were so new – and apparently so scary – my high school did not allow them. Fountain pens or pen and ink (so old fashioned!) only.

His eyes met mine and he gave me what I could only describe as an engaging smile before using that mouth to pull the cap off the pen, holding it between his front teeth as he turned his attention to my scaly arm. "Now, as I was saying," he began, spitting the pen cap into his lap, "or, as I was shouting, I think I came up with an idea for your cover story." He knit his eyebrows and studied my arm, placing the pen against one of the more chapped spots and pulling toward him in a deliberate, wavy stroke, stopping at a dark red bump.

I was so frozen I wasn't sure what to do or say. Even though I had gotten pretty comfortable around Henry, in this moment, I was anything but. "OK," I finally stammered.

"Your friend Maggie is a working girl, right?"

"Yes," I replied, watching him draw another wavy line to the left of the first, connecting one scaly patch to another.

He absentmindedly tucked a loose curl behind his ear – which was becoming my favorite thing in the whole world – and went back to making more lines, this time short and purposeful, moving quickly from bump to inflammation to patch. "So, it wouldn't be unusual for her to be interested in moving from Philadelphia to, say, San Francisco, especially if it was for a glamorous job, right?"

"Like to put on fashion shows for a highly respected department store?"

"Now, you're cooking," he said, continuing with the little lines down by my wrist, in what looked like an arc.

"And since Navy ships were coming and going from San Francisco to the Pacific during the war, it wouldn't be outlandish to assume a Navy officer might have spent time in San Francisco."

I leaned toward him, my heart pummeling my chest. "Henry Winters, you're brilliant." He stopped drawing, raising his head to meet my eyes. He must have dropped the pen, because that hand was now grabbing my free arm, pulling me into him. Our lips came together, almost on accident, but we purposely kept them there, those soft, full lips of Henry's finally on my own. He pulled back, long enough to give me another one of his dazzling smiles, before dragging both hands into my hair, his palms resting softly against my cheeks, and pulling me back into his kiss. With my own hands now free, I was able to lean over the arms of our chairs and wrap my arms around his waist, pulling him as tight to me as I could get. That's when he opened my mouth with his tongue, and all that activity in my heart shot like a locomotive in a direct line past my stomach and between my legs, nearly lifting my body off the chair.

When we finally released, we were both so exhausted we had to lay back in our chairs and rest, neither of us having enough energy to talk. Henry kept a tight hold of my hand though, even after his breathing got deep and rhythmic. I wanted nothing more than to lay there and watch him sleep, but my eyes were too heavy to fight. Before succumbing to sleep, I remembered my left arm, and shook back the sleeve that had fallen during our ardent kiss. My rash had been replaced by a seahorse, fragile and fascinating. Just like Henry.

CHAPTER 7
MEANWHILE, BACK AT THE RANCH

A week later, I got the reply I was hoping for from Maggie: She was in on the plan. (And super excited for my first kiss, too!) She filled in the blanks for me, specifically identifying the naval officer, who would unknowingly be feeding us information. His name was Benjamin Fowler, an old school chum of her oldest brother, Frankie. Ben was a Lieutenant Commander, who served during World War ll on the aircraft carrier USS Lexington, one of the Navy's first aircraft carriers. The USS Lexington, when not active during wartime, had spent a good deal of time on California's west coast during Ben's service on the vessel, and there was a good chance he would be familiar with all that was happening in San Francisco, at least where the military was concerned.

Maggie assured me Ben had made it clear that, when it came to her, he liked what he was looking at, during the multiple occasions that Frankie had brought him to the family home for holiday dinners. While he was too old for her – twelve years to be exact –

he wasn't bad looking, with a strong jaw and dark, deep-set eyes. But never having married, Ben had that desperate edge to him, a sweaty mix of loneliness and hope, that Maggie found off-putting, but not so much that she couldn't put up with it temporarily for the good of the plan.

Maggie had set up a family dinner for Sunday, confirming with Frankie that Ben would be in attendance. She was holding nothing back, stocking the fridge with beer and planning a menu of steak, mashed potatoes, and creamed corn. Between the heavy food and frothy drink, Ben wouldn't have the will to do anything but comply with Maggie's wishes. And that wasn't even considering the red wiggle dress she would be wearing.

I immediately replied to Maggie's letter, begging her to telephone me after Sunday's dinner, promising to find some way to reimburse her for the expensive long-distance call. It would be impossible to wait for a written account of the evening.

Telephone calls were not common at Trudeau, as many of the patients' loved ones lived far enough away for the calls to be considered long distance, but every so often, a lucky patient would find a nurse with a wheelchair next to his or her bedside with news of a waiting telephone call. The only telephone accessible to patients was located in the hallway just before the Visitors Room, housed in a little cutout in the wall that was covered in a walnut wood and finished with a ledge to rest your elbow or jot down a note. There was always an urgency to transport the patient to the phone, and it was only during that time that the nurses moved with any speed at all. Everyone understood the expense of wasted minutes as the telephone sat off the hook, waiting lazily for the recipient.

Nurse Betty posted my letter and got it into the afternoon's pick up. I couldn't get over how pretty she was looking. Not that she wasn't attractive before. It was just more obvious now, with the shorter haircut showing off her bone structure and the red lips lighting up her smooth skin. I knew without a doubt there was a man behind this change. There always was. No woman wakes up on a random day and says, "I want to overhaul my appearance" on her own. It's because she wants to catch a certain man's eye. Otherwise, she'd just go about her day as usual, not concerned with going beyond good hygiene and a neat appearance. The important things.

While Nurse Betty was dispensing my afternoon medication, I decided to keep my bold streak going and inquire about her appearance.

"You sure are killing it in the looks department these days." I was spreading it on thick, but it was also the truth. And I wanted her to tell me about it.

Nurse Betty handed me the tiny cup holding the big pills and knitted her brows while reaching up to feel for her hair, as if checking it was still as she remembered. "Oh," she said, clearly flabbergasted. "Why thank you, Marilyn." She pushed the glass of water into my other hand and looked away. Had I embarrassed her?

"I just mean, you're doing a heck of a job impressing whoever you are itching to impress." Now I just sounded stupid. How could I be so bad at flattery?

She turned back to me, her expression so tense I'm ninety-five percent sure I saw her nostrils flare. "Is there someone in particular you think I am trying to impress?" She didn't sound angry, but she didn't sound amused either.

Sharing my theory about girls only making changes for the sake of men suddenly sounded juvenile, so instead of making up some cockamamie story to cover my foolishness, I threw the pills down my throat, lapped up the water like a dog in August, and coughed for the next five minutes until the awkward conversation was traded in for soft pats on the back and a water refill.

That week was one of the longest of my life. Sunday felt like a year away as opposed to mere days. Plus, I felt so dumb around Nurse Betty that anytime I saw her nearby, I would slide under the covers and roll onto whatever side was opposite of her direction, faking sleep. I thought I was quite good at it, actually, making my breath deep and rhythmic like the immense woman in the bed to the right of me, who moved so infrequently from her back, I was convinced her neck had been replaced by her many chins. I also managed to keep my eyes fully closed during my fake sleep stints, as opposed to trying to peek out from the smallest of slits, which would make my eyelids flutter and give me away. That was not easy, as I really wanted a looksie at Nurse Betty, to see if her regular face – the one that always exuded warmth and compassion – had returned.

Both Henry and I had exams that week with Doctor Whitlaw. I didn't think much about my exam, but I sure was worried about Henry's. The very first thing we did at an exam was get weighed, and if the doctor couldn't see Henry's weight loss with his own eyes, he would be certain of it when he read the number on the scale. For all my newfound boldness, I was too afraid to ask Henry about it. The truth was, I didn't want to hear the answer. He was far sicker than me, and for all my moaning and groaning about Mildred VanHoosen and how much she set me back by not caring enough about me when it mattered, at least I did eventually get the care I needed. Outside of having to live in the infirmary at Trudeau, and having almost zero contact with my parents, I was doing okay. Henry, on the other hand, had it pretty tough, with disabled parents who were unable to see him – one literally – and an advanced disease that I didn't understand. And yet, he never seemed affected. By any of it. Why did he accept his lot in life so willingly? Did that make him an unusually lucky person, or a weak one?

My exam was ordinary, as expected. A weigh-in that showed I had gained two pounds pleased Dr. Whitlaw. I knew he was pleased because, when he read the updated weight entry on my chart, he nodded once and continued scanning. Yes, that Dr. Whitlaw sure was an emotional man. It was funny to be actively trying to gain weight, as I was one of an odd lot of folks who never lost her appetite when sick. My school friends, in contrast, would come down with the mildest cold and drop five pounds each, all equally plagued with "no ability whatsoever" to eat. I remember once, when I was in sixth grade, I had a virus so severe, every time I tried to lift my head a wave of nausea hit me like a dinghy in a Nor'easter, and I had to roll to the edge of my twin bed as fast as I could to throw up in my pink plastic waste basket. Every single time, after I had cleaned up the edges of my mouth with a tissue and my stomach had resolved itself, I would call out to Mildred VanHoosen for food. Any food at all, to be clear, I was that hungry, which I would only receive after I called out long enough and loud enough. She would begrudgingly whip up either a ham sandwich, bacon and scrambled eggs, or waffles with syrup. I could see the disgust in her face as she watched me inhale the contents of the plate she had placed in front of me on a wood tray, usually pivoting on a pricey pointed pump and exiting the room before I reached the point of licking the dish clean.

I pointed out to Dr. Whitlaw that lying around all day with

nothing to do but eat and sleep would eventually take my successful weight gain to the extreme, turning me into a pudgy bowl of pudding. I assumed he would ignore my comment, as usual, so imagine my surprise when, after scanning my chart again and listening to my lungs with his stethoscope pressing along my back – I still felt like there was something resting on my chest, but now it was more like a handful of pebbles rather than a boulder – he said with absolutely no emotion (shocking), "Looks like one more month and we can start you walking again. Slowly." He looked down at me with his mouth half open, as if he'd had a genius thought and then lost it. Pushing his thick glasses securely onto the bridge of his nose, he handed my chart to the nurse who had been standing quietly beside a tall cabinet, and exited without a goodbye or handshake, leaving the nurse and me looking at each other uncomfortably. I kind of wanted to hug her, I was so ecstatic to hear I'd soon be back on my feet. But, considering I had never met this one before, didn't even know her name, and the most contact I'd had with Nurse Betty was feeling her hand on my head, I kept my arms, and my excitement, to myself. It would keep for Henry.

Henry's exam was scheduled for later that afternoon. I thought it might be a nice idea to have lunch together in the dining room prior to his appointment. Neither of us had taken a meal anywhere beside our beds, and with how little alone time we were able to muster – outside on the chairs, a few stolen moments in the infirmary – it would be a kick to sit upright and talk over a meal together. Like normal people do.

I flagged down Nurse Betty and made my plea, careful not to mention her hair or her lipstick or make prolonged eye contact, I was so anxious to not screw up this opportunity with Henry. She gave me a little nod, her stiff nurse hat like a kid's paper boat dipping in a creek, and even smiled slightly. I desperately wanted to apologize for what I had said about her trying to impress someone, but I couldn't form the words. I didn't want her to hate me all over again. At the moment, she was the closest thing I had to a present family member. There was no sense messing with that.

She disappeared for a few minutes, returning with a nurse named Maude, who sported chin-length, ink-black hair that curled wildly only at the temples, and had one of those cherub-type faces that made old aunts and grandmothers want to pinch her full cheeks. Each of them was pushing a wheelchair. Nurse Betty sauntered over to Henry, bent over him with her womanly, half-moon derriere pushing back at me, and whispered in his ear. His head peeked out from behind her hourglass-shaped body to grin at me for a split-second then vanished again. As Maude was helping me into my chair, I couldn't stop watching Betty and Henry across the way. The way she expertly helped him into his robe, sliding a hand across his bare wrist, her fingers hooking underneath to gently guide it through the armhole. And then how closely she held him while transferring him from the bed to the chair. Their faces were as close as Henry's and mine were the day we kissed on the porch chairs. I couldn't explain why Nurse Betty suddenly felt like my competition, but she did. What chance did I have with Henry, when a real woman – a serious looker at that – with a filled-out body and red, red lips was an option?

Was it possible the person she was trying to impress was Henry?

We rolled along the hallway single file, Nurse Betty, her round bottom, and Henry in the lead. I couldn't help but wonder if she chose to go first so I would have to watch her hips sway from side to side as she pushed my fellow, maintaining all the control while I sat helplessly at the rear with no control – or much rear of my own for that matter - at all.

I was relieved once we had been parked at a small square table for two along the windowed wall. All the blinds had been pulled up to the very top, and the view from here was really quite pretty. The cottages dotted the landscape like a mini-village, similarly sided with white wood slats trimmed in forest green, and bottoms wrapped in smooth stones. Each cottage had a dark, multi-peaked roof and a paved walkway that led to the steps of the front door. Those steps were the only sign needed that the patients housed inside were in much better health than the lot of us in the infirmary. We would never be allowed to walk up and down a stairway. Not even a short one.

"Together at last and you're a million miles away."

Henry's voice snapped me back to my immediate landscape in the dining room. While I had been gazing out the window lost in thought, someone had placed in front of us plates of piping-hot macaroni and cheese with a side of wilted broccoli. And, of course, a filled-to-the-rim glass of milk. No meal at Trudeau went without a heaping serving of milk. What I would give for a root beer. Better yet, a root beer float. I wondered if Henry could see me drooling at the thought.

"Better eat up for your weigh-in today." I shoved a heaping forkful of my entrée into my mouth, horrified at my incessant need to blurt out stupid shit.

"Ah, is my Dolly worried about me?" Henry teased while poking at the macaroni and cheese with his fork.

I tucked my chin, finished chewing, and looked up at him

sheepishly. "Well, kind of."

I kept eating, but Henry set his fork down and leaned back in his wheelchair, his expression amused. "My best girl doesn't need to worry about me. I'm going to be just fine."

I eyed his plate suspiciously. "Then why haven't you taken a single bite yet? I've already wolfed down half my lunch."

Henry leaned forward, now clearly studying my plate. "It appears you have the appetite of a barnyard animal that also harbors a grudge against limp vegetables."

"Henry!" I grabbed one of the broccoli florets in question and flung it at him, missing him by a mile and instead whacking the back of the chair behind him. A stiff-looking gentleman, who had the presence of wealth with his perfect posture, neatly combed hair, and cashmere cardigan draped over his shoulders (which lucky for him, hid that ugly robe), turned and glared at us. "I beg your pardon," he said with what sounded like a hint of a forced English accent. Henry and I burst out laughing, sliding down in our chairs to get as out of view as possible.

Once we had regained our composure and wiggled back up to our normal sitting height, I went back to devouring my lunch while Henry sat and watched me pig out, that amused look of his ever present.

"You know," he said, reaching across the table for my hand, "it really is sweet how much you care about me."

My macaroni-and-cheese-stuffed cheeks went crimson, and yet, I kept my grip on his hand. Even when mortified, I wanted to be as close to Henry Winters as possible.

A subject change was sorely needed. "I think I'm going to burst waiting for Sunday to get here," I said with a much-too-full mouth.

"Because of all the mac and cheese?"

I rolled my eyes. "Honesty, Henry! Because of Maggie and her grand plan with the Lieutenant Commander!"

"Do you really think she'll be able to get any kind of secretive information out of him?" He stroked my rashy arm, which was surprisingly calming.

"If anyone can, it's Maggie," I replied with absolute confidence.

"She is a looker."

My heart hitched, and I pulled away from Henry's hand. I knew how pretty my best friend was, but I sure didn't like Henry having the same knowledge. But where did he get that knowledge? "How do you know what Maggie looks like?"

He smiled shyly. "My folks telephoned me that afternoon she came to visit you. After the call, I convinced Nurse Betty to wheel me down the hallway a bit further so I could see what you were up to. I told her I had been wanting to see what the Visitors Room looked like. Pretty good cover, eh?"

"Do you think Nurse Betty is a looker?" Oh God, I could not believe that came out of my stupid, stupid mouth.

He paused for a moment. "Sure, she's fetching."

My heart, my body, and my face all simultaneously sunk.

He looked around and leaned forward. I stayed back in my chair. Anything he had to say next I was sure I did not want to hear. "But don't you think she's really been pushing it lately?" he went on in a low voice. "I mean, with the new hair and all the makeup? Who do you think she's doing that for?"

My eyes welled up and my lips trembled. "You Henry. I think she's doing it for you."

To my surprise, Henry threw his head back and shrieked. "Oh

Dolly," he cried, his own eyes tearing up, but not from sadness. "You really are a hoot. And you are obviously, unequivocally in love with me to think such a thing. Are you really that thick? Nurse Betty is clearly over the moon for Dr. Whitlaw."

CHAPTER 8
WHAT, ARE YOU WRITING A BOOK?

It's amazing how life can change in the blink of an eye. The world goes to war. Your dad goes missing (twice). Your mom stops loving you. (And now I'm wondering if she ever did.) You get tuberculosis. You're forced to leave the only home you've ever known (by yourself). You start loving someone else. You realize you aren't losing that person to someone else. You realize you still might lose that person.

The whole stupid thing was a shitty, never-ending roller coaster with no safety harness. Now I know why I always preferred the unchanging stability of the Ferris wheel. At the very top of the wheel, I can see everything. There are no buried secrets. No medical unknowns. Each time I am smoothly transported from the bottom to the top, the view is the same. The landscape is understood. The horizon is unchanging.

It's my version of Heaven.

For the ride back from the dining room, Nurse Betty had taken charge of my chair, and upon inspecting me while helping me back into bed, declared I was looking peaked, and insisted I close my eyes and nap for a while. I quickly obliged, certain she was right, having been positively thrown by Henry's declaration of Betty's love for Dr. Whitlaw, and the realization that I had, in fact, declared my own love for Henry, even though the actual words had never escaped my mouth. I had given it all away in my tears and misery. Now both Henry and I knew that I loved him. I wondered who was more shocked?

I woke to chaotic sounds coming from across the way, and quickly pulled myself up to see what all the commotion was about. My stomach instantly knotted when I realized it was Henry, wailing his refusal to get out of the wheelchair and back into bed. Clearly, his appointment had not gone well. His face, the part I could see anyway, said it all: his half-opened mouth turned down hard at the corners, and tears streaming past the loose hair that had tumbled over his eyes. Nurses Betty and Maude were bent over either side of him, trying to coax him into bed in matching soothing yet no-nonsense tones. But Henry just kept shaking his head wildly, clutching the arms of the chair with the little strength he had.

"Please Henry," I heard Nurse Betty say, "you need to stay calm. Fighting us will only make you weaker. And make your head hurt worse."

Henry threw his head back, clearing his hair away just long enough to make eye contact with me. "Dolly!" he cried out. "Dolly!" It felt like a knife repeatedly stabbing at my heart, determined to lodge itself there.

I scrambled out of bed and stood too fast, which made the room all wobbly. Keeping my hands on the edge of the bed to stabilize myself while waiting for my equilibrium to catch up, I inched my way to the end of the bed, beads of sweat gathering at my temples and above my upper lip. Normally a sweat mustache would make me terribly self-conscious, but I was too alarmed to give it a second thought. The bed seemed as long as a football field. Finally reaching the end, I paused to wipe above my lip with the sleeve of my nightgown, and struggled to both catch my breath and quiet it. The last thing I wanted was a nurse dragging me back to bed before I could reach Henry. I took the deepest breath my lungs would allow, let go of the mattress, and hobbled the six steps it took for me to make contact with the end of Henry's bed, once again, leaning all my weight into the thin mattress while I caught my breath.

"Marilyn, you should not be out of your bed," Nurse Maude scolded. Ignoring her, I slowly worked my way to the side of the bed where Henry was waiting for me in the wheelchair, his arms outstretched like a distressed toddler.

"Let it be," Nurse Betty said to Maude, pulling her back out of our way. Finally, within arms' length of Henry, the most I had exerted myself while at Trudeau, I set my backside on the bed and leaned forward into his embrace, circling his head with my skinny arms. He sobbed into my chest while I focused on slowing my breathing, wondering which of us would be most likely to pass out first.

I don't know how long we sat like that, but to say it felt like a lifetime was only a slight exaggeration. During that time day had turned to night, and Henry's sobs had turned to weak whimpers, which were drowned out by the clinking and clanking sounds of dinner being served to the infirmary patients. When he finally went silent, I pulled back, placed a bare foot on either side of his wheelchair seat, and held his head in my hands. "Boy, you really put up a stink when you're missing me," I said, deadpan. The smile that took over his face was the best response I could have asked for. "Now would you get into your damned bed so we can have a proper conversation without attracting the attention of all the Trudeau gossips?"

He nodded weakly and I scooted down so Betty and Maude, who had been standing silently by the entire time, could get into position to lift him. It was like moving a sack of potatoes – not a particularly heavy sack, of course – but once they got him nestled under his covers, he looked like regular ol' Henry again. Just how I liked him.

"Is it okay if I stay for a bit?" I asked Nurse Betty.

She placed a hand on my head and flashed me the most compassionate smile I had ever seen. "Of course, Pet." In that instant, I knew we were back to normal. I smiled up at her, never wanting her to take that hand away, but also desperately wanting to be alone with Henry. Seeming to read my mind, she let her fingers run gently through the back of my hair, a new move which I immediately adored, and without another word left us to ourselves. Feeling like I could do just about anything in that moment, I swung my legs onto the bed and laid on top of the covers beside Henry. I was careful to stay on my back with my hands clearly folded on my stomach, so no one would think there was any funny business going on, but with our faces turned toward each other, it was the closest I had ever been to him in the infirmary. It was glorious.

"Want to tell me what happened?" I prodded, trying to keep the mood light while practically desperate for answers.

He sighed and closed his eyes for a moment, as if to gather strength. "Doc said surgery." His voice hitched on the last word. As

70

did my heart.

This was not what I was expecting. I thought Dr. Whitlaw would be focused on Henry's inability to gain weight and putting together a strategy to get food into his body, maybe even resorting to force feeding him. Or using a blender to turn all his food into runny goo and making him drink it down with a straw. Both vile options, but understandable if he wasn't going to eat on his own. My dad's Uncle Jack got sick when I was little, and he had all kinds of trouble swallowing, so my Aunt Kay blended all his food into lumpy, puke-worthy drinks. He drank roast beef and noodles, chicken kiev and rice, pork and potatoes. You name it, he drank it. Or at least tried to. I left the room the second the blender was pulled out of the cupboard. The site of Uncle Jack burping and gagging while he worked to get down that goopy mess really rattled my cage.

Suddenly, drinkable food sounded dreamy compared with surgery.

I wanted to be strong for Henry, but inside, I was in pieces. Operations were meant for the truly sick. The dying. Last resorts to fix something that wasn't self-fixing. The very thought of Henry not being alive, when he was normally so full of life, even while bed-ridden, shot a pain from my throat to my belly that felt like a massive tree trunk had taken root in my intestines. While everyone at Trudeau was technically "sick", I'd bet the bulk of us didn't see ourselves that way. Tired and breathless? Sure. But really sick? Nah. Save for walking, or anything else that sucked our energy, we were normal. We ate our meals and read our books and wrote our letters and lived for gossip. We weren't what the world thought of as sickly. Were we?

I didn't want to clue in Henry to my fears. I was the only one here he had – the nurses didn't count, at least I sure didn't want them to count in Henry's eyes – so it was my job to be strong for him. No matter how I felt inside. Swallowing hard, I pushed down my fears far, far below the roots of that growing tree trunk and flashed Henry a smile so fake, I was sure he would burst out laughing at my feeble attempt to act like this whole ordeal was no sweat. I could benefit so much from theater classes.

"This is funny to you?"

The glare he gave me wiped that false smile off my face in an instant. I shook my head.

"Then why were you grinning like the Cheshire Cat?"

"Oh, I love Alice in Wonderland," I blurted out like an idiot.

Henry frowned. "That's very informational, but it doesn't answer my question."

I sighed and rolled my eyes. "I have no idea. I want to be strong for you, but..." I flipped onto my side and folded my arm under my head. "Honestly, I don't know what to say or do. You said surgery and I seized up like all the oxygen in the world had disappeared." I felt my lips quiver. "I'm scared, Henry."

He stroked my cheek, his eyes glistening with fresh tears. "Me too."

"So, what do we do?"

"Go forward, I guess," he said. He reached for the hand I was trying to keep visible up on my hip and pulled it in to him, nuzzling it under his chin. "What other choice do we have?"

❖

Henry's surgery was scheduled to take place somewhere in the neighborhood of ten to twelve weeks. During the time leading up to the operation, Dr. Whitlaw wanted Henry to undergo steroid therapy in an attempt to reduce inflammation in his central nervous system, and also minimize brain damage, a potential outcome that completely threw me, the possibility instantly becoming more terrifying than the actual surgery. It was only then that I realized just how little I knew about Henry's form of tuberculosis and how serious it really was. Dr. Whitlaw, with his shameful bedside manner, informed Henry that steroid therapy could significantly reduce mortality but the effects were predominately noticed in children only. And Dr. Whitlaw made an exaggerated point to remind Henry that at eighteen, he wasn't what they would consider a child anymore (what an ass). But Henry said he would rather have the steroid therapy and have a chance at improvement prior to surgery – he was careful to omit the subject of brain damage – rather than take nothing and have no additional opportunities to get even a little better.

Nurse Betty informed both Henry and me that there were side effects to steroid therapy, including mood swings. She told me it was my job not to take anything personally that Henry might say to me during the time he was taking the medication, no matter how hurtful it might be. As if I didn't have enough to worry about, now I was spending my alone time in bed creating mini movies in my head of any and every bad thing Henry could say to me, especially, "You're ugly," and "I could never love someone like you." I could even see the disgusted expression on his face as he hurled insults at me that I could not return. In my movie, I was standing in the middle of the infirmary, naked, too thin, trying to hide myself behind a cart as Henry shouted words of hate at me for everyone to hear, his full lips wet from the saliva that spat out like arrows. Disgusting, but less penetrable than hearing him scream, "You are nothing to me!"

With Henry's impending surgery, potential last days on Earth, and hammering moodiness running rampant in my mind, I hadn't noticed that Sunday had already arrived. I was lying on my stomach in bed, trying without much success to pen a love letter to Henry, which I would give to him the morning of his surgery. I wanted him to know how I felt. How he had become my entire world. How his smile was all I needed to be peaceful. How I didn't even hate Mildred VanHoosen all that much anymore. I mean, I still kind of hated her, just with less evil thoughts all roped about in my wrath. I didn't want to spend a minute in the same room with her, but I also stopped contemplating the sweet chance of timing that would place Mildred VanHoosen into the path of an oncoming bus. (I mean, one step at a time, right?) But when I tried to put my feelings onto paper, it was a giant hunk of beating around the bush and stupid attempts at sarcasm. These are not the qualities that make up a classic love letter.

I was gnawing on the end of my pencil, trying to focus on writing one single sentence that would, just the littlest bit, express the depth of my love, when Maude appeared at the side of my bed with a wheelchair in tow.

"Telephone, Marilyn," she said, clearly excited for me. "Let's get to it."

Before she could reach to help me, I slithered off the bed and plopped my bottom into the pliable seat. "Let's go!" I cried out. I couldn't believe this day had come. I couldn't believe I had forgotten what it was like to look forward to something as opposed to wanting so badly to stop the future from happening. Maggie was waiting. If this wheelchair could fly, we wouldn't have been able to get to the telephone fast enough.

CHAPTER 9
WORD FROM THE BIRD

"Maggie." All it took was the uttering of her name to pump my well of tears.

"Why, hello to you, Mari-boo! Have you missed me?" Her bouncy demeanor was a strong contrast to my sad, worn self.

"You have no idea," I whispered, wiping away the waterfalls that had sprung from both eyes.

"Marilyn, what's happened?"

"It's Henry." I swallowed away a sob that tried to escape, but couldn't refrain from the horrifying snot sucking that gave away my sorrow.

"That hep kid you've been digging on?"

I couldn't help but smile by her cool depiction of my sweet Henry. "Yes. He's sick."

"Uh, aren't you all sick?"

I wiped my running nose with the sleeve of my robe, sorry I hadn't thought to stick a tissue in my pocket. "Technically, yes, but some are sicker than others."

There was a pause on Maggie's end. "Is he dying?"

That was the first time anyone had said that word out loud in relation to Henry. I had thought about it – more than I cared to – but the possibility of him dying had never actually been discussed.

"Honestly, I'm not sure. I think he could if he doesn't have surgery. But there's a chance he won't make it through the surgery. It's all a bunch of unknowns and it's so scary." Admitting all this to Maggie started up the waterworks again, and I had to switch to the other sleeve to keep up with the flow.

"That's heavy, Marilyn. What can I do to help?"

"You can take my mind off of all this by telling me what you found out about my dad."

"Oh, Mari-boo, that's one thing I can absolutely do."

I adjusted my position in the wheelchair, settling in for what was already the longest long-distance phone call I'd ever had. Crossing one leg over the other, I winced from the feel of all the hair that had sprouted from my ankles to my knees. Shaving your legs during a sponge bath is not an option. And I didn't think I had the energy to get a leg up on the sink in the bathroom, much less stay propped up in that position long enough to get a razor up one strip of skin. It was horrifying to imagine Henry getting an accidental feel of what could easily pass as Viking boots. Thank God both the nightgowns and the robes were long, and I could pull my socks up high. My legs needed all the camouflaging they could get.

"How did the dinner go with Ben?"

"Well, it started off kind of shaky..."

It turned out the day of the big family dinner, Maggie's brother Frankie came down with a nasty cold, and wasn't feeling up to company, or even eating for that matter, which was impossible to imagine, given Frankie's imposing size and penchant for resting a half hour after dinner before starting to feel hungry again. When Ben heard about his friend's unexpected illness, he suggested rescheduling the dinner for the following Sunday, but Maggie wouldn't hear of it. It was a bigger commitment than she had intended, but she saved the day by suggesting that Ben take her out on a "proper date", a proposition he was certain not to turn down. And he didn't. He picked her up in his brand new red Chrysler Windsor Deluxe Convertible – it was a little too chilly to put the top down even though spring was around the corner – and took her to Don's Drive-In, a popular joint in our town with rims of pink neon lights circling the top of the round façade, where friends gathered together for food and fun, and teens going steady sought out for a little time away from their parents. It was typical burgers-and-milkshakes fare, which was fine with Maggie, who never met a meal she didn't like. It was a wonder she stayed so slim. And another reason why I liked her so much. (Her great love of food, not her trim figure.)

Ben surprised Maggie by parking at an outdoor stall – which understandably, was more popular in the warmer months – rather than getting a table inside. "Isn't it a bit cold?" she questioned, pulling the collar of her sky-blue car coat close at the neck. Imagine her surprise when Ben turned a dial and warm air flooded the car. She had never been in a car that had a heater. "Oh, it's wonderful!" she exclaimed, removing a tan leather glove to feel the cozy warmth on her bare hand. Even when Ben rolled down the window to give their order to the carhop, a pretty girl sporting short bangs and a high ponytail, with rosy cheeks and an attitude that was anything but, the temperature in the car remained comfortable.

Maggie found herself looking at Ben differently. Much differently than how the carhop was looking at him, complete with narrowed eyes and chattering teeth. Ben was certainly handsome. But that desperation she used to see in him wasn't there anymore. He seemed to possess such confidence now. And his older status suddenly didn't seem much of an issue. Remembering why she was out with Ben, Maggie shrugged off her thoughts and refocused. She had to be the one in control if she was going to get any answers. She could think about Ben later.

"So," she said, batting her long eyelashes in Ben's direction as she leaned toward him, hoping to simultaneously dazzle him with the scent of her Yardley English Lavender, "I understand you spent some time in California. I just love California!" She hated how simple and downright girlish she sounded, but she also knew what it took to fluff up a man's feathers. If she wanted him to tell her everything, she had to ensure him she knew nothing.

Ben's eyes lit up at the mention of California. "I sure did. Been up and down the coast multiple times."

"Oh, how exciting. I am just so jealous!" She laid the tips of her fingers on the back of his hand for a jarring second before gingerly placing her hand back in her lap, never breaking eye contact with him. "Was there a city you liked best?"

Ben's mouth was hanging open just enough for Maggie to know her tactic was effective. "Um..." He paused as if stumped. Or downright dumbfounded.

Maggie flashed him a dazzling smile. "What's the matter, cat got your tongue?"

He blushed then, tucking his chin and looking up at Maggie

sheepishly. He never looked more handsome to her than in that moment. She reached for his hand again, but this time, she left it there. "Go on," she encouraged. "Tell me all about California."

"San Francisco and Los Angeles," he sputtered.

"What's that?"

"I have two favorite cities there," he said, his voice stronger this time. "San Francisco and Los Angeles."

"I see." Maggie tugged on one of her pin curls playfully. "I've never been to either, but I would just die to go to both!"

The carhop returned with their order, and Ben rolled down his window then turned up the heater to combat the outside air. As the carhop secured the tray to the car and Ben paid for the meal, Maggie sat quietly, thinking as fast as she could for a way to hone in on the military's interest in San Francisco. How was she going to get him to share such specific information with ordinary, first-date conversation?

Ben passed Maggie her milkshake, which she greedily sucked down until the front of her head started to hurt from the cold. "You're a pretty tough girl," he joked, watching as she kept one hand on her forehead to ward off the pain while she turned her attention back to the milkshake. "I bet you could handle life in the Navy on a big ship, too."

Maggie lifted her head to meet Ben's gaze, a smile playing on the corners of her mouth. "Oh, I don't know about that. You're so big and strong and fit for life on a ship. But you get to spend time on land, too, like in San Francisco, right?"

He took a big bite of his hamburger and washed it down with a Coke. "Tons of time on land in San Francisco. In fact, I bet I could tell you just about anything about that city. Go on, ask me."

Gingerly biting into her hamburger, Maggie looked up at the ceiling of the car, as if really pondering Ben's challenge. "Oh gosh, I don't know. Um, did any of the fellows in the Navy like San Francisco so much that they stayed?"

Ben lowered his burger and knit his brows. "What's that?"

"Oh, you know, the city being so wonderful and all. I would imagine some people wouldn't want to leave. Did you want to leave?"

"I sure did. Don't get me wrong, it's a fine place to visit. The steep hills, the statuesque Golden Gate Bridge, and the bay so calm it's like staring at glass. But I'm an East Coast fellow. I couldn't wait to get home. And, see you again, of course."

It was a simple statement, and yet, it made Maggie's heart flutter.

"But yes, to answer your original question, a lot of guys did decide to stay."

"Hmm," Maggie purred, sliding her fingers into Ben's palm. "In that case, maybe you could help me track someone down."

As Maggie explained to me on what was now surely the most expensive phone call ever, she had no real reason why in that moment she decided to stop acting coy and be straight with Ben. She just knew she could. She told him everything: my dad's lengthy lag time in returning home from the war, the name change, Mildred's odd behavior (that one could have taken her all night to recount), and my father's latest disappearing act. And, according to Maggie, she did it all from the passenger seat of that warm, warm car, never once moving those fingers away from that palm.

Who knew my scheme would light a love match?

CHAPTER 10

CATS LIKE US

It took less than a week before the mood swings kicked in. The first one happened while Henry was writing a letter to his folks. Having such issues with travel, understandably they were frightened over the state of their son's health and his impending surgery. Their only lifeline to Henry's official medical care was Dr. Whitlaw, and his frank and indifferent delivery put no one at ease. Ever. As a result, their letters were arriving daily fraught with concern. Henry hated it.

While attempting to compose a lighthearted reply that would temper his parents' distress, Henry broke character, whipping the pencil he was using across the infirmary. It bounced off the wall a few feet over my head and landed smack into a bowl of water that was on a cart in the middle of the room. Under typical conditions, which for us would be our standard-issue tuberculosis maladies, Henry and I would have become hysterical over the impossibility of that pencil shot until our breathing became too strained for us to remain conscious if we didn't immediately curb it. But all I could do was sit in silence, watching with trepidation for what would come next, which turned out to be Henry crumbling the letter he had been writing, and crying out just loud enough for me – and everyone around us – to hear, "Dammit!"

I had never heard Henry Winters swear before. It didn't suit him.

Nurse Betty may have warned me about the mood swings, but she didn't tell me how to react to them. Was I supposed to act like nothing unusual was happening? That Henry's sourpuss expression was commonplace? If I responded in my favorite fashion – with sarcasm – would he still find me amusing or would it make things worse? Was I supposed to remind him the mood swings were as normal as they were temporary? I had no idea how to act, or for that matter, how to help, so I did nothing. I kept my mouth closed and my body horizontal. The simplest way not to engage with Henry was to pretend I was sleeping. It was weak, I know, but I was scared. And so unbelievably helpless.

I passed the time leading up to Henry's surgery in one of three ways: writing letters to Maggie, and a couple to my grandparents – which were getting harder to compose, having to mask my entire life while trying to get a few upbeat lines onto paper – reading dated magazines that Nurse Betty kindly gifted me from her personal collection, and eating every morsel of food placed in front of me so I would have the maximum strength possible once I was allowed to start walking. Writing letters and flipping through magazines allowed me to remain horizontal for much of the day. It had been days since I had looked Henry Winters in the eyes. I felt like a coward, but then again, it wasn't like he was making any effort to communicate with me, either.

Nurse Betty read a lot of magazines, but clearly her favorites were Vogue and Harper's Bazaar. For Mildred VanHoosen's expensive taste in clothes – purchased only for her, of course – I had never seen one of these utterly glamorous fashion magazines in our house. She read My Home and Woman's Own, like all the rest of the ladies in our neighborhood. I tried reading an issue of My Home once and couldn't get past an article that, I swear, was something about not being a wet blanket to your husband. Why would I want to waste my time on something so banal when I could be paging through bewitching magazines dedicated to the most unreal threads I have ever set eyes on? There was no comparison. While I loved Henry with all my heart, if being a wife meant dedicating my days to becoming a better wife, maybe we could just date forever.

I wondered if it was the influence of these fashion magazines that inspired Nurse Betty's glamorous new look. They were certainly inspiring me. Or was Henry, right? Was Betty in love with Dr. Whitlaw? And if she was, why? There was nothing heart-pounding about that man, from my experience. He was only a little handsome, and the bit he possessed disappeared in an instant when he dismissed the patients like we were keeping him from better things he could be doing with his time.

Keeping my distance from Henry had left me feeling as lonely as I did during my first month at Trudeau. The only other person I had to talk to was Betty. And I was dying to know what was going on with her. If only I had a clue how to start the conversation without insulting her again.

As if on cue, Nurse Betty was at my bedside with a little cup holding my pill in one hand, the standard cup of water in the other, and a tube of salve peeking out of her pocket, thank God. With all the extra time on my hands, my hands had been spending it scratching at my rashes. Henry really had a way of taking my mind off the itchiness.

She sat on the edge of my bed, handed me the Isoniazid and water, then closed the Vogue I had been paging through, examining the cover. "This one's from November, Pet. We finally broke fifty degrees today. Last thing I'd want to do is look at winter fashion."

I considered the captivating woman on the cover, wrapped in a sumptuous fur coat with a smart red hat and matching lipstick. She resembled Betty, especially the wideset eyes and porcelain skin. Although Betty's hair was an even lighter shade of blonde.

"I don't mind. I could look at that fur coat all day. Mildred has a fur – actually she calls it a mink – but I'm not allowed within ten feet of it."

"Mildred?" Nurse Betty tapped the back of my hand that was holding the pill, her gentle reminder to take the damn thing.

"You know, my *mother*," I replied, emphasizing the word "mother" to ensure my sarcasm was clearly understood.

"You call your mother by her first name?"

Her surprise was, well, surprising. "How do you not know that? I've been here four months already."

She straightened her little white nurse's hat that already looked perfectly in place. "I don't know. I guess I never heard you say it before. Why don't you call her Mom?"

"Because she doesn't act like one." I threw back the pill without any additional coaxing, but only because the full cup of water had gotten too heavy to continue holding. Betty rubbed clockwise circles on my back while I hacked and hacked and hacked. "I am never going to get used to that," I sputtered.

Betty flashed me a smile that could only be described as angelic. "No, I suppose not."

She took the empty water cup and the little pill cup from my hands and stood. It was apparent she didn't want to push the subject of Mildred, but I didn't want her to leave, either.

"Her lipstick looks like yours," I tried, holding up the Vogue cover for her to see.

She nodded, set the glass and cup on my bedside table, and pulled out the salve from her pocket. "Almost forgot."

As she carefully rubbed the salve up and down both arms, I carefully kept the conversation going. "Did that cover inspire you to wear red lipstick?"

She paused, and I suddenly regretted pushing the subject.

"I didn't mean anything by it."

"It's OK." She went back to applying the salve, and my body relaxed. "I think we're inspired every day, but that inspiration isn't always felt immediately. Under the right circumstances, our mind remembers that thing it had filed away until that very moment it becomes relevant, when it is presented as new thought."

"Whoa, you are a deep cat."

That statement got me the best gift ever from Nurse Betty: a deep belly laugh that doubled her over and caused a tear to run down her cheek. It was ever better than salve.

That was the first time Betty and I connected as friends. Maybe it was stupid of me to think that a beautiful nurse at least ten years older than me would enjoy spending time with a mousy juvenile thing like me, but then again Maggie wanted to be my friend – best friend, actually – so I felt like anything was possible. And with

Maggie so far away and our friendship primarily limited to letter writing for the time being, it was nice to have another friend close by. Sure, Henry was my friend, but he was also kind of my boyfriend, and that fact placed limits on our friendship.

❖

A week into my Avoid Henry Campaign, Nurse Maude stopped by my bedside to deliver a letter. I snatched it from her hands, eager for an update from Maggie. It had been nearly two weeks since there'd been a progress report on the "San Francisco Situation." That's what I was calling it now. It sounded much cooler than, "Where the Hell Is My Two-Named Father?"

I turned over the enveloped and was surprised to see it had no address written on it. With brows knit, I tore it open and removed a thick piece of stationery. I couldn't help but grin once I unfolded it and realized it was a letter from Henry.

My Dearest Dolly (that's you, Marilyn!),

It occurred to me that, while I consider you my gal, we haven't had what one would consider to be a conventional courtship. In fact, we've never had an actual date! Or have I met your parents (har har). So, I thought, if I can't take you on a date, or do some of the other romantic or just plain normal things that couples do, the least I can do is write you a love letter. So please accept this declaration of my love, your first corny letter of many, from your dear ol' Henry. I'm sorry I've been such a crab. I don't blame you from keeping your distance. If you were to pay me a visit, or have lunch with me again in the dining room, I sort of promise to be on my best behavior. What do you say, Dolly? I sure do miss you being around.

Yours (seriously),

Henry

It was the most wonderful thing in the whole world.

Of course, I considered writing back to him, but based on the original letter I tried to compose for Henry, I knew it would be nothing short of a failure. Besides, how could my letter ever compare to the sweetness and perfect timing of his? So, I did something I could do better than Henry: I slowly made my way over to his bed to pay him the visit he wanted, and to accept his invitation to the dining room. Truth be told, I was also hoping for a kiss. Just a little one. But damn, I missed those full lips.

I slid my arms into my unflattering robe, tying the belt tight at the waist, and stepped into my slippers, holding onto the headboard with one hand while carefully reaching down to pull up the back of each slipper onto my heels. Slowly I slid off the bed until all my weight was on my feet. I stood like that for a minute, surprised how amazing it could feel to stand unsupported. In fact, I felt so amazing, I decided to try walking without holding onto anything. It was a scary yet exhilarating plan. Sliding one foot in front of the other, I started my journey across the infirmary floor. My arms wanted to dart out to the sides to steady myself like a young gymnast on a balance beam, but I curbed the inclination so as not to draw any attention to myself. Last thing I needed was a nurse turning me right around and sending me back to bed. Turned out, this trip to Henry's bed was easier than the first. It was exciting to recognize how the pressure on my chest had lightened, and that, even though I was moving like a tortoise, when I finally reached my destination – where I was rewarded with one of Henry's blinding smiles – I wasn't completely zapped of all my energy. I didn't even need to lay down. But I did it anyway.

I was proper, of course, once again staying on top of the covers with my hands in plain view. Although Henry did take one of those hands, clamping his around it and bringing it up to his cheek.

"Thank you for the letter," I tried. I didn't know the state of Henry's mood swings and what might set him off.

"My pleasure, Dolly. Thanks for the effort to get yourself over here."

I turned my head to Henry, my eyes wide, excited to share my progress. "It was actually easier than I thought. I didn't even hold on to anything. This is the first time I feel like I'm getting better. Isn't that the most?"

Henry responded by letting go of my hand and turning his head away from me. "Well, aren't you the most special patient at Trudeau."

If my chest didn't hurt before, it did now. I was an ass to boast about myself while Henry wasn't progressing at all, and facing surgery to boot.

"I'm sorry, Henry, that was stupid of me."

"Nice to hear something smart finally coming out of your mouth."

"Henry!" Desperate to go back to my own bed, I sat up quickly, too quickly, and a dizzying wave came over me, forcing me back down. Clutching my head with both hands, I turned on my side. If I couldn't leave Henry's bed, at least I wasn't going to look at him.

I felt him shift his weight, then a hand on my shoulder. I was relieved for it, and yet, didn't want to give in to it after the way he treated me. "Ah, Marilyn, I'm sorry. It's the steroid therapy. I overreact to the littlest things. You know I didn't mean what I said. Of course, I'm happy you're feeling better." He moved his hand into my hair, instantly calming me. "I love you, Dolly."

My breath hitched and my body tensed, but in the most wonderful way. I closed my eyes and made a silent plea to not roll over and find it was all a dream. Warily, I turned until we were face to face. Henry's face showed worry. I'm pretty sure mine showed deliriousness. "Oh Henry," I said, fighting like mad to hold back the happiest of tears, "I love you, too."

It was the most perfect moment of my life. Right up until I heard the unmistakable voice of Mildred VanHoosen bellow, "What the hell kind of institution are you running here?"

CHAPTER 11
GET BENT

Nurse Maude pushed me into a small, plain office that was outfitted with a wooden desk, a tall metal filing cabinet, and three chairs. The walls were bare save for a Girl Scout calendar. The only real clutter was on the desk where a mass of papers barely left enough room for a telephone, lamp and ashtray. Perched at the front of the desk was a nameplate that read J Mahoney. I didn't have a clue where we were. In fact, I'd never been in this particular part of the building, but if I had my direction right, we were somewhere on the east end.

I could hear Mildred VanHoosen's heels getting louder as she approached. If I could run, I would have. She entered the room, surveyed the space, and pushed one of the chairs out of the way before taking a seat in the farthest one. Nurse Maude moved me into the open space and activated the wheelchair brake with her foot then disappeared. Lucky Maude. Mildred VanHoosen did not speak or look in my direction. I focused on tearing at the skin alongside my nail.

After a few of the longest minutes of my life, in walked a portly man with a deep side part and the thickest hands I've ever seen who I could only suppose was J Mahoney. He went straight to the filing cabinet, thumbed through a number of manila folders, and pulled one out, tossing it onto the paper pile on his desk. He sat down and began paging through the file, his dexterity seemingly not affected by his chunky fingers.

"Mrs. VanHoosen, I understand you have an issue with your daughter's care here at Trudeau?" He folded his hands on top of the file and looked at her with disinterest.

"You're damn right I do," she snapped, crossing one trim leg over the other. "I arrived here today to visit with my only child to find her in bed with a boy. A boy! How could you allow such an immoral thing to happen? Do you know how much money I give to you in return for her care?"

J Mahoney pawed at his forehead, clearly uncomfortable with Mildred VanHoosen's barking. "On behalf of Trudeau Sanitorium, I apologize for the shock you experienced upon seeing your daughter in what could easily be perceived as an indecent situation. However, I spoke with the nurses on the floor at the time and they all assured me that absolutely nothing immoral was happening between your daughter and, uh..."

"Henry," I said, causing Mildred VanHoosen's head to whip around at me.

"You don't get to talk."

"Yes," he went on, "Henry."

"Of course," Mildred VanHoosen interrupted. "Because they're watching my teenager's every move twenty-four hours a day." She opened an off-white purse with a clear top handle that I had never

94

seen before and pulled out a cigarette. J Mahoney leaned over to hand her the pack of matches that was sitting in the ashtray. I couldn't close my mouth as I watched her coolly place the cigarette between her lips, strike a match, and set the end ablaze. She inhaled deeply, her chin lifting as she did so, and blew out the smoke in my general direction.

"You smoke?" was all I could think to say.

She ignored me and went on with her ranting. "I want to know how you can allow any patient to get in another patient's bed. This is a hospital, for God's sake."

"Technically, it's a sanitorium," J Mahoney mumbled.

"I don't give a damn what it is," she said, tapping ashes on the floor instead of the easy-to-reach ashtray. "You have a responsibility to your patients and their families." She took another big drag and exhaled directly at J Mahoney. "Now, what are you going to do about it?"

J Mahoney sat back in his chair, which groaned with his weight. "I'll send out a memo to the staff that patients may not get into each other's beds or else there will be disciplinary action. Will that satisfy the situation?"

Mildred VanHoosen smashed the rest of the cigarette into the bottom of the ashtray, and leaned her arms on the desk. "Not even close."

I sat up in my new bed with arms crossed and expression even more cross. My new location? The farthest bed in the infirmary, set mere steps away from the bathrooms – close enough to be disturbed when toilets were flushed. And close enough to smell every vile odor wafting from underneath the doors. Apparently, this satisfied the situation for Mildred VanHoosen. Rather than allow me a little happiness while convalescing at Trudeau, which let me reiterate was *her fault* in the first place for not getting me the medical care I needed when I first needed it, she'd rather have me lonely, angry, and smelling rank shit all day.

Mildred VanHoosen was the biggest witch who ever walked the Earth.

Nurse Betty woosh-wooshed in my general direction, and I turned my head toward the bathrooms, hoping she wouldn't notice me, or if she did notice me, would get the hint that I wasn't up for friendly banter. It wasn't really that I didn't want to talk to her. I was afraid if I opened my mouth I would start crying and I'd never be able to stop.

"Marilyn, what are you doing down here?"

No luck. I was going to have to answer. I turned in her direction, and when our eyes met, my eyes welled with tears. With tight-pressed lips, I shook my head as my cheeks dampened.

She frowned. "Don't move; I'll be right back." Pivoting on her heel, she took off for the doors of the infirmary with impressive speed.

I adored Nurse Betty and knew without a doubt she saw herself as my protector. But neither her concern nor her fetching looks were going to get me out of this one.

Somehow, amidst my fury and resentment, I managed to fall asleep sitting up. I suppose hatred takes a lot out of a tuberculosis patient. Thanks to sleeping in such a screwy position, my neck was now stiff down the left side, and while attempting to stretch it out, I made eye contact with the woman in the bed next to me. She was about thirty and hard looking, with short, black hair that curled just a little at the ends, and deep-set eyes that seemed suspicious of everything. She was thin and pale and staring at me.

"Can I help you?" I wanted to be the first one to be combative. I didn't care how much older than me she might be.

"Your mom is one hell of a bitch."

I had found my new best friend.

Her name was Joan, which suited her. She had been at Trudeau for exactly one week and was just as miserable as I was when I first arrived. As miserable as I was again. She was a poet and a musician, and was the lead singer in a band with four men, touring the East Coast in a station wagon towing a trailer that held their instruments.

She was living the coolest life ever. I was sure she would be enthralled to learn about my ridiculous little life. Although I had finally kissed a boy. Huge for me, but pathetic for a worldly woman like Joan, who had probably kissed every guy in the band.

I don't know what made me share my life story with Joan, but I did. Maybe she felt trustworthy. Maybe I hoped to impress her with the screwed-up lives of the VanHoosens. All I know is, once I got through the telling, it didn't much matter that I had never danced with a boy and only just had my first kiss. My life was as dramatic as one of Mildred VanHoosen's soap operas. Based on Joan's wide, less-suspicious eyes and gaping mouth, having your own mystery to solve really makes a girl more interesting.

A half hour of enjoyable, sarcastic banter with Joan and I was feeling better, despite Mildred VanHoosen still being somewhere on the premises. Despite being sixteen beds away from Henry. At least I would be able to see him later that afternoon on the porch chairs. That was better than nothing. And while my new neighbor, the toilets, were a literal crappy situation, maybe it would make things easier between Henry and me to have a little distance. I loved being able to look at him any time I wanted – sometimes a flash of his smile was enough to get me through itchy rashes and harsh sponge baths and choking on pills. But it also meant he could see me scratching my rashes raw and clumsily trying to cover up my partially exposed body and dry heaving horse pills. Not real attractive moments. And even though it was weak of me, it was kind of a relief not to be center stage for Henry's mood swings. It was awful not to be able to do anything to help him, and watching him go into a tirade only made me remember why it was all happening: to prepare him for a dangerous surgery.

My thoughts were interrupted by the clicking sound of Mildred VanHoosen's heels. I could only pray she was coming to say goodbye.

I looked up to see Betty with a wheelchair keeping time with Mildred VanHoosen. "Am I going home?" I was part-joking, part-wishing, and part-terrified that I could be parting ways with Henry with no preparation.

"Dinner time," Mildred VanHoosen said, her voice devoid of pleasantries. She scanned my new location and nodded. At least somebody was pleased. "The nurse," she started, indicating Betty, who was standing at attention behind her.

"Betty," I noted, hating her knack for dehumanizing people.

Mildred VanHoosen clicked her tongue at me. "I said the

nurse..."

"Her name is Betty," I said, rather proud of my defiance.

"Marilyn Louise VanHoosen, be quiet!"

Her eyes locked on something then, deep trenches materializing between her eyebrows. I followed her line of vision to see Joan giving Mildred VanHoosen a look that would have given me chills had it been directed at me. Mildred VanHoosen scowled and dipped her chin. "May I help you?" I immediately disliked how much I had sounded like that the first time Joan looked at me.

"I would never ask for help from you," Joan replied dryly. "You might break a nail."

I suppressed a giggle, ducking my head and pretending to cough.

Mildred VanHoosen turned her attention back to me. "The *nurse* will take you to the dining room. Let's go. *Now.*"

Joan and I made eye contact. She rolled hers. I crossed mine. I couldn't wait to introduce her to Maggie.

The ride to the dining room and the parking of the wheelchair occurred in silence. It was odd for Nurse Betty not to say anything at all to me, especially after I defended her, but I was also well aware that when it came to Mildred VanHoosen, silence was golden. The less you had to interact with her, the better.

Once our meals were placed in front of us, Swedish meatballs and noodles for me, salad and cottage cheese for Mildred VanHoosen, she got chatty. Which is never a good thing.

"The rest of your time at Trudeau will be very different from what you've been allowed."

"Great, so no more rough sponge baths and daily freezing spells on the porch?"

She tapped the tines of her fork on the little bowl of cottage cheese. "You're not as clever as you think, Marilyn."

"I don't think I'm clever at all," I managed with a mouthful of noodles.

Mildred VanHoosen cringed. "As I was saying, your stay here will come with new rules. Most importantly, no more alone time with that boy."

I stopped chewing, and held my mouth half open for maximum disgust. "Define alone time."

"You and that boy will not be in the same space without adult supervision. And yes, that includes close proximity on the porch."

"That's not fair!" I threw down my fork and it bounced across the table, landing on the floor.

"I don't need a tantrum out of you," she hissed. "You want to talk about what's not fair? Try dealing with an ungrateful child with tuberculosis, whose medical care is draining my bank account."

I crossed my arms and stared her down. "We have medical insurance to pay for that."

She crossed her arms, too, clearly mocking me. "No, we don't."

I let my arms fall and leaned forward in the wheelchair, momentarily forgetting my anger. "Why not?"

She sighed and pushed her tray of food away. "It's none of your business. All you need to know is there's no medical insurance. We're going to be in the poorhouse by the time you're finished with your treatment here."

I took a deep breath and let it out slowly. There were things I needed to know and I had to handle it the right way. "What's Dad going to do about it?"

Her eyes darted away and she shifted in her seat. I had never seen her look so uneasy. "Nothing."

"I don't understand."

In a snap she was back to her fierce self. "What's there to understand? Your father isn't going to do anything about it."

"But why not? Doesn't he have a job? Doesn't he get some benefits as a serviceman? Why can't he get us insurance?" I banged my fist on the table, jarring the dishes. "Just tell me what's going on? Where is my father? Where has he gone to again?"

Mildred VanHoosen took her napkin from her lap, dabbed at either side of her mouth, set the napkin on the table and stood. "Your father has left us, Marilyn. We're getting a divorce. Are you happy now?"

CHAPTER 12
THINK FAST

My head was reeling, and I had no chance of sharing it with Henry. Not allowed to be in the same space without adult supervision. What bullshit. In fact, Mildred VanHoosen's whole trip to Trudeau was bullshit. The crap she was feeding J Mahoney about her concern for my care and my morality was just that: crap. If she had cared for me so much, she would have gotten me the vaccine. And taken me to a doctor before I was coughing up blood. And visited more than one time in four months. Or called me, ever. She was an excellent fraud, which I suppose she had to be, having married a man named Pierre who was really named Paul. She had to have known. Paul was my father's legal name. If it was on his birth certificate, then it also would have been on their marriage license. I'm pretty sure she would have had to see it. So why go along with the fake name? Why never tell me? And why would he leave us now?

I may have been paranoid, but I swear the nurses were collectively avoiding me. Every time I tried to make eye contact or wave at one, eyes would unmistakably divert and direction would swiftly change. I didn't blame them. After the browbeating I'm sure Mildred VanHoosen gave to each and every one, I would keep my distance from me, too. But they wouldn't be able to stay away for long. Somebody had to dispense my giant pill. I wondered if they would draw lots to determine who would have the misfortune of delivering it to me.

Worn out from the day's drama, I tried to take a nap, but I couldn't quiet my mind. It kept jumping from one image to another, one thought to another, one jarring truth to another. I missed Henry. I wanted to tell him about Mildred VanHoosen not only smoking – which I had never seen her do before – but also having the audacity to drop the ashes on the floor of J Mahoney's office. I wanted to tell him about seeing her in yet another pair of new pumps that looked expensive to me, though I'm no expert on the subject of fashion. I wanted to tell him how she declared we would soon be in the poorhouse, because we had no medical insurance, and how she claimed she was paying the Trudeau bill herself. And then one single question took over the rest of my mind: why was Mildred VanHoosen buying expensive shoes when we were going broke?

I spent the next two days with no contact whatsoever with Henry, save for low-energy waves to each other while Nurse Doris wheeled me out to the porch to sit in a chair situated on the opposite end of where he was placed a few minutes later. It felt like I would never smile again. Meanwhile, the sun was certainly grinning from ear to ear, spreading its rays like a comforting hug to all us feeble beings lying immobile on a sanitorium porch.

It really was a glorious day, and I wanted to feel something –

anything – good. Closing my eyes, I breathed in as deeply as my lungs would allow without breaking into a coughing fit. They held more oxygen than I expected. I didn't want to give myself false hope, but I was pretty sure my health was improving. In fact, I felt I could probably start walking. At least a short distance. A glossy black bird cawed as it glided across the meadow, ducking for a moment onto a high branch of a towering oak tree that was just sprouting its first spring leaves, before taking off again toward the north. To have that kind of freedom. To answer to no one. To have no rules. No parameters. No Mildred VanHoosen.

I could be like that bird.

With the weather being milder, we were no longer covered with blankets, as that would defeat the purpose of cold cure, and that made it easier for me to sit up and look around for any sign of Trudeau nurses. Fortunately, the nurses really only appeared on the porch to escort patients to and from their beds, meaning a lot of time without supervision. All was quiet on the porch, so I made my move. Slowly, carefully, I pushed myself to a standing position from the low-lying lounge chair. A frail woman stationed next to me with a thick braid wrapped around her head opened her eyes at the sound of my motion, frowned and closed her eyes again, seemingly content with ignoring my obvious rule-breaking behavior.

Feeling steady enough and determined not to hold onto anything for support, I slid one foot in front of the other, getting the feeling of fully supporting my body weight. It was hard, but I wasn't going to stop. I slid my way past three lounge chairs, ignoring the clicking tongues and obvious sighs, before feeling brave enough to actually lift my feet and really walk. It felt like a lifetime, and it was miraculous I didn't get caught along the way, but eventually I stopped at Henry's chair. I tapped the leg of the chair with my foot and Henry opened his eyes, first squinty, as the full force of the sun flooded his vision, and then wide when he realized I was really there.

I put my finger to my lips to keep him quiet, and sat down on his chair by his feet. "I'm sorry we're being kept apart," I said, my voice cracking on the last word.

He reached out for my hand. His arm looked scrawnier than ever. "It's not your fault. When we get out of here, I'm going to have to marry you to get you away from that woman."

I burst into tears and buried my face in my free hand. "That's not funny, Henry." I was terrified he was never going to get out of this place and be able to do anything normal, ever again, but I sure as hell couldn't tell him that.

"I'm not trying to be funny."

Peeking at him through my web of fingers, it was clear he wasn't being funny at all. In fact, I had never seen him look so serious. I kind of understood. If I was facing something as scary as death, I'd want to continue planning my life as if nothing bad was happening. Even if it was fantasy-type stuff. I knew he was being ridiculous, but I had so little to give him, I could at least let him pretend. I could give him that.

I wiped my eyes on the sleeve of my robe and put on my biggest smile. "Well then, I'm going to hold you to that, Henry Winters. When we get out of here, you are going to marry me and take me far, far away from Mildred VanHoosen."

We sat there like that, our fingers intertwined and staring at each other's faces as if desperate to memorize them, until Nurse Betty appeared beside me. Without a word, she put her arm around my

106

back and gently hoisted me up, and surprisingly, allowed me to walk all the way back to the infirmary, with a couple of silent stops along the way to rest. It was in that moment that I knew I loved her. I loved her like a mother. Like I had never loved Mildred VanHoosen.

Betty and I never discussed what I had done, but the next day a friendly man with a dent in his chin and deep set dark eyes appeared at my bedside as I was finishing my lunch and declared we were going for a walk. In my excitement, I nearly knocked my tray to the floor. He held out an arm for me and I gingerly wrapped my hand around it and got to my feet.

"I'm Freddy Flores," he said. He stepped to the side, revealing a strange three-sided thing made out of metal with two small wheels. It was as tall as my belly button. "Isn't it neat?" he asked. "It's called a walking frame. It's a brand-new piece of equipment that, well, guess what it does?"

I was perplexed. "Um, helps me walk?"

He pointed an enthusiastic finger up into the air. "Correct!"

He was really excited about this walking frame. I didn't get what the big deal was since I already knew I could walk. Henry could do a better job getting me to walk than this thing, but I wasn't going to tell Freddy that.

"What's so exciting," he went on, oblivious of my indifference, "is that Trudeau is one of the first places to get one. That's how new they are! Now, let me show you how you'll use it to practice your walking."

I nodded enthusiastically, because I really didn't want to curtail Freddy's excitement. He was so proud. He placed the walking frame in front of me so I sort of stood inside of it, and then he instructed me to place my hands on the side bars and lean my weight into it, slowly pushing it forward and moving my feet behind it. I had to admit, it really did make walking easier.

I shuffled my way through the infirmary with Freddy on my heels, enthusiastically rooting me on, as if I needed any encouragement. When I got to Henry's bed, I stopped and flashed him a bright smile. "Kind of like my first car," I teased. "Am I a good driver or what?" But Henry just frowned and went back to reading the book that was on his lap. I chalked it up to his mood swings and moved along, Freddy chatting away about other exciting new medical inventions that I wasn't listening to at all.

That day, I walked back and forth in the infirmary twice. I was tired but exhilarated when I got back to my bed. Joan said she was envious that I was getting back on my feet while she was begrudgingly trying to get used to being on her back in bed. She admitted that with all the touring her band had been doing, she didn't bother getting the vaccine, a decision she was now deeply regretting. As were her bandmates, as her tuberculosis diagnosis put the tour on hiatus until further notice. Although on a positive note, the fellows in the band were now newly vaccinated and doing just fine.

The next day, right after lunch again, Freddy and the walking frame were ready and waiting for me. This time we walked all the way to the dining room, which was just starting to quiet down from the lunch rush. He suggested we stop in for a rest and picked out a table for us right near the doorway, holding out my chair for me in a way that made me blush. "I'll be right back," he declared and took off in the direction of the double doors that led to the kitchen.

That Freddy sure was a sweet one. He could be a great catch for Maggie, now that I know she likes them older, if she didn't go and fall in love with Ben first, an idea I had been teasing her about in every letter I had written since they had their "proper date". But then again, Maggie was in Philadelphia, and Freddy was all the way up here with me in Saranac Lake, New York.

Freddy returned a few minutes later with two tall glasses of Ovaltine. I nearly drooled at the site of them. Ovaltine was my absolute favorite drink in the whole world. While the other girls in my class dreamed of drinking champagne, I entertained fantasies of Ovaltine at breakfast, lunch, and dinner. It was that delicious. I drank it down without stopping to breath, huffing and puffing once the last drop was gone. Freddy looked amused.

"I guess I picked the right drink."

"I didn't know it was available here!" I gasped, stifling a hiccup.

Freddy looked around then leaned forward. "Don't tell anyone I gave it to you. It's only for the staff. But you did such a good job with your walking, I thought you deserved a little treat." He winked at me and damn it if I didn't blush again.

The day after my big dining room walk, something miraculous happened. It wasn't as miraculous as Henry suddenly getting well, but it sure made me wonder if God not only existed, but also was on my side. Betty was getting me into a wheelchair for cold cure therapy, which at this point was more like room temperature therapy, curing absolutely nothing. I wasn't allowed to walk there, which seemed silly to me, because the only person who could oversee my walking was Freddy. Even though I was still smarting over Mildred VanHoosen's visit and heavy hearted about my forced separation from Henry, getting to walk around a bit had lifted my spirits. Even the sporadic smell of feces seeping from my neighboring bathrooms was less offensive.

As Betty pushed me through the infirmary, I was going on about cold cure therapy in milder weather. "I'm thinking the docs are going to stick all the patients in the kitchen freezers to get us to the temperature necessary for the therapy to be effective."

She chuckled. "Now that's an idea."

We passed by Henry's bed, but he didn't look up, so I didn't call out to him.

We were heading down the dim corridor toward the east porch when Betty stopped the chair, opened a door on the left and pushed me in. It was an empty office with no light source other than the sunlight squeezing its way in through closed metal blinds. "I'm sorry, Pet. I left something behind. I'm going to park you in here while I go fetch it so you'll be out of the way. Just one minute."

Before I could utter a word, she had slipped out the door and closed it behind her. I couldn't imagine what was so important that she couldn't get me out to the porch first before abandoning me. I considered deserting. Now that I could walk, I could get myself out to the porch. Hell, if I rested periodically, I could get myself away from Trudeau. Maybe I could find a family in one of the neighboring houses, claim I had been abandoned on the side of the road by a man who said his name was Pierre but it turned out it was really Paul, and they would take me in and make me one of their own. But Betty was so good to me, I didn't want to scare her, or worse, get her in trouble. And I knew I most likely couldn't yet make it off Trudeau property.

I was getting bored so I decided to work on my strength by using my arms to wheel myself around the office. Clearly the room hadn't been occupied in a while as the walls were dingy and the blinds were covered in a layer of dust. My back was to the door when I heard the

110

handle turn and I whipped my head around, ready to read Betty the riot act. I clapped my hand to my mouth when Henry wheeled in, powered by the one and only Nurse Betty.

"Ten minutes," she said then slipped out again and closed the door. That little devil.

"Hi," I said, suddenly feeling shy. We had never been all alone before.

"Hi yourself," he said, giving me the smallest of grins that quickly disappeared.

I wheeled over to him so we were face to face. "Henry, I miss you so much," I blurted.

He cocked his head. "Do you?"

My jaw dropped. "Of course, I do. Didn't I walk all the way to your chair just a couple of days ago?"

"And ever since, you've been walking on by with ol' Freddy."

I burst out laughing and was rewarded with a scowl. "Is that funny to you?"

"Oh Henry! It's hilarious! You're jealous!"

He put his hands on the wheels of his chair. "That's it. I want out of here." He tried to turn his chair but didn't have the strength to move it more than a couple of inches. Sighing, I pushed up from my chair, walked over to Henry, and lowered myself into his lap, having the good sense (for once!) to plant my feet enough to support the bulk of my weight. "What the hell?" he snapped.

Taking his face in my hands, I boldly kissed him on the mouth. As long as I had all the strength, I was going to make good use of it. "Henry Winters, didn't I recently agree to marry you? How could any girl engaged to a handsome boy like you have eyes for anyone else?"

That brought back the smile.

He reached his hands up and cupped my cheeks, pulling me toward his lips. His tongue encircled mine, instantly warming all my parts. I pulled him as close to me as I could possibly get him, our hearts thumping to a mismatched beat, his knocking harder and faster than mine. Feeling his rapid heartbeat scared me a little. Reminded me of his fragility. Worried me that we wouldn't always be able to make out this way. Push our bodies together this way. So I gave him a little present, loosening my robe and pulling down my nightgown so he could see my breasts. I had never done anything like that in my life and was practically giddy. He eyed them hungrily and reached for one, stroking it gingerly at first then becoming more accustomed, using his whole hand to hold it, massage it. My giddiness turned to excitement. My breath became heavy. When he gently twisted my nipple, I cried out in bliss. I could feel him get hard underneath me, and I couldn't help smiling, proud of what my body could do to Henry Winters.

A light knock at the door startled us, and I pulled up my nightgown and leaped into my chair, frantically pulling my robe closed before Betty's head appeared. "All clear in here?" she asked lightly.

"All clear," I said. I was pretty sure my heart was now racing as fast as Henry's. Henry smiled sheepishly at Betty, his hands strategically placed in his lap.

"Well then, we better get you both to the porch." She pushed open the door to reveal Nurse Maude standing beside her. "Shall we?"

CHAPTER 13
REAL GONE

That whole next week was one of the best weeks of my life. What a thing to be able to say, trying to recover from tuberculosis, the love of my life facing serious surgery, and stuck in a sanitorium, with the mystery of Mildred VanHoosen and my father still looming. But it was true. Every day I got to walk a little bit farther. Every day it got a little more spring like. And every day Nurses Betty and Maude snuck Henry and me into that empty office for brief make-out sessions and very short but very honest talks. It was heavenly.

I didn't want to say I was getting used to Henry's kisses, but by day four I had experienced enough of them to be okay with foregoing making out to instead discuss the plethora of bizarre happenings that occurred during Mildred VanHoosen's visit to Trudeau.

Henry, on the other hand, wasn't as enthusiastic about a day without French kissing (and other stuff), so I placated him by half-sitting in his lap again, but this time letting him slide his hand up my nightgown while I caught him up on everything.

"So, let me get this straight," he huffed while kissing my neck, which made me writhe, "Your mom was smoking."

"Yep." I shrugged his mouth from my skin, hoping to keep him focused.

He frowned at me. "But you never saw her smoke before."

"God no."

His hand squeezed at my bare thigh. "And she was wearing expensive new shoes."

"Uh-huh." God, it was getting hard to concentrate.

"And yet she claims to be running out of money." He inched his hand closer to my underwear.

"Oh yes." At that point I wasn't sure what I was agreeing to.

"And there's no health insurance because your dad has left and now they are getting divorced."

"Mmm hmm." My heart was palpitating, I was so ready to be touched there.

Henry yanked his hand out from under my nightgown and grabbed my shoulder. "That's baloney."

My jaw dropped, half from his reaction and half from knowing I wasn't going to get touched there after all.

"Medical insurance doesn't disappear just because your dad is no longer living under the same roof as you. Even if they got divorced, you as his daughter would still be eligible to receive medical benefits through your father's policy."

I leaned back to get a better look at Henry. "How in the world would you know any of this?"

He pressed those beautiful lips together. "I have one parent who is blind and one with cerebral palsy. I've spent my life in doctors' offices." I tried to stop him, not wanting to cause him more pain from remembering all the hardships, but he waved me off. "Once I was old enough, I filled out all the forms for my folks. I also overheard many conversations between doctors or nurses and patients regarding insurance eligibility, premiums, making insurance claims, and so much more it would bore you right to sleep. But it kind of intrigued me. I realized how hard it all could be to navigate. How scared sick people were over the cost of medical bills. In fact, sometimes I think I'd like to become a lawyer so I could help people with legal matters related to their health issues."

I threw my arms around him. "You never cease to amaze me."

Henry peeled me away and held my wrists, giving me that look I love. "As much as I love to have a beautiful girl hanging on me, we've got to figure out this insurance thing. Why would your mother say you don't have health insurance when her only reason would be that Pierre? Paul? What am I supposed to call him?"

"I guess call him Pierre since that's more familiar to me. Although his name really is Paul."

"I'll call him Pierre. When her only reason would be that Pierre left you both. That would not stop your health insurance."

I bit my lip and thought about that for a minute. "Could he have stopped paying the bill?"

Henry nodded. "That's a possibility. But again, why would he when he knows his only child is in a sanitorium for months, and he knows the magnitude of that expense if there was no health insurance?

I slid back over to my wheelchair, certain my weight must be killing Henry by now, though he would never admit it. "He could have lost his job."

"True, but there are programs in place to ensure medical insurance continues while between jobs. You have to make your payments, but once again, my previous argument still holds. What did your father do for a living?"

"He was in the Navy."

Henry adjusted his position, clearly more comfortable now that I wasn't crushing him. "I mean before and after the war."

"He was in the Navy. He always was in the Navy."

"If he's a service man, then there's no way he's without health benefits." He ran a hand through his silky locks. "Can you ask Maggie to grill...what's his name?"

"Ben. Actually, Lieutenant Commander Benjamin Fowler." My arms were starting to itch again. I had gone too long between salve applications. I hated tearing at them in front of Henry.

"Yes, ask Maggie to grill Ben about health benefits. A fellow serviceman will know."

I leaned forward and grabbed his hands, forgetting the itchiness for a blissful moment. "Henry Winters, you are a genius."

After a woefully boring stint on the porch that at least came complete with a rubdown of salve for my arms, I was back in bed, scribbling a letter to Maggie. The mail had already arrived, so my letter wouldn't be on its way until morning. By the time Maggie received it, executed the next stage of the plan, and wrote back – or even better, called – it could be a week. Or more. And then it would be only a few more weeks until Henry's surgery. That was a lot of waiting and anticipating.

Even though we were hopefully going to get some answers regarding this health insurance mystery, we still had no starting point to explain Mildred VanHoosen's expensive shoes. Two pairs, at least that I knew of. Logic told me if there were two, there were probably more I hadn't yet seen. What the hell was that about? How could she be broke but still buying expensive shoes? My breath hitched just then because I remembered something Maggie said when she came to visit me. There was also a new dinette set in my house. The entire time I lived under that roof, I don't remember my parents ever going out and buying new furniture. What we had wasn't scrappy, in fact it was up to par with what I saw in all my friends' houses, but it had been there as long as I could remember. I get admitted to Trudeau, my father disappears, and Mildred VanHoosen goes on a spending spree. Why?

I needed Maggie to go back into that house and go through the bills.

Taking out another sheet of stationery, I wrote yet another letter to Maggie. She was going to have a busy week. And I owed her big time. When I got out of here, I was going to get a job and buy her the prettiest dress at Macy's.

I knew the next week would move slower than Nurse Doris' sense of humor, so I pledged to keep myself as busy as I possibly could in a tuberculosis sanitorium filled with little action. I convinced Freddy to extend my walks and take them outdoors. In actuality, I still wasn't going all that far, but for me, it felt like crossing a football field. Getting to walk down two whole steps to get off the side porch – with Freddy in charge of my walking frame and me holding onto the railing for dear life – and then onto the back lawn was heavenly. And to walk in the grass, which was still more brown than green (but I wasn't complaining), well, there were no words. Had I been allowed to take off my shoes and squeeze the blades of grass between my toes, I surely would have passed out from the exhilaration.

I worked on my friendship with Joan. Though I knew if we had met outside of Trudeau, she wouldn't have given me a second glance, in here we'd rather hit it off. The moment she confessed she had attempted – and failed – beauty school, I asked her to give me a makeover, to make me look less girlish. When she asked me why I would trust a flunky with my looks, I was reminded how Mildred VanHoosen never allowed me to sport a stylish hairdo or mess around with her makeup, even though every day she was impeccably put together, with regular trips to the salon to have her hair set, and a face that never lacked lipstick, rouge, and powder. She preferred me plain and pale – the exact opposite of her. You'd think I'd be thrilled not to be like her, but it sure would have been fun to play dress up with my mom like other girls did.

I sighed. "How much worse could it be than what I have now?" Thankfully, Joan eagerly agreed. We paged through magazines from Betty's collection, trying to figure out the right hair style for me. Joan also promised to teach me how to apply makeup, though she warned she wouldn't let me "overpaint my face" as she said I was too much a natural beauty to go and cover it all up. That made me grin like an idiot. A natural beauty, ha!

I also made the most of every make-out session with Henry, and by that I mean I gave up on chatter altogether, save for an "I like that," or "Try up and down like this," so we could dedicate all our time to kissing and experimenting. To say I was trying to remain virtuous and not think about having sex with that boy would be a lie. In fact, I was thinking about it every minute I wasn't thinking about Mildred VanHoosen and my father, or Henry's surgery. I knew there was a chance Henry wasn't going to survive the surgery.

He was so weak and the operation was serious. That meant there also was a chance I would never get to have sex with Henry Winters. And that didn't seem fair. Because based on the way he kissed me; the way he touched me that was both gentle yet commanding; the way I responded to him – I knew going all the way with him would be the most. Henry Winters was the most. Life was too fragile to save myself for an idea that may never have existed in the first place. Since Henry was the one who brought out my boldness, giving myself to him would be the boldest thing I would do. But before that happened, I would have to do one more bold thing: tell Betty what I was planning to do, and convince her to help me make it happen.

I waited, restless, jittery really, in my bed for Betty to come around with my medication and salve. And hopefully a primer on the birds and the bees. Oh, I had picked up some stuff, mostly in the girls' bathroom at school, but I wasn't sure I could trust it. What girls said in public bathrooms were often puffed up to unbelievable proportions. And, ironically, while I was here at Trudeau, the girls in my grade were getting their etiquette class, which typically happened in springtime. The teachers must have figured all the kids were especially primed for blooming right in time with the flowers. Etiquette class – I heard – was embarrassing as hell but useful, with lessons on dating, what to say to a boy when he walked you to your door, and the like. I had no experience with any of this stuff, and now I was having to fumble through it on my own. Marilyn's Crash Course for Hitting All the Bases. And I was due for a home run.

"OK, I have given this a lot of thought, and I believe your best hairstyle is Audrey Hepburn," Joan said, startling me from my thoughts. "That pixie is cute as can be and you would be, too."

I made a sour face as my response, and Joan let the magazine close in her lap as she shifted onto her side to better glare at me. "Are you doubting me?" she asked, her tone mocking.

"Me with hair that short? Might as well change my name to Mark, because everyone is going to think I'm a boy."

"Fine, girl with her own mind." Joan tossed the magazine onto my bed. "What do you think?"

I picked up the magazine and examined it. It was a recent issue of Vogue with no dog ears or torn pages. It was practically a treasure. Flipping through pages of spring fashions and the newest red lipsticks, I landed on a blurb for an upcoming film called "High Noon" with a photo of the elegant and bewitching Grace Kelly. I first saw her on screen last year when my father took me to see "Fourteen Hours". Her role was small, and I was already suffering the symptoms of tuberculosis. (Mildred VanHoosen said it was a cold and to grow up.) But even unwell, I was dazzled by Grace Kelly's beauty. Her presence. Her gracefulness. Never was there a woman so appropriately named. Now she had a new movie and a larger role. There was no doubt she was going to be a big movie star. And she had enviable locks, shorter, but still feminine with a bit of a bouncy curl at the ends. I wanted my hair to look just like hers, but how would I ever pull that off on my own? Joan may be able to give me the right cut, and I'm sure she would show me how to style it just so, but expecting me to replicate it? That was as messed up as my Isoniazid dreams.

Still, I showed Joan the picture and she nodded her approval. "A most elegant choice. You'll look like a dream."

"Will it be hard to maintain?"

She took the magazine from me and examined the hairstyle. "A little, but it's all about getting the hang of pin curls. Once you get comfortable doing them, you'll be able to pin your own hair with your eyes closed."

"Might have better results that way."

Betty wooshed in our direction, making all the blood drain from my face. There was concern in her eyes when she made eye contact with me.

"Are you okay, Pet?" She placed a soft hand on my forehead. "You're not warm, but you are pale."

I flashed her my biggest smile to reassure her. "I'm fine." I leaned forward to whisper so Joan wouldn't hear. "But I kind of need to talk to you."

Betty sat on the edge of my bed. "What is it?"

I looked around, feeling unsure. "Is there a more private spot? This is kind of embarrassing."

She nodded, helped me out of bed, and led me the few steps to the girls' bathroom. Like I said, all the sex talk happens in the girls' room. Once inside the peach-colored cramped space that held a tiny shower stall, toilet and sink, she locked the door. "Now I'm curious."

I sat on the toilet seat to conserve my energy. My heart was racing, but it wasn't from the brief walk. Saying the words was terrifying. I took a deep breath, closed my eyes, and then opened them, staring directly at Betty. "I want to have sex with Henry before his surgery."

She had to steady herself using the porcelain sink before she could respond. "Oh, boy."

"Betts, it could be my only chance."

"To have sex?"

I sighed. "To have sex with Henry."

Her expression relaxed. "Oh, honey. You must be so scared." She leaned over and embraced me so lightly, she pulled me up from the seat.

"I love him, Betty."

She tucked one side of my hair behind my ear. "I know you do, Pet. But that doesn't mean sex is the only answer. What if you got pregnant?" Her eyes got misty and my bottom lip started to quiver watching her become emotional over me. "I would never want you to have to rely on your mother if there was a baby. You'd never be free of her." She wiped away a tear, and in watching her do so, I became the baby. A sobbing, brokenhearted baby, who would never have the mother she wanted.

CHAPTER 14
PUNCH IT

Much to my surprise, Betty agreed to help. But only if I agreed to use a condom. Learning how one of those things works was nothing short of mortifying, especially watching Betty carefully slip it over the top half of a rather large banana. There was a piece of produce I'd never look at the same way again. She would supply me the condom and a spot more private than the empty office Henry and I had been using for our make-out sessions. After that, I was on my own.

She also agreed to find me some sharp scissors so Joan could cut my hair, and a razor so I could finally shave my legs and armpits. I was not going to have sex for the first time and be hairier than the boy.

It's possible I was more excited for my haircut than I was to have sex. The idea of having sex was enthralling, intimidating, and terrifying, all at the same time. The haircut, on the other hand, was a good and necessary idea. I was preparing myself to do something so adult-like, it was time to say goodbye to my childish looks.

I asked Joan to do it before I had to head out to the porch in case today was the big day. The less people who knew I was getting ready to lose my virginity, the better. This was not going to end up sanitorium gossip.

I went over to Joan's bed for my haircut, since her energy level was low enough to rival Henry's. I felt bad that my clipped hair would most likely get all over her sheets, but she didn't mind.

"Are you ready for this, Marilyn?" Joan's voice sounded week but there was energy in her eyes.

"You bet." I forced myself not to cry out when the first lock of hair fell onto the bed beside my hand. I hoped this wasn't a mistake. She took her time, barely saying a word to me except for "Turn a little to the right," and "Try not to fidget." I don't know how I could have been fidgeting, when I felt like I had been holding my breath for the entire length of the cut.

She had me turn once more to face her, so she could work on the front. It was only then that I could see how hard and fast her chest was rising and falling. "Are you sure you want to keep going?"

She smiled, but I could tell it was fake. "Sure," she assured me, "why wouldn't I?"

"You're exerting an awful lot of energy. I don't want you to get sicker over a stupid haircut."

She set the scissors on the bed and cocked her head. A drop of sweat escaped from her hairline and slid the length of her face. "You calling my haircutting stupid?"

"Oh...no, I..." I liked Joan way too much to insult her.

She offered a slight grin. "I'm fooling with you, kid. Although you don't look like a kid anymore. Now you look like a sexpot." She breathed in and out deeply. "Go take a look."

I scurried as fast as I could scurry to the bathroom, locked the door with the light still out, counted to three, and then flicked the switch. The mirror reflected back a stranger; a more mature, certainly more experienced woman. And that was without the added charm of pin curls and setting spray to hold it all in place. Once those were set, Henry was going to have to be fastened into his wheelchair to hold back from me.

Whipping open the bathroom door, I sauntered back to Joan, trying to move with a sophistication that matched my hair, hoping I didn't look as awkward as I felt, my hips sashaying like Betty's. But when I reached Joan's bed, I could see she was in distress. She was on her back, dripping in sweat and her eyes didn't seem able to focus. "Joan, can you hear me?" I screeched, placing my palm on her perspiring forehead.

A crotchety man two beds down, who obviously didn't approve of my hysterics, snapped at me to keep it down. If I wasn't so panicked, I would have pointed out to him that his yelling rivaled my own and maybe he should take his own advice, but I was so worried for my new friend, I didn't have the heart to lash out.

Our combined noise drew the attention of Nurse Maude, who scurried over and asked me to step aside. "What happened to her?" she asked me.

"I'm not sure." My heart felt so high in my throat that I could swallow it back down. "She was cutting my hair and breathing kind of heavy. I went to the bathroom for a split second and when I came back, she was like this."

Nurse Maude loosened Joan's nightgown and then took her pulse. When she was done counting, she scowled at me. "She's too sick to be cutting your hair. What a foolish thing to do."

A sob stuck in the back of my throat. "I didn't know she wasn't supposed to do that. Nurse Betty gave her the scissors." As soon as the words spilled from my mouth, nasty as vomit, I desperately wanted to take them back. Tears streamed down my face, as much for Joan as they were for my cowardly finger pointing at Betty. Betty, who had done so much for me. Betty, who was about to give me the greatest gift of my life. I gave her up to spare me a slap on the wrist. I was a terrible person. Maybe I was no better than Mildred VanHoosen.

Dr. Whitlaw sped toward us, sliding an arm into the empty sleeve of his white coat as he arrived. In his grasp was an oxygen tank, and I watched in silence as he secured the nasal catheter around Joan's head and turned a knob on the tank to release the flow.

While Dr. Whitlaw leaned in to examine Joan, Nurse Maude grasped my shoulders and gently pointed me in the direction of my bed. "You should lay down," she commanded with a whisper. "You've had plenty of excitement for one day."

I obeyed and got into bed, but I never took my eyes off of Joan. I was responsible for her condition, not Betty. It was me Joan was taking care of when she should have been taking care of herself.

After a few minutes, Dr. Whitlaw straightened up and pulled the nubs of his stethoscope from his ears. "She needs the iron lung. Prepare to move her."

"Yes Doctor," Nurse Maude said, scurrying away as Betty came onto the scene. She didn't look herself. Then I realized her hair was flatter than usual. And she was missing her red lipstick. Maybe she had taken a nap or wasn't feeling well. I hoped she wasn't getting sick. I needed her to help me with my plan for Henry.

God, I was a horrible, horrible person.

I lay as stiff and still as a wooden board, watching as Nurse Maude returned with a gurney and two men with nice muscles. The men were in charge of carefully lifting Joan and setting her onto the gurney with the gentleness of a kindergarten teacher. As they moved her, long strands of my hair flitted from the sheets, landing about their feet. I hoped they were too focused on Joan to notice. Once they left the infirmary, I planned to scoop it all up and trash it in the bathroom wastebasket. Who didn't want to hide their guilt?

I may have had my new hair, but suddenly I couldn't bear to think about sex with Henry while Joan was stuck in some iron lung. What the hell was that, anyway? It sounded heavy and terrifying.

Just then, Freddy came bounding over, walking frame in hand. "Why hello there, Miss Marilyn. Whoa! Look who got herself a new hairdo!" He actually stopped talking for a whole minute to really focus on my hair, which wasn't mortifying at all. "Very flattering, if I do say so myself," he announced, his expression fixed in a smug grin. "So, glamour girl, are you ready to go a little farther today?"

I scratched at my arm and sighed. "Can we skip it today, Freddy? I'm not in the mood."

Freddy's never-ending state of euphoria wasn't bothered in the least by my lack of desire. "Nonsense. A good dose of sunshine will do you good. We're going to walk over to one of the cottages today."

That got my attention. I sat up in bed. "The cottages? Why"

He put his hands to his mouth like a megaphone and whispered loudly, "I hear somebody's getting sprung from the infirmary soon."

A shock of panic stabbed me just below the breastbone, radiating from the top of my breasts to a good two inches below my navel. I must not have looked so good because Freddy's overarching smile vanished. "You all right, Marilyn? You're a little green."

That was my cue. "Not really, Freddy." I moaned for good measure and laid back down with great effort. "Not feeling well at all. Can I get a raincheck?"

"Well, sure thing. Don't want to push you if you're under the weather. But let's definitely plan to get over to a cottage tomorrow. You're going to love it there. It's like another world from the infirmary!"

"Sure Freddy. Tomorrow." I closed my eyes. I couldn't stand to talk about it a minute longer.

I kept the under-the-weather thing going for the rest of the day. I couldn't see Henry; was too scared to talk about Joan. And I sure as hell didn't want to know about the cottage and my relocation there. When I first got here, all I wanted was to be placed in one of the cozy-looking cottages. I would have been housed with a smaller group of girls in less sterile-looking conditions. They seemed less like a place for sick people and more like a resort. I could easily have pretended I was on a vacation away from Mildred VanHoosen. But because I was so ill, there was no choice but to put me in the infirmary, filled with the sickliest patients, men and women, mostly old. Sponge baths and weird sounds in the middle of the night. Over the course of five months, however, it had, surprisingly, become my home. It was where Henry was. It was where Joan was. My God, it was where Betty was. I couldn't be without all of them. I just couldn't.

That night, after most of the infirmary patients had gone to sleep, a woosh-wooshing announced that Betty was still here and coming to see me. I was pretending to read by the dim light of my little lamp, but really I had been lost in thought ever since Joan was wheeled away. I hadn't seen Henry or made it to the porch that day, which was how I wanted it. While I wasn't into acting like a martyr – that was Mildred VanHoosen's preferred persona – I truly felt like I didn't deserve to have anything good happen to me for the rest of the day.

The weight of her body settling onto the edge of my bed was her only hello. It wasn't like her to be so quiet. For that matter, it wasn't like her to hang around Trudeau after her shift. What if she had gotten fired and was here to say goodbye?

Unable to stand the silence anymore, I flopped onto my back and reached for her hand. "Did you lose your job because of me?" My lower lip was already quivering.

Her head jerked back. "What? No, Pet. What would give you that idea?"

"Well, it's way past the end of your shift and I told Nurse Maude you gave Joan the scissors." I squeezed her hand. "I'm sorry I ratted you out like that. I didn't mean to."

Betty pressed her lips together and looked at me for a moment, as if she was trying to take in all of me. Making sure she wouldn't forget. "You didn't rat me out. You told the truth. Nurse Maude was wrong to scold you. It's not your job to know the health of every patient."

The relief made my body feel light. "You didn't get fired."

Betty pulled away from my grip, which I realized had gotten much too tight, and patted my hand. "No. And I didn't get into trouble, either. There wasn't anything wrong with me giving Joan those scissors. Cutting with scissors is considered minimal activity and Joan was allowed minimal activity." She leaned in while keeping a watch for any prying ears. "Between you and me, I don't think any of us knew she was that sick. Even Dr. Whitlaw."

I pulled myself to a seated position. "That makes me feel better. But what about Joan? What will happen to her now?"

"Joan will have to stay in the iron lung for a while." Betty unpinned her paper cap and laid it and the bobby pins between us on the bed.

"I don't know what an iron lung is, but it sounds awful."

She nodded. "It's kind of awful, but it has a very important job. When breathing becomes too difficult, an iron lung can do the breathing for you."

My eyebrows jumped at that. "Really?"

She smiled. "Really. It's a long chamber shaped like a tube that you lie in, with your head sticking out one end. It's not very fun and you really can't do much of anything, but it will do the breathing for Joan while her lungs rest and she gets healthier. Once that happens, she should be able to come out of the iron lung and breathe on her own again."

"Should?" My voice hitched.

Betty's expression turned grave. "There are some people who have to spend the rest of their lives in iron lungs." She ran her hand along my rashy arm as I nervously played with her paper hat. "But that's typically in polio cases. Specifically, people with permanent paralysis. I don't see that being the case with Joan at all. Would you like to visit her tomorrow?"

I beamed and nodded. "Do you know how many times since I got here that I've wanted to give you a hug?"

Without hesitation, Betty pulled me toward her and bestowed me the greatest hug I'd ever been given. "I'll take one of your hugs anytime, Pet." She stood, straightened her skirt, and picked up the hat and pins from the bed. "Now you get some sleep, you hear me? You have a big day ahead of you. First, you have a visit with Joan, then you have to practice your walking, and then...you will receive your wish."

Joan may have been the one to need the iron lung, but in that moment, I wasn't sure I'd ever be able to breathe again.

CHAPTER 15
ROYAL SHAFT

The next morning was a Friday. The only way I was able to keep track of the days of the week at Trudeau was by Betty's schedule. She had enough seniority that she didn't have to work most weekends, unless she was covering another nurse's shift, which she did from time to time. It occurred to me that I really knew nothing about Betty: I had no idea where she lived, who she lived with – I didn't even know her last name. What did that say about me that I knew nothing about one of my favorite people in the world? I promised myself I would learn at least one thing about her life before the day was over.

That day was the first I was allowed to start taking my meals in the dining room. A cute candy striper pushed me over there for breakfast. I still didn't understand why I could walk every day with Freddie, but otherwise I still had to use that stupid wheelchair. But there were a lot of things I didn't understand about Trudeau, like why a teenage girl could have a cranky old man gassing up the bed next to her

Eating in the dining room had its pros and cons. The big pro was monumental: No trying to swallow down my food while surrounded by sickly people getting sponge baths or pushing out their bowels on a bedpan. But the major con was that I didn't have anyone to eat with, and eating by yourself in a dining room was way lonelier than eating by yourself in your bed. If only Henry were healthier. As I scooped up a forkful of fluffy eggs, I thought about the one time Henry and I had lunch together here, when I tried to hit him with a broccoli floret that missed and pegged the chair of some wet rag. We laughed like idiots over that guy's reaction. It seemed like a lifetime ago. In some ways, so much had changed since then. And then some things hadn't changed at all.

After breakfast, I got to visit Joan. She was located in a small, windowless, all-white room with one other girl who was also stuck in an iron lung. It turned out to look exactly as Betty had described it. The iron lung was like a mini submarine with Joan's entire body inside save for her head, which rested on a little ledge. Joan and the other girl were having a lively chat when I rolled in, and I was grateful she had good company and was in decent spirits.

"Marilyn!" Joan called out when she noticed me. I half expected her to hold her new prison sentence against me and never speak to me again. My sigh of relief must have been vociferous, because Joan and the girl looked at me then at each other and laughed. "I told Dotty you were probably blaming yourself for my new outfit," Joan chuckled.

I looked at them both and swallowed hard. Why was it bothering me that they were both in such good moods?

The same candy striper that had gotten me to breakfast parked my chair just in front of Joan's head so she could see both Dotty and me without having to turn her head.

"How are you?" I asked. It was the only thing I could think to say.

Joan and Dotty looked at each other and burst out laughing. My level of comfort was plummeting.

"Don't you worry yourself, kid, I'm fine. I was a little frosted when they first locked me up in this tin can, but then I understood that it's only for little while, and it might actually speed up my lung healing more than just hanging out in bed all day. Which means I can get sprung from this joint even faster. Isn't that a gas?"

"A real gas," I agreed.

"And in the meantime, I get to hang out with Dotty, who's into music like me."

Dotty's response was to break into song, softly crooning Rosemary Clooney's "Come On-A My House." Before I could say anything, Joan joined in, singing the harmony, the sound surprisingly full considering their matching armor. I sat there picking at my nails and feeling stupid while they worked their way through the entire song. Clearly, this duet wasn't going to expand into a trio. Not that I could carry a tune anyway.

I couldn't believe it. I was jealous. Again. This time of people relegated to iron lungs. It was all I could do not to blurt out that I would soon be engaging in secret sex with Henry, just to get some attention. But I didn't. It seemed juvenile and I wanted so much to be sophisticated and experienced.

I passed another half hour with Joan and Dotty, mostly smiling pleasantly while they completed each other's sentences, before excusing myself for my daily walk. I was annoyed in there, but also still convinced I singlehandedly landed Joan in that sardine can, so

I really had no room to complain that Joan had found someone whose friendship she preferred over mine. They were closer in age and had that musical connection, so I shouldn't have been surprised, but Joan was the first real girlfriend I had found at Trudeau. I didn't include Betty in that category as she had become more of a parental figure, although she may not be too enthused about that, being too young and beautiful and single to ever be confused as the mother of a pain-in-the-ass, foul-mouthed teenager.

Even though I had no desire to explore the potential cottage phase of my imprisonment at Trudeau, I knew perfectly well if I didn't take that walk today, a far bigger (and more life changing) step would not happen for me later that afternoon. I was sitting on the edge of the bed with robe tied tight and slippers securely on when Freddy arrived.

"Somebody's eager to visit the cottages," Freddy sing-songed as he positioned the walking frame for me.

"Somebody's eager to see Henry naked," I sing-songed in my head.

We shuffled through the infirmary, past a sleeping Henry, down the long hallway, and out the back doors without stopping once. That was progress. I agreed to rest only after climbing down the two steps to the grounds. I wanted to walk through the grass, but Freddy insisted we take the walkway to the cottage. Trudeau procedure, he said.

That extra distance to get to the closest cottage was the farthest I had walked with Freddy. And it was taking a toll. I wanted desperately to be back in my shitty little bed. I was worried I would use up my remaining energy getting back to the infirmary and not have any gas left in the tank for sex. While I had no real point of reference, I was fairly confident that act was going to be draining.

The cottage we were visiting was really quite lovely, with hooded gables and rows of thick cobblestone reaching up from the foundation. Orderly white columns effortlessly bore the weight of the low roof that covered the front porch, giving the building a cozy, intimate feel. It would be my dream house if it weren't on the grounds of a tuberculosis sanitorium.

What surprised me – other than the seven stairs I was expected to climb to get into this cottage, which Freddy told me was called Ladd – was the imposing stone chapel set two buildings to the right. From my limited perspective from the infirmary porch, I never saw this view. Or a few of the other buildings from diminutive to imposing that dotted the landscape.

"That's Baker Chapel," Freddy noted, following my gaze. "It's just as grand on the inside." He turned back to me and dipped his chin. "I could take you there sometime."

Was it my dopey imagination or did this guy like me a little?

"Maybe sometime, Freddy," I said, having no real intention of stepping foot in that, or any, chapel. God wasn't exactly my best friend at the moment. I wasn't in the mood to do him any favors. Or let Freddy think I liked him back, although I had to admit he was somewhat dreamy. His only downfall was not being Henry.

It took all the effort I could muster to get up those stone steps to the cottage, even with Freddy's arm lodged under both my armpits for support. Freddy knocked on the door while I leaned against a column to catch my breath. We were met with a grinning nurse I never saw before. It hadn't occurred to me there was another set of nurses tending to patients in all the cottages. They must like their jobs way better than the nurses stuck with the super sick in the infirmary.

The first thing I noticed upon entering the cottage was that the women living here were dressed. In their own clothes. They didn't even look like patients. Two of them were set up at a card table in the middle of the room playing bridge, while two particularly lively women, both around Mildred VanHoosen's age, I assumed, sipped tea from delicate cups while engaged in a game of checkers at a wood table, which must have been where they took their meals.

None of them took notice of me, which is good, because I must have looked off my rocker the way I was gaping at them. "Are you sure they're not just on vacation?" I whispered to Freddy.

"Nah," he said, stifling a laugh. "This is what your next months at Trudeau will look like. Isn't it exciting?"

"Months?" My chest tightened at the thought. "But I thought I was getting better." I slumped into a stiff wood chair next to the door. A woman at the bridge table with a too-short haircut that didn't flatter her round face rotated in my direction just long enough to take me in, before turning her attention back to her cards.

Freddy crouched down next to me. "What's wrong, Marilyn?" His genuine look of concern evoked a floodgate of tears I wasn't expecting.

"I don't know!"

It was the truth. I didn't know what was wrong. Or perhaps, I didn't know where to start identifying every single thing that was so, so wrong.

I had already been at Trudeau for five months. How much longer would it take for me to get well enough to be released? Once I was released, how would I see Henry? All I wanted in the entire world

was to be with Henry. I could give up my house, my high school –
even Maggie, if I had to. But God, I did not want to give up Henry.
Not ever. If he meant it, I would marry him. I would marry him
tomorrow in that great stone chapel at Trudeau Sanitorium. Then
we would never be parted.

"Marilyn." Freddy's voice pulled me back to the cottage.
He pulled a hanky out of his back pocket and handed it to me.
"Look up."

Patting my cheeks dry with the hanky, I lifted my eyes, expecting
to see something remarkable. "What am I looking at?"

Freddy pointed to two large windows so far up on the walls they
were practically touching the high ceiling. "They're called clerestory
windows. More usual to see them in a big cathedral rather than a
cozy cottage. Before electricity, those windows were responsible for
lighting the room."

I wrinkled my nose at Freddy. "And?"

"In the darkest of moments, there is always a solution that will
bring the light."

Normally I would have scoffed at such a goofy sentiment. Instead
it earned Freddy the biggest hug I could manage.

On the way back to the infirmary, which we took at a much
slower pace so I could make it, Freddy distracted me by pointing out
other buildings we could see, including "Little Red", a tiny one-
room cottage that was the first built on the grounds, the large
Nurse's Cottage, and the Doctor's Cottage, where Freddy said
Dr. Whitlaw lived with his family. Did Betty know Dr. Whitlaw
had a family? I just had to find out. Or at least get information on
her behalf.

"Dr. Whitlaw is married?"

"Oh sure," Freddy said, placing a hand on the walking frame to make me stop and catch my breath. "He and the Mrs. have three teenage daughters. They're away at prep school, but they come around from time to time, mostly at the holidays."

I tried to imagine Dr. Whitlaw having a normal family life, with dinner around the table with the girls, lively conversation and teasing ensuing. I couldn't see it.

Sure enough, by the time I made it back to my bed in the infirmary, I only had enough energy left to haphazardly pull my blanket up before nodding off where another Isoniazid dream was waiting for me.

I was back in front of my house, at the moment where my father and the handsome man emerged from the taxi. Except this time, the handsome man was Henry. A healthy Henry, all filled out with his hair slicked back and skin glowing. Again, our eyes met, but this time the message was different; it was an invitation to go into the house with them. With a slight nod, I followed them inside and straight up to the attic. Why would we come here?

There were three tall chairs set up in a half circle. My father and Henry sat, and Henry motioned for me to take the last chair. I timidly moved to the chair, knowing their eyes were on me the entire time, and perched on the end of the seat. There was no sense in trying to get comfortable.

There was a large box on the floor in front of us that I hadn't noticed before. I knew that box. It was the PRIVATE box. The box I was never supposed to see. The flaps were wide open like an invitation. I peered inside. It looked like the same pile of papers I had seen before. There was a crinkled yellow paper that was folded in quarters, stuck against one side of the box. I glanced over at my father and Henry. My father was staring straight ahead, as if Henry and I weren't there. But Henry's gaze was fixed on me, and he nodded just slightly – my encouragement to move. Leaning forward, while trying to keep my butt in my seat – as if losing contact with the chair would zap me out of the attic and away from answers – I gingerly snatched the piece of paper and unfolded it. I could only focus on a single word: Undesirable.

A hand on my head shook me from the dream. Betty. I was in a fog but I knew something wasn't right about her.

I rubbed my eyes and sat up. "What time is it?"

"Just after six." She fluffed my pillow with a firm hand then motioned for me to lean back, which I obeyed. "You need some dinner."

"But Henry," I started, my pulse suddenly racing.

"Not tonight, Pet. Too much exertion today." She pulled my sheets taut, and then sat beside me.

For the second time that day, I cried.

Betty embraced me in that way every mother knows how to do. Or should. She held me tight while my body shook. "Shh," she coaxed. "You have tomorrow. He's not going anywhere."

"Yet," I blurted, hating myself for being so weak and needy.

Betty took my face in her hands, her expression stern. "Now you listen to me," she whispered. "He needs you. You are the strong one. You must be strong for him. You give him something to live for, don't you understand that?"

I nodded, not wanted to say anything for fear it would be nothing but blubbering. I hated my stupid bed next to the stupid bathrooms. Joan's bed was now empty and Henry felt like a million miles away. The only good thing was I didn't care about any of the people in the beds around me to worry about what they thought of my sniveling.

CHAPTER 16
GET WITH IT

One would think, on the day that one is going to have sex for the very first time, that having sex would be the first thing on one's mind when one woke up. Instead, I couldn't get the word "Undesirable" out of my head.

Once I noticed the razor on my bedside table, however, everything else fell away. Peering around to make sure no one was paying attention to me, I swiped the razor and slid into the bathroom. Every once in a blue moon, it's handy to have the girls' room within arm's reach.

Letting the water run so it would get hot, I set down the razor, which was rather handsome with its gold head and Bakelite handle, so I could use two hands to lift my leg to the sink. I had used Mildred VanHoosen's razor once before, so I had some idea what I was doing. Including soaping up my leg really well and running the razor along ever so slow and light so I didn't bleed to death on the cold tiled floor.

I took my own sweet time shaving both legs up to the knees, and my armpits, too, which were ghastly to look at in the mirror. While I wanted to do a good job, and be smooth and feminine for Henry, I also wanted to be damn sure that I had plenty in reserve to actually get to Henry this time.

By the time I had rinsed and patted everything dry, taking care to clean every last hair from that beloved, borrowed razor, a good half an hour had passed. My stomach was growling for breakfast – although I had slept in and really it was getting closer to lunch – and I was hoping to take either meal in the dining room with Henry.

A new person was getting moved into the bed next to mine. A man, because, why wouldn't you put a grown man next to a teenage girl in an infirmary? He didn't look like a wet rag or anything, but he did look weak. He was also wearing dog tags around his neck.

I flagged down Maude and put on my robe for breakfast. She arrived with a wheelchair. "No Henry," was her greeting.

I tried to turn back to look at her while feeling my way into the chair. "Where is he?"

"Having a hard day," she answered, while briskly maneuvering me through the infirmary, her shoes squeaking on the linoleum. "He's in with the doctor."

How fun. I would be eating alone, Henry wasn't well, and I would bet a thousand dollars there would be no sex today. I reached down to feel my bare leg and wondered how long it might stay that way.

With all the bad news of late, I didn't have much of an appetite. My eggs got cold and my toast turned soggy while I sat quietly, listening to other patients' chatter in the dining room. It was funny I never considered that other friendships, maybe even love matches, were being made in this sickly place. I was so consumed with my

144

relationship with Henry, and then my budding friendship with Joan, I guess I assumed all the other patients of the infirmary were forsaken and friendless here. Sure, I saw them eating together in the dining room, or sometimes with their ears pressed firmly to the telephone receiver in the hallway. But I guess I never truly *saw* them. They were like extras in a Hollywood movie: surely not the stars or even the supporting cast. They were nameless, not worthy of being listed in the credits. And not worth my attention. I was a terrible human being. Maybe that's why bad news had overtaken even the smallest hint of good news.

Surprisingly, I really missed having Joan in the next bed, for the very short time that she and I had bonded. Now that she was locked up with her songbird sister, our friendship may as well have never existed. The only thing I had to show for it was a good haircut, even if I hadn't yet tried to style it. A haircut that Henry had not yet appreciated, either. Hard to believe when I'd had my new hair for two days and Henry and I existed within the same infirmary. But he'd been sleeping constantly or with the doctor and our paths had not crossed. He hadn't even turned up on the porch.

Maybe he wasn't just having a "hard day." Maybe he was getting worse.

A body slipped into the chair across from me. Betty!

"What are you doing here?" I demanded, knowing darn well it was her day off.

It was possible I wasn't at my best to make observations, but I swear she looked sheepish. "I wanted to check on you, Pet. I know Henry isn't available to you and thought you might be blue."

She placed a brown paper bag on the table, unwrapped it, and gingerly pulled out a white box held shut with twine. Giving it a

145

nudge in my direction, she said, "Open it."

I couldn't help but smile a little. Pulling at the bow, I unraveled the twine and lifted the lid of the box, smelling what was inside before I could see it.

"Chocolate cake?" I said, not meaning to question the gift.

"Not just chocolate cake, but the thickest slice of chocolate butter cream cake you can get from Ebingers's in Brooklyn."

She unfolded the box and handed me a fork. I dug in for a big bite, savoring the sweetness of the icing and the delicate flavor of the sliced almonds that decorated the side. It was a dream.

Betty sat in silence while I devoured that giant piece of cake. Once I had come up for air, I realized I had all but ignored her during my gluttony. Now I was the one looking sheepish.

"Thank you for doing this for me." I couldn't help but to push a little. "When were you in Brooklyn"

Betty untied the red and blue printed scarf that had been keeping her hair in place and ran a hand through her pale blonde hair. "Um, overnight."

I squinted to see the clock on the far wall. "It's not even noon. Why did you come back so soon? How long of a train ride is it from Brooklyn to Saranac Lake?"

Her eyes darted about. "Oh, it's a few hours. Nice trip."

My eyebrows popped up. "I think it's more than a few hours. You would have had to board your train very early this morning. You had enough time to stop at a bakery?"

I had no idea why I was grilling Betty this way, but I knew she was hiding something, and I guess I desperately wanted her to confide in me. I would keep her secret. Just like Mildred VanHoosen kept my father's secret. It was in our blood.

146

She grabbed her scarf and stuffed in it her coat pocket, then stood fast enough to knock her chair over. "I bought the cake last night, if you must know." She picked up the chair and returned it to its proper state. "I had to get back early because I had things to do." She shoved both of her hands deep in her pockets. "Are you satisfied, Marilyn?"

If I could have melted into that chair, I swear I would have welcomed it. Anything would be better than being the focus of Betty's contempt.

"I'm sorry," I whimpered. Scrambling out of my seat, I took off out of the dining room, at my quickest possible pace. Once I was around the corner and out of sight, I leaned all my weight into the armrest of an empty wheelchair that was parked against the wall, my chest heaving from overexertion.

Plopping my backside onto the soft seat, I lifted the break and wheeled myself back to the infirmary, where Maude caught sight of me, grabbed the handles, and pushed me the rest of the way to my bed, refusing to let me stop and see Henry, who was back in his bed and clearly awake. Welcome to sanitorium punishment for being too independent.

Maude put me into bed without a word, then deposited a paper cup of pills into the hand of the new patient next to me before rushing off to fetch him some water. After ensuring he swallowed them all, Maude switched off his light and left us, clearly expecting us to sleep.

I thought about the dog tags he was wearing, and turned on my side to face him. "If I say 'undesirable', what do you think of?"

"My ex-girlfriend," he smirked. "She dumped me for my cousin, Frank."

"Oh, Ha-ha Uh, could it be a word used in the Service? Like, maybe you got a bum leg in the War and can no longer serve?"

His lips pursed as he considered my question. "Well, the one thing that comes to mind is something called Undesirable Discharge. Why do you ask?"

I pressed my palm to my forehead, trying to will my memory to work. What had I seen in that PRIVATE box?

❖

Maude woke me from a deep sleep to transfer me to the chairs on the covered porch. I had to keep myself from crying out when I realized Henry was in the chair next to mine! Once we were alone, we fervently grasped for each other's hand, me having to stretch, as there was no Betty to push our chairs together. We also didn't want to attract too much attention, as most of the nurses were still on high alert after Mildred VanHoosen's visit, and if any of them remembered Henry and I weren't supposed to be near each other, we surely would be separated.

"Dolly I missed you so much," Henry whispered, clearly straining to talk. There was passion in his eyes, but his expression was pained. His body so limp. His hand felt breakable in my grasp.

"I missed you, too." I blinked back tears. "Terribly."

"I could...use a distraction," he huffed. "Got any news?"

"Do I." I inhaled pretty deep for a girl with tuberculosis (and was instantly grateful for the ability to do so), and vomited everything that had happened over the past two days. "I made Joan cut my hair, but that was too hard on her, so Dr. Whitlaw put her in an iron lung, but she doesn't mind because she found a new best friend, also in an iron lung, and we're probably not friends anymore, and now there's a new guy, who took over her bed, and he's wearing dog tags, and he said that discharge goes after undesirable, which is the word I saw on a paper in the PRIVATE box, but only in my dream – I think – and I believe Betty is hiding something, and that something may be in Brooklyn, but I did a bad job trying to get her to confess and as a result she's really mad at me. After she brought me chocolate cake, too."

I panted a bit waiting for Henry to respond, but he was still as a statue, his eyes fixed on my mouth.

"Henry, are you ok?"

He pressed his lips together, suppressing a smirk. It was the first glimpse of cheerfulness out of him in what felt like ages.

"Henry Winters, are you laughing at my expense?"

"Never." He tried to cover a grin. I would have dispensed a playful smack on his arm if he weren't so fragile. "Now," he panted, "let's start with that sexy hairdo." His chest was heaving. "You sure look all grown up, Dolly."

I blushed. That boy did affect me.

It was a good thing I had a lot to say, because Henry needed me to do the majority of the talking. Wanting to entertain him as much as I hoped he might have insight into the Undesirable dream, I didn't leave out a single detail in my storytelling. It turned out, Henry did have advice, but it was like playing Charades to get it out of him.

"Dad."

"My dad?" Henry nodded. "What about him?"

"Assume...discharged...without honor."

"Fine. I can do that. But why?"

He shivered, even though it was June. I let go of his hand, tucked his arm next to his body, and covered him as tightly as I could with the blanket.

"That's...the question."

"Figure out why he was undesirably discharged and solve the mystery."

His chest continued to heave. "Yes."

"I know just who to ask." I stroked his hair and leaned in as far as I could, just enough to plant a light kiss on his cheek. "Get some sleep Henry. You've earned it."

We dozed for a few hours on the porch, but only one of us was rudely awakened to practice walking.

Freddy and I muddled along the grounds, me too lost in thought to carry on a conversation, which Freddy seemed fine with. It was oddly foggy out, everything clear enough from the ground up to about our knees, but then nothing but a thick cloud cocooning buildings and trees alike. It was like walking through a spooky story.

We stayed to the path, of course, me barely needing the walking frame anymore. It was only useful when Freddy made me go farther than I cared to, and I needed the support to keep me upright. Just to see what would happen, I stopped, let go of the walking frame, and stepped around it, continuing along the path.

"Nice try, Marilyn, but it's Trudeau policy that you use the walking frame while practicing."

I turned back with fists to hips. "I'm done practicing, Freddy. Let's see what I learned, shall we?"

I continued, despite Freddy's protests. What was he going to do, tackle me and carry me back to the infirmary? I couldn't hear the sound of the walking frame dragging along the ground, which meant he was either carrying it or gave up on it, too.

My footsteps were slow but determined. It was damn good to be completely upright while in motion. Then right in front of me Betty scurried out of Dr. Whitlaw's cottage and into the side door of the Nurses' Cottage, and I tripped over my own feet, tumbling hard to the concrete below.

Turned out it was me who tackled myself, and Freddy did, in fact, carry me back to the infirmary.

Maude gasped when she saw me, which was only slightly worrisome. She ushered Freddy and me into one of the examination rooms, and then hurried back out, promising to return with supplies to clean me up.

I sighed. "How bad is it?"

Freddy grimaced. "The truth?"

"Nothing but."

"You've looked better, Marilyn." He picked what turned out to be a pebble from my skin at the jawline.

"Ow! Freddy! Can you leave that to the professionals?"

"Oh, I'm sure Maude is going to pick rubble from your face much more professionally than me."

I punched Freddy. He deserved it.

"I hate to state the obvious, but if you had listened to me, you wouldn't look like you'd been creamed by a car."

Oh good, now I felt even more foolish. "You're right, Freddy. From now on I will never question your judgment."

Freddy clapped his hands, the sound so loud it reverberated around the small, sterile room. "Excellent! In that case, my judgment says we should be jacketed."

I choked on my own spit, coughing so arduously, I feared I would slip off the table and hit the ground for the second time in one day. Freddy jumped into action, placing an arm in front of me to hold me in place, while lightly patting my back rhythmically. Maude had already returned and was pouring rubbing alcohol onto a towel when I finally caught my breath and shouted, "You want to go steady?"

Maude gasped. "Freddy! You know the rules." She tsked as she went about putting me back together, her eyebrows knitted and lips pressed tight. With rubbing alcohol-filled towel in one hand and tweezers in the other, she set about excising all the stone and debris that had lodged itself into my face and forearms. As she removed, she dabbed the area with the towel, trying to keep me from getting an infection, she said.

Freddy never left the room. He also never said another word.

My mind bounced between Freddy declaring his feelings for me (while I thought he might like me, I also thought it was his job to be nice to all his patients), and Maude's insistence on the rules. If there were such strict fraternizing rules at Trudeau, did they apply to everyone except Dr. Whitlaw?

I was returned to my bed looking like a wounded soldier. The only thing missing was a ribbon of white gauze wrapped around my head and strapped under my chin.

"Fight?" came a voice from the next bed over.

"Eh?" I was feeling a little lightheaded from the pain medication Maude gave me. For once I got to take a pill that wasn't wider than my throat.

"You look like you were in a fight. Did you win?" The guy with the dog tags said.

"I fell on the concrete outside."

"That'll do it." He took a laborious breath. "I was in the war and never looked that bad. Even the time we hit rough waters and I hit the deck. Literally. Lost a tooth, though." His smile was his proof.

"Did you spend any time in San Francisco?" My fingers were crossed under the sheet.

"Nope." He played with his dog tags; the rhythmic scraping of metal almost hypnotic. "I was in Reykjavík."

"Is that some kind of prison?"

The man chuckled. "In a way. It's where I was sent to set up an air base in Iceland."

"It sounds cold."

"It can be. It's not frozen all the time, like you might think from the name. But it doesn't get very warm."

"I think I'd rather be in San Francisco."

"Me too. Or, at least my base in South Carolina. That's even warmer than San Francisco, usually. Why you got that place on your mind?"

I didn't know his name, yet somehow, I felt I could trust this person. There was something about him that made me feel safe.

"What do you have to do to get an undesirable discharge?"

He didn't respond. I sat up to make sure he was still awake. His kind-looking eyes were fixed on me. "That's a big question for such a young thing," he finally said. His shaggy beard covered most of his face, but he looked somewhat young himself. At least not nearly as old as my father.

"I'm seventeen," I said defensively. "Wait, what's the date?"

"Uh, June the fourteenth, I believe. Might want to check with that nurse to be sure."

"My birthday is in three days. I would have missed my own birthday. Missed turning eighteen."

"That's an important one."

"Yes, it is." And then it hit me that I did, in fact, miss something. High school graduation. Which meant I also missed my senior prom.

I had been looking forward to my graduation ever since attending Maggie's the year before. It was a grand occasion, marching in twos out to the football field, while the band played the Pomp and Circumstance March, and the parents waved madly from the stands. The boys wore handsome suits and the girls turned out in pale dresses that hugged the bodice and flared to the knee. I wondered what dress I would have chosen for my own graduation. Maybe a pale blue sleeveless with layers of tulle. I might have looked fetching with my new hairstyle pin curled. And a swipe of red lipstick.

I couldn't even think about senior prom. It was a monumental affair that I had dreamed about since I was fourteen. Who would be my date? What couple would we go with? What would I wear? How would we pose for pictures? I couldn't wait for that day. Couldn't wait for a handsome boy to twirl me around the dance floor, and hold me close for the slow songs. Refill my punch when my cup ran low. Pull out my chair so we could sit and gossip with our friends when we needed a rest from dancing. I had never experienced romance, and was sure prom would be one of the most romantic evenings of my life.

Instead, I spent that day, whenever it actually was, in my thin nightgown in a tuberculosis sanitorium. And there was no place else

I would have rather been.

"It's not the best answer, but an undesirable discharge would include most anything that's not honorable that doesn't cross a line like murder or something," he said, pulling me from my thoughts. "Why'd you ask about San Francisco again?"

"It's where my dad was sent after the war."

"Sent?"

"I guess so."

"Oh."

"Does that mean something?"

He sat up as much as he could and reached out his hand. "I'm Jimmy, by the way. We've never introduced ourselves."

"Oh. I'm Marilyn."

"It's a pleasure, Marilyn." I pretended to shake his hand as I was too sore from my fall to reach. "How long have you been in here?"

"It's my sixth month."

"God help me, I hope I'm out of here in less than a month."

"Don't count on it. I've been told most people stay closer to a year."

"I don't think I could bear that." He let himself sink back into the bed; his eyes cast to that nothing of a ceiling. "How do you get through?"

"Friends," I said without hesitation. "All it takes is one."

CHAPTER 17
WATCHING THE SUBMARINE RACES

Days, even weeks, can fly at Trudeau, which may seem impossible, being stuck mainly on your back day after day in a stark-white sanitorium far from home. But honestly, we slept so much, sometimes we could miss an entire day. Blink, and a week was gone.

Henry was sleeping so much lately, I didn't know how we were ever going to have sex. That and his frail state. My knowledge of sex was limited at best, goodness knows I had no real idea who did what and what went where. Well, maybe I had some idea after my sessions alone with Henry, but I imagined he would need some sort of strength to take part in the act. Then again, as the much healthier one, maybe I could be the one to exert the most energy. At least then, losing my virginity to Henry would still be a possibility.

I was going to need some help.

Betty was acting like nothing had happened between us, so I asked her to take me to Joan and her iron lung for some girl talk. I failed to mention what the talk would be about. I also failed to mention seeing her rush out of Dr. Whitlaw's cottage. She wouldn't tell me why she cut her hair or started wearing red lipstick. I was fairly certain she wasn't going to reveal that she was having an affair with a married man.

What I wasn't certain about was how I felt knowing what I knew about Betty. She had gone from being a parental figure to me – a much, much improved version of any parental figure I had ever known – to another woman with secrets which, if exposed, would damage other people's lives.

Maybe there was a little Mildred VanHoosen in us all.

Thankfully, Joan was alone when we reached the room. Her face lit up when she saw me. Then it turned concerned when she saw my healing face. Betty applied the wheelchair's brake and left us.

"Concrete fight," I explained to get it out of the way. "Where's Dotty?"

"That cat is gone, Marilyn."

My breath hitched. "Dotty is...she died?"

Joan roared. "Marilyn! No! She left. The ol' iron lung really came through for her. Got her well enough that her family transferred her to some other facility closer to home to finish her treatment. I can't tell you how jealous I am."

"Oh." Relief flooded through me. I was glad to have Joan to myself again, and happy it wasn't because her new best friend was no longer on Earth.

"So, what's new, kid? How's that fellow of yours?"

I blushed. "That's what I wanted to talk to you about. Joan. Can you keep a secret?"

"Sure, what's up?"

"I'm planning to have sex with Henry. Here, at Trudeau."

158

"That's no easy feat, but I'm with you so far."

"Henry hasn't been doing so well. He has a serious surgery coming up and, uh..."

"You want to do it before then. Just in case."

"Yes." I paused, refusing to cry. Or outright sob. "Just in case."

"I get that. So, why are you telling me about it?"

"Well, Henry's pretty weak right now..."

"Ah." Joan nodded. "If you want to do it, it will literally be you doing it."

Had I ever been more mortified than this? No. No, I was certain never in my life.

"Yes."

"And..."

"I have no idea what to do."

"Marilyn, you've come to the right person."

❖

I went from Joan straight to the porch until dinnertime, where I stared out at the Adirondack Mountains, carpeted with lush vegetation in every shade of green imaginable, and tried to picture myself doing all the things Joan had instructed. I wasn't a prude. Henry had explored my body with his hands multiple times. And I had done the same to him. I never felt uncomfortable or hesitant. Really, just the opposite. I relished what we did to each other. How our bodies reacted to each other. But to initiate sex – and not just the act itself but all the things Joan told me to do with my mouth –

I felt like a bashful schoolgirl. Which I guess I still was seeing how I didn't graduate with my class.

Joan had asked me to visit her again the next day, and I promised I would. I was going to need more reassurance from her; that was certain. Now that I had trusted her with a secret, maybe I could also trust her to help me figure out just what Betty was doing and why. It was bothering me so much that she could carry on with Dr. Whitlaw the way that she was. I may not have known much about her, but I thought I had an idea about who she was as a person. She was a comfort to me and made me feel less alone, especially in the beginning when I truly was alone, but she shared nothing about herself with me. I decided that would be my focus until the opportunity arose for Henry and me. Uncovering what Betty had been doing might keep my mind off what I would be doing to Henry.

As soon as she retrieved me for dinner, I dug in.

"Where did you grow up, Betty?" I asked while moving from porch chair to wheelchair.

"Florida. But my folks moved to Brooklyn when I was twelve."

I was surprised to get that out of her so easily. Maybe banal questioning was the way. As long as she was being open, I would keep going.

"Was it hard for you to move away from your home?"

She wooshed as she pushed me down the long hallway. "It was hard to get used to winter, that's for sure."

"But you did, eventually."

"Sure. With enough time, we can get used to pretty much anything."

She was right about that. I had gotten used to living in a sanitorium amongst complete strangers. I had gotten used to not

160

having parents around. I had even gotten used to not knowing my father's whereabouts.

"How did you end up here?"

She stopped the wheelchair just before the dining room entrance; the steady sound of dishes clanking over lively chatter telling me it would be hard to find a table of my own. "At Trudeau? That's a story for another time." We started moving again. "Now, let's get you some dinner, Pet."

Could she have come to Trudeau for Dr. Whitlaw? Had their affair been going on back in Brooklyn, now where they escaped to be alone with each other? If I couldn't solve my father's mystery, then damn it, I was going to solve Betty's. One way or another, I was getting to the bottom of something.

The next day was a good one. It began with a letter from Maggie. Her correspondence had been few and far between as of late, and I was desperate for news from back home.

My Dear Friend,

Please forgive me for my silence. After receiving your last letter that described your vivid dream and the word undesirable, Freddy and I went to work to understand how undesirable and the military might go together. And Mari-boo, we found something! There is an undesirable discharge category in the military, including the Navy, which means Pierre.

The good news is that if he was undesirably discharged, it means he didn't do anything really serious like commit a crime. But most likely, he had some sort of misconduct. It's possible he just got in a really bad fight.

It would have to be really, really bad, but I guess that's not the worst thing, right?

Anyways, Ben looked into it, and if Pierre did get an undesirable discharge, then he would not receive veteran benefits. And that would mean Mildred is telling you the truth.

Of course, we had to check it out! Ben and I snuck back into your house. We climbed up to the attic and...

Did you guess it, Marilyn? The PRIVATE box was gone. Do you think Mildred is onto us? I swear we didn't leave anything out of place any time we snooped around the house. But she must know. Why else would she remove the box?

And another thing, Marilyn: Mildred's parents are rich. Really rich. Why would they allow her to struggle, especially with her husband missing and her only child in a tuberculosis sanitorium?

Tune in next week as Maggie and her handsome beau Ben try to solve Mildred's mystery and produce Pierre. Ha ha!

Hugs and kisses from your very best friend in the whole world,

Maggie

The more I learned, the more confused I became.

I did have one idea, though. Try to get some answers from my grandparents. Maggie was right: they were really rich. My grandpa owned hotels, for Pete's sake. They were always generous at Christmas and birthday time. And, my birthday was in one day. I could care less about getting a present. From anyone, really. The only thing I wanted for my birthday was answers.

I reached under my bed and grabbed blank sheets of Trudeau

stationery from the top of my suitcase, and a pencil from my bedside table. Starting the letter was not easy. I had always liked my Grandma and Grandpa Baker, but now I was suspicious of them. They would never let Mildred VanHoosen struggle.

Before I got sick, they visited us just about every month, Grandpa Baker always enjoying a long drive in his Alfa Romeo. He loved to brag that it could go ninety-six miles an hour, and Grandma Baker admitted – her eyes looked terrified during the retelling – that he proved that speed more than once on the Pennsylvania Turnpike.

One time, when I was fourteen, they took the three of us to the Jersey Shore for my first real vacation, and we stayed in *two* rooms in a towering hotel set right on the beach that was dotted with striped cabanas. I felt like a Hollywood starlet, and wore a white scarf around my head to protect my hair from the wind as we walked up and down the Boardwalk in Atlantic City. I was also trying to look like one of the contestants in the Miss America Pageant, which was taking place during our stay. The week included a magnificent parade with the glamorous contestants showcased on puffy floats, waving gracefully to the crowd, their smiles wide and bright.

My grandparents were good to us. Just because I didn't like Mildred VanHoosen did not mean they felt the same way.

My letter couldn't sound suspicious. I needed them to share. Better yet, I needed them to call. I would know by my grandma's voice if something was up.

Dear Grandma and Grandpa,

How are you both? I sure do miss you! As you might expect, it gets pretty lonely in a sanitorium far from home. I hear I'm getting better, and

I do feel somewhat better, and get to walk every day to work on my endurance, but I still haven't been told when I'm going to get sprung from here.

Mom was here for the first time a month ago, just for the day, and my best friend Maggie has visited once, and that's all the visitors I've had. Dad hasn't come at all, and while I know Grandpa's health prevents him from a visit, it would be so good to hear your voices. Do you think you could call me?

I was thinking today about our trip to Atlantic City. Do you remember how fun that was? What do you think about all of us going on another trip once I'm better?

Tomorrow is my eighteenth birthday. I know you won't get this letter until my birthday has passed, but hearing from my grandparents would be the best belated birthday present in the world.

Fondly from your granddaughter,
Marilyn

That was a short letter packed with tall lies. I hoped it was also packed with enough guilt to earn me a phone call.

CHAPTER 18
ON THE STICK

I woke up on my eighteenth birthday feeling no different than I had the day before. Wasn't eighteen supposed to be magical? Shouldn't I feel womanly? More confident in my skin? I would've been perfectly satisfied to look in the mirror and discover myself a mere ten percent more like Maggie. But I was still me. An underweight, flat-chested girl who couldn't do her own hair. Maybe it was impossible to achieve magic cloaked in a thin nightgown with rash-covered arms.

Betty was waiting with an empty wheelchair when I emerged from the girls' bathroom.

"Happy birthday, Marilyn. Let's get your day started off right, shall we?"

She motioned to the chair and I got in. "Where are we headed?"

We rolled past the rows of beds. The patients too ill for the dining room were well into their breakfasts, most with books propped on the edge of their trays. I looked for Henry, but he wasn't there. I hoped he wasn't back in with Dr. Whitlaw first thing in the morning. An early-morning appointment always meant something serious was going on.

Betty rolled me into the dining room, which wasn't the special morning I was hoping for. In fact, I was going to request a breakfast in bed rather than having to sit alone in the dining room on my birthday. That just sounded depressing.

Imagine my surprise when I spotted Henry Winters at one of the tables, waving to me! That was more like it. And he was clearly in good spirits, too.

Betty parked me and left to get our food. Henry immediately reached for my hands across the table.

"Happy birthday, Dolly. Eighteen and never been..."

"Henry! You certainly are promiscuous this morning! And you seem better, too. Are you better, Henry?"

He flashed me a warm smile. "As good as I'm going to be until the surgery. But at least I'm feeling well enough to spend your birthday with you."

The ability to feel joy and pain in the exact moment – if there wasn't a word for it, there should be. That's how I felt. Beyond joyful to have a day with Henry Winters. Utterly pained that his surgery was still looming. There was a moment, seeing him look so good, that I believed he was going to escape it. Experiencing those emotions simultaneously felt like they were going ten rounds inside me, their jabs compressing my lungs, fluttering my heart, and contracting my abdomen. But I refused to focus on the bad for one day, so I swallowed my fear, straightened my posture, and pretended I was a different Marilyn, a model-turned-actress whose undeniable sex appeal and good looks were turning her into the most talked-about starlet in Hollywood.

"As the birthday girl, I do get a present, right?" I looked straight at Henry with lifted chin and half-open eyes, to elicit some sex appeal of my own.

"Dolly, are you tired?"

I clicked my tongue and let my eyes return to their normal level of openness. "No, Henry, I'm just fine."

Betty returned with two trays and set them in front of us. The thick, smoky aroma of bacon was like inhaling comfort. It's funny how a scent can transport you to another time and place. My father got into the habit of cooking big Sunday breakfasts after coming home from the war. Or wherever he was. He could make the most perfect pancakes. Big and round and fluffy. He would cut slices of butter to set on top of each stack, and then drizzle the syrup like it was an ad in a magazine. The best was when he poured powdered sugar into the sifter and made it snow over our plates. There was always a side of the thickest bacon, cooked just well enough not to be wobbly. And a pot of fragrant, steaming coffee, which I took with enough cream and sugar to turn it into dessert.

I recalled the scene, the smells, but no other content. Did my parents converse with each other like other married couples? Did they interact with me? Did we laugh or eat in silence? I couldn't even say for sure if we all were at the table at the same time. I was old enough to remember. A teenager, in fact. So why didn't I?

Betty removed the lids keeping our meals warm, said, "Eat up, you're going to need your energy," winked at us, and sauntered away.

I raised my eyebrows at Henry. "We're going to need our energy?"

The depth of his blush was the cutest thing ever. "Today's the day, Dolly. Nurse Betty has it all set up."

I could now attest to the fact that it's possible to be alive when your heart has stopped.

My fork was in my hand, but it seemed I couldn't recall how to use it. Which was fine, because I was confident chewing and swallowing were no longer second nature either.

"Do you still want to do this?"

Henry's voice brought me back to my senses. Yes, I wanted to do it! And he did, too, thank God. "Absolutely," I said, poking at my scrambled eggs to prove I could. "Today, really?"

He nodded. "Instead of going to the porch. If we're not there the nurses will assume we're in bed. They never check."

"Where will we be?" I still couldn't bring a forkful of food to my mouth. Henry, on the other hand, had already inhaled his eggs and was on his second piece of bacon. Clearly, he was heeding Betty's advice.

"So, there's a tiny bedroom off the exam rooms that Dr. Whitlaw would use if he had an emergency in the infirmary and needed to stay close by for the night. That's where we'll be." He reached for me with his free hand while the other kept putting food back. He was eating!

I slid my hand in his, running my fingertip along his wrist. His grasp gave me the grounded feeling I needed to focus on my food. We sat in silence, both of us lost in thought. I was wondering how much hair had grown back on my legs, and which pair of underwear I had put on that morning.

I'm pretty sure Henry was having very different thoughts.

After breakfast, Betty and Maude appeared to whisk us to a room we had not yet visited: The Game Room. It was one room past the dining room, which would explain why I was not aware of its existence. It was a cozy space, dotted with several sitting areas, and a bookshelf opposite the windows filled with board games and puzzles. It was empty saved for two older ladies with matching permanent waves, hunched over a myriad of puzzle pieces.

"How come you've never brought us here before?" I asked.

"You have to be at a certain level of wellness," Maude explained, stopping Henry at a round wood table just in front of the bookshelf. "You are officially allowed in here now, Marilyn, but Henry still has a little way to go." She patted him on the shoulder as she set his brake. "Except for today, of course."

Betty set checkers, Monopoly, Rich Uncle, and The Game of Life on the table. "You two can stay put in here until lunch. We'll check in to make sure everything is okay."

"Thanks, Betty." She was going way above her normal consideration for me, which already was pretty great. I had to admit I was touched.

Now we just had to get through the next few hours so I could really be touched.

It was good to spend time with Henry after so many days with barely any contact. It was also good to do normal-people things – something we never got to do, if you don't include eating – like beating Henry in three games of checkers. But it all felt like an act, like performing a scene in the most boring play ever penned. Neither of us wanted to while away the hours in The Game Room. We were scheduled to have sex. Scheduled! And it was the only thing on my mind. From the way Henry kept placing his forearm across his lap, it was the only thing on his mind, too.

It took two lengthy games of Monopoly and a completed puzzle of Big Ben to get us to lunchtime. Thank God. I needed to get back to a noisy environment. The Game Room was so small and deathly quiet, the two old bitties sharing space with us would have heard all our business had we tried discussing anything of greater importance than it finally being summer or our hopes for Trudeau's menu to change.

We landed at the same table where we had taken our breakfast, and were presented with plates filled high with roast turkey, mashed potatoes pooled with brown gravy, and soft carrot circles. This time, the fork easily found my mouth. After toying all day with the idea of having sex with Henry in Dr. Whitlaw's emergency bedroom (and shutting down the notion that he and Betty had already christened the space), I was resolved that the most wonderful moment of my life was right in front of me and I was going to embrace it fully. I inhaled my food in preparation.

To be safe, Betty and Maude split us up after lunch. Betty came for me first. We made a pit stop in the girls' room where I took one last look at my virgin image in the mirror as I washed my hands.

Betty peered down a couple of hallways before steering me to the modest bedroom. I climbed out of the wheelchair and situated myself on the bed, feeling so uncomfortable, only Nurse Doris' public sponge baths were worse. Betty put her hand on my head. She looked like she was about to say something, but instead bit her lip and pulled her hand away. I wondered if she was thinking about being with Dr. Whitlaw in this very room. As she backed the wheelchair through the doorway, she gave me a wink. I understood her silence. Having sex isn't like getting ready for a big football game. What do you say to someone you know is about to lose her virginity? "Get in there, and get the job done!" A wordless exit is as graceful as it gets.

The mind races when sitting alone in darkness in a strange room. I pondered body hair, the diminutive nature of my breasts, the current state of my breath, whether we would be fully naked or just bottomless, and how Betty and Maude would know when we were done (and not walk in on us!). I was thrilled when Henry finally arrived so my stupid brain would shut up. And so we could have sex, of course.

Maude helped Henry onto the bed beside me before fishing in her pocket for a condom, which she handed to me. I blushed so hard I was grateful the room was dim. As soon as Maude shut the door, I leaped up to lock us in, and tucked the condom under the pillow for safekeeping.

Henry and I sat beside each other, unable to see much more than our outlines from the strip of light coming in from under the door. I was happy about that. He tucked a lock of my hair behind my ear and grasped the back of my head, pulling me into his kiss. My heart hitched and I knew without a doubt how much I wanted this. I turned my body to face him, winding my bare legs around his torso, my right thigh greeted with a stroke from Henry's free hand. He kissed my neck, unbuttoning my nightgown until it fell away as his mouth moved lower and lower. His tongue found my left nipple; my back arched in response.

He gave my shoulders enough of a nudge to understand he wanted me to lie back on the bed. I obeyed. His fingers explored my body, encircling my naval, following the outline of my cotton panties. His fingers locked on either side of the fabric, and I lifted just enough for him to easily slide off my underwear. I felt so bold, so free, so grown up to be sprawled naked across a bed in front of a boy. His focus was now between my legs, his hand tracing, massaging, cradling. He slid two fingers deep inside me and I writhed with pleasure. I didn't think anything could feel this good.

It was the strained amplification of his breath that brought me back to my senses. With a kick to the bed I shot myself backwards, away from his reach.

"What's...wrong?" He was breathless.

"We can't do this, Henry."

"Oh, believe me," he sucked hard for air, "we can." He leaned toward me, so I scooted farther back, sliding right off the bed. I landed with a thud on the cold floor. "Marilyn, what are you doing?"

I put my head in my hands. "I can't do this, Henry."

"I thought...you were ready," he whimpered.

"I am."

He lowered himself onto his back, the bed springs moaning in response. "Then why?"

I sighed. "You're too weak, Henry. I can't be selfish and risk putting you in a worse position before your surgery." I slid my half-naked body along the floor until my face was again next to his. Planting a light kiss his sweaty forehead, I tasted the saltiness of his skin. "The truth is I'm scared. I don't want to lose you, Henry. Not from the surgery, and certainly not from overexerting you."

He leaned his head into mine. "I really wanted this."

"Me too."

"Marilyn, I don't want to die a virgin." His voice cracked on the last word.

It hurt my heart to hear him talk about himself dying. What did either of us understand about his impending surgery? Could he really not survive it? Since the first days of knowing this boy, the severity of his illness has weighed heavily on me. Before I loved him. Before we knew he wasn't getting better. I wanted to believe we had a future, somehow, somewhere outside of this place. But he had to stay alive for that to happen. He just had to.

"Well, then, Henry Winters," I said with the most authoritative tone I could muster. "I guess you better not die."

We sat in silence like that, our heads together, until Henry's breathing slowly returned to normal. Tuberculosis normal.

I was fumbling with the buttons on my nightgown when Henry finally spoke again. "I love you, Marilyn. I didn't want you to leave this room without knowing how much I love you."

My heart swelled. "You know you've been calling me Marilyn since you got in this room."

"I wanted to demonstrate the seriousness of the occasion." I couldn't help grinning. My Henry was back.

"Then you should have included my middle name," I teased. "Everything is more serious when a middle name is invoked."

"You're going to have to tell me your middle name if I am to invoke it."

"Still so much to learn about me. It's Elizabeth. Like the new queen of England."

"Very regal." Henry reached an arm around my neck, and I pulled it tight around me. "I love you, Marilyn Elizabeth Queen-of-England VanHoosen. Don't ever leave me."

"No chance in hell of that happening," I said, silent tears springing to life. "My love for you is forever, Henry Winters. That I can promise."

CHAPTER 19
KNUCKLE SANDWICH

Being separated from your true love is dramatic. Especially after pouring out your hearts to each other. But then finding out your separation is due to a phone call from Maggie suddenly makes the theatrics less "Gone With the Wind" and more "The Wizard of Oz." Except I wasn't so interested in finding my way home quite yet.

Betty was so hasty to get me to the phone, I don't think she bothered to look out for anyone who might catch our exit from the little bedroom. Luckily, the hallway traffic was sparse for midday, and Maggie didn't have to wait long to get me on the other end.

"Mari-boo, my birthday girl, I miss you sooo much!" she cried. "While I will admit I have been spending quite a bit of time with Ben – do you know he has hinted at engagement – it's still not the same as a girl having her best friend to really talk to about all the important stuff."

"Engagement?" I don't know why I got stuck on that word when Maggie was laying it on thick with all the love and attention a girl

175

could ever hope for from her best friend.

"Oh, not yet, of course. My parents wouldn't like it if we were looking to get married so quickly. But he has stated his intention, and that's all I need to know."

"You want to marry Ben?" I shifted in the wheelchair, not able to curb my uneasiness.

"Yes, Mari-boo, I do! I can't believe I'm saying it out loud but I really do. Are you happy for me?"

I burst into tears.

"Marilyn? Marilyn, darling, are you alright? I hope I haven't upset you, my dear. Marilyn, it's your birthday! Please stop crying and tell me what the devil is wrong."

"I don't want to miss it!" I wailed.

"Miss what?"

"Your...wedding," I stammered. "I've missed everything in here: senior prom, graduation. I can't bear the thought of missing my best friend's wedding."

Maggie giggled. "Marilyn, you are so daffy. Do you really believe I would ever get married while my maid of honor is stuck in a tuberculosis sanitorium?"

"Maid of honor?" I sniffed.

"Well, of course, silly."

I wiped at my eyes. "Wow, Maggie, I...I don't know what to say."

"How about you say yes now, and then we don't have to go through all this again when it really happens."

The tears squeezed out from the corners of my eyes, a mix of emotions finding their escape. "Okay. Yes. Yes, yes, yes! Oh, and Maggie?"

"Yes?"

"I almost lost my virginity. Like ten minutes ago."

"You what?"

"I'm going to save those details for a letter, as I know how expensive this phone call is going to be."

"Holy cow, Marilyn, you *almost* had sex? I haven't let Ben do more than kiss me, and I'm practically engaged. Okay, I guess I am going to forget you just said that for now and focus on the reason I called you."

"Oh yeah." I didn't want to throw her into a complete lather by admitting I was practically engaged, too.

"Ben has reached out to a number of guys from the Navy, and every time he mentions San Francisco as a drop-off point during the war, he's met with silence."

I ran my hand through my hair and sighed. "Why?"

"He doesn't know yet. No one will budge with information. But he's not letting this go. He's determined to get to the bottom of Pierre's mystery, and so am I."

"Please thank Ben for me. And Maggie?"

"Yes, Mari-boo?"

"I'll have your letter in tomorrow's mail."

"You sure as heck better."

I hung up the phone and looked around for Betty with no luck. My head was racing. I wanted to get back in my bed and think, so I wheeled myself to the infirmary. Henry was already fast asleep in his bed. Miraculously, no nurse snapped at me for handling my own wheelchair. Maybe they all knew I was getting better, and their time would be better spent on sicker patients.

My bed came into view, and with it, Jimmy in the next bed, who was thumbing through a newspaper. I halted my wheelchair as I fixed on him, remembering his reaction when I told him my father had been sent to San Francisco after the war. "Oh," he had said. And then he changed the subject. Jimmy knew.

I rolled to a stop beside his bed and crossed my arms. Jimmy looked at me over his newspaper, then set it in his lap like a nest of newsprint.

"You look like you have something on your mind," he said, removing his reading glasses and propping them on his head.

"You're right, I do. Tell me what you know about San Francisco."

"I said I hadn't been stationed there, remember? I was in South Carolina."

I shook my head. "Jimmy, I'm not a dummy. I saw how you reacted when I told you my father had gone to San Francisco after the war. He didn't come back for a long time. Didn't talk about it either. In fact, I had no idea where he was during that time. Didn't know anything at all, really. I was lucky to overhear him talking to a neighbor about it, otherwise I'd still be in the dark."

Jimmy sighed and folded the newspaper neatly, setting it at the end of the bed as if it would be some time before he'd be able to return to it. "Kid, I don't know that I'm the one who should tell you any of this."

"Any of what?"

"How much do you know about your father?"

"Apparently, I don't know him at all."

"You're still young, kid, but one day you'll understand. Adults learn to bury the truths they can't assimilate, and adopt new truths they can."

I wrinkled my nose. "I have no idea what that means."

"It means if you can't accept who you are, you can always become someone else."

"Jimmy!" I huffed. "Enough of the riddles. Just say it."

He closed his eyes and pinched the bridge of his nose. His shoulders slumped. "Fine. I can't say this with any certainty, but from what I know, and what I have heard from you, my guess is your father is a homosexual."

I was frozen. I couldn't move my head. My mouth. My body. My brain felt fuzzy, like the circuits of a television going haywire.

"Are you okay, kid?"

Still, I could not react.

"Kid?" Jimmy leaned forward, his expression puzzled. "You still in there?"

I had to concentrate just to get my lips to press together and then open. I attempted a whisper. "A what?"

Jimmy cleared his throat and awkwardly folded his hands in his lap. "Well, a homosexual is..."

"I know what a homosexual is," I murmured. "Why do you think my father is...one?"

"San Francisco," Jimmy said. "That's where they dropped them off. If they were found out."

"If they were found out."

"Yes."

"You're telling me that during the course of the war, my father did something with...with another man, was caught, and to punish him, instead of getting him home when the war ended, the Navy ship sailed to San Francisco, made him get off, and left him behind?"

"That's correct."

"Is there any other reason he could have gotten off in

San Francisco?"

"I s'pose he could have decided not to go home."

"That hardly makes more sense. Why wouldn't he want to go home?" I folded my arms, as if defiant. "My father was perfectly happy with my mother and me."

As soon as the words tumbled out, the memories also began to tumble. And then they crashed, really, really hard.

How often do kids pay attention to their parents? When I was young, I didn't know anything about my folks. They were there to feed me and bathe me and make sure I went to bed at the same time every night. They were caregivers, not people with identities and hopes and fears and desires.

Once I became a teenager, I thought about them even less. I had boys to think about. And spending as much time as possible with my friends. Not to mention schoolwork and football games and dances. Parents do not figure into the lives of teenagers.

And yet, I see them now. It wasn't until my father came back from the war – a year after it ended – that I could first remember my parents interacting with each other. Or in their case, not interacting with each other. They didn't talk to each other, unless it was that necessary married-couple dialogue: "Pick up a quart of milk;" "There's a stain in that shirt," "The car's making a funny noise." They never gossiped, never discussed their days, never shared a clever story. I remember conversations now. At dinner. But only my father speaking to me, asking about school or mentioning a new movie that looked good to him. He had no trouble talking to me. Why did he refrain from talking to her? Maybe he and I were similar creatures; I didn't like talking to Mildred VanHoosen, either.

And then there was the bed in the guest room that was never made.

Mildred VanHoosen wasn't the model housewife. She didn't spend her days scrubbing the house from top to bottom. But she wasn't a slob, either. The beds were made, the carpeting typically sported vacuum lines, and dishes didn't pile up in the sink. Yet the guest room was never put together. The shades were drawn and the bed was unmade. Every day, I guess. I hadn't thought much about it. The guest room was one room past mine, directly across from my parents' bedroom. I rarely went into their bedroom, so I rarely passed by the guest room. I was a teenager. Life existed either in my room, or outside of the house. Who paid attention to a mussy guest room?

Had my father been sleeping in there all along?

Maybe he didn't want to come home after the war. Maybe he hated Mildred VanHoosen as much as I did.

But I was pretty sure he loved me. Would he have been willing to leave me, too?

I shook my head at Jimmy. "I just can't believe my father would abandon me."

"Then you need to consider my original hypothesis."

As crazy as it sounded, there was a chance Jimmy was right. And there was only one way to find out.

I flagged down Maude, who rolled me to the telephone in the hallway, and then I placed a collect call to Mildred VanHoosen. I waited with fingers crossed that she would be home and accept the charges. When her curt voice came over the line, I almost lost my nerve.

Almost.

"I know about my father. You better get your ass to Trudeau."

❖

It's funny that on the day I almost lost my virginity to the love of my life, I was consumed with thoughts of my father. I had expected to spend the rest of the day reliving Henry's hands on my body, how womanly I felt half-dressed sprawled across the bed. Until I was certain the excitement was about to lead to his collapse. But I was sure I could tuck that part away for a bit and focus on the good stuff.

Oh, what Mildred VanHoosen and her pack of lies could do.

I had hung up the phone before she could speak. Who wants to hear more tales from a chronic liar? Plus, I didn't want to give her the chance to place any doubt in my mind. She needed to be the one who was unsure for a change. To wonder what I might do with the information I had. What would I do if she didn't come? The easiest way not to face a problem is to avoid it altogether. It was feasible she could cut off all communication with me. Typically, I would say that wouldn't be the worst thing that could happen to my life. Unfortunately, this was one of the rare times that I needed her. I needed her truth, if she was capable of providing it. Whatever that truth might be.

Back in bed, I could feel Jimmy glancing over in my direction. Probably because I was trying so hard not to look at him. His eyes were practically searing my skin. "What?" I finally said.

"Are you okay, kid?"

"You don't have to be concerned about me, Jimmy. I'm fine."

"It's a lot of information for a girl to process."

"I'm eighteen, Jimmy. Today, in fact. I'm not a girl anymore."

"Oh, hell, it's your birthday? I'm sorry to have laid all this heavy stuff on you when you should be celebrating."

"Oh yes, so much to celebrate all alone in a tuberculosis sanitorium with no cake or presents or party." I knew I shouldn't be directing my flurry of emotions at him, but I still managed to be an ass.

"Marilyn..." he trailed off.

I sighed. "It's not your fault, Jimmy."

"It's not yours, either."

To pass the time, I put all my focus into fake sleeping. I faked sleeping when Freddy came to take me walking. I faked sleeping when Betty came to get me for dinner. I was far too nervous to eat, anyway. If only I could see Henry. That would give me some peace, just to look at him, even if it was only to watch him sleep. But my new bed was just far enough away, and he was usually flat on his back, so the patients and the nurses and the bed covers kept him hidden from my view.

At some point in the evening, I finally slept for real; a fitful slumber that featured close-ups of both my parents' faces, their expressions tense, or maybe I was seeing the look of mutual spite. I startled awake sometime during the night. The infirmary was dim and quiet, save for the faint footsteps of a nurse squeaking from the far end of the room. As my eyes adjusted to the darkness, I noticed something had been placed on the little table beside my bed. It was a cupcake with a candle in it. I pulled myself up to inspect it. Vanilla with pink frosting. My stomach growled at me, clearly unhappy with my choice to skip dinner. Setting the unlit candle on the table, I raked my finger across the frosting and shoved it in my mouth. Delicious was a weak word to describe the sugary confection. It only took two bites to finish it off, and I gave a silent thank you to whoever was kind enough gift me with a proper birthday treat.

It hit me then that neither my parents nor my grandparents had contacted me for my birthday. Not a phone call, not a card, not a present. Nothing. That was more than strange. I had come to terms with the fact that my parents had all but forgotten me. But my grandparents? They've never missed a birthday. Never. Never!

Where the hell was everyone?

CHAPTER 20
LAY A PATCH

I agreed to get out of bed and go to the dining room for breakfast only if Maude promised to take me to see Joan right after. You had to do what you had to do to get what you wanted, I was learning. Maude sat with me for a few minutes and made small talk, but I couldn't fake wanting her to be there, so she quickly made her excuses and left. I had nothing against Maude – she was the sweetest nurse at Trudeau – but my mind was running so fast, I could barely keep up with it myself, much less try to shut it down temporarily to focus on anything else.

Almost sex with Henry, Maggie's impending engagement, me being a maid of honor, the sheer neglect of my entire family, and what may be the truth about my father was more drama in one day than I had encountered in my entire life. How could I be expected to be good company?

I gobbled up my breakfast, clearly in need of sustenance after going without dinner, and looked around fervently for Maude to flag her down for a ride to Joan. I had a hunch that Joan would be able to provide me some clarity on the issue of my father. She was in a band that toured around the country. She had met every type of person imaginable on the road. If anyone was enlightened enough to know a thing or two about people, I expected it would be Joan.

She was right where I had last seen her, horizontal in her trusty iron lung. Her dark hair had grown since arriving at Trudeau, now fanned out as far as her chin on a direct course for her narrow shoulders. Considering her current state, she looked amazingly well, with bright eyes and her customary smile for me.

Once we were alone and had exchanged our pleasantries, I got right to it.

"I need to ask you something, and it's a little awkward," I started, raising the wheelchair break to move closer to her head. This wasn't the type of conversation that you wanted overheard.

"You got my attention," she replied.

I bit my knuckle, trying to decide how to begin. "In your travels, have you come across many homosexuals?" I hoped she didn't think I sounded as idiotic as I did.

"Okay, was not expecting that, and I'm not sure where you are going with this, but sure. I don't know if I'd say many, but I've known a couple. Not that it's easy to tell. They don't wear nametags, you know. Why in the world do you ask?"

My eyes closed, I inhaled deeply, searching for the words. "My father." It was all I could manage.

"Oh." She paused. "Are you sure?"

"I don't know," I said, shaking my head. "It's a guess, based on a few nuggets of information."

"It's risky to hedge your bets on minimal information."

A lone tear ran down my cheek. I wiped away the evidence and dried my fingertips on my robe. Crying was not part of today's plan and needed to stop immediately. I needed to be strong. To learn the truth. To grow the hell up.

"The little information I have is pretty reliable. His Navy ship dropped him off in San Francisco after the war instead of taking him home. It was done to men that were, you know."

"I see. Did you have any indication otherwise?"

"No. Other than the fact that he's gone by two names, I never would have suspected anything. But I've been thinking that I was also a self-consumed teen, giving very little thought to my parents. Or their sexuality."

Joan mulled that over a bit. "Makes sense. Like I said, it's not like they wear a scarlet letter. And it's not that unusual for a homosexual to try to live a life that isn't true. You know, get married, have a few kids. It must be hell to bear on the inside, but it can be way less painful than revealing the truth. The world is cruel, Marilyn. That's the lesson here."

I tried to imagine my dad living a life that wasn't authentic. Marrying a woman he didn't love. Maybe having feelings for someone that he could never admit. Feeling lonely. Keeping everything inside. It made me so sad for him. He loved me. Of that, I was sure. Even if he hadn't contacted me one single time since I got here, I knew he still loved me. I also was certain I didn't want him to be miserable. He was a good dad. He bought me ice cream cones, and bandaged me up when I fell. He talked to me like a real person, as opposed to barking a few words at me when absolutely necessary like Mildred VanHoosen. He was gone a long time while

I was growing up, but I remembered him. I remembered the love.

I had to find him and help him.

Betty came into the room with Joan's medication and a glass with a straw so she could swallow down the pills while lying on her back. Joan and I stayed perfectly quiet throughout the interruption. I eyed Betty as she worked, practically fixated on her pouty red lips and the way her backside wiggled when she walked. It made no sense, but in that moment, I felt betrayed. She was supposed to be one of the good ones, the only woman in the world who truly cared about me, but the truth was she cared more about sneaking around with Dr. Whitlaw. She kept everything under her hat; sharing barely any details about her life with me. Nearly every question I posed to her was met with silence or diversion. Now that I thought about it, pretty much everything with Betty was a secret, and if there was one thing I could no longer allow in my life, it was secrets.

"Boy, that Betty is a looker," Joan commented once we were alone again.

I clicked my tongue. "When you're someone's mistress, you're supposed to be all done up like that." As soon as I said the words, I was shocked I would say such a thing about Betty, but the truth was it felt kind of good.

"Betty is having an affair with a married man?" Joan's voice rose. "I'm impressed."

"Joan!" I roared.

"Aw, relax a little, kid. It's just sex. So, you know who the Big Daddy is?"

"Joan!" I swear if she weren't in that iron lung, I would have slugged her. "How can you be so nonchalant about this? And yes, as a matter of fact, I do know who it is."

"You better sing, sweetie. You can't deny the wishes of a girl in an iron lung."

"Okay, okay." I looked around sheepishly, knowing full well this was the very definition of gossiping. "Don't say a word, but it's Dr. Whitlaw."

"Whitlaw?" she cried out way too loud.

"Shh!"

"Sorry," she whispered. "How do you know?"

I inhaled deeply then told her everything: the haircut, the lipstick, how Betty dodged my questions about her new look, the odd overnight trip to Brooklyn that she wouldn't talk about, and catching her sneaking away from Dr. Whitlaw's home.

Joan's eyes were wide. "Whoa, Betty and Whitlaw. What do you think she sees in him?"

I shook my head. "I have no idea. It's clear he was born without a personality."

"He's not dreamy, but love is blind, kid. None of us have control over who we fall in love with."

After my talk with Joan, I went back to my bed to write the letter I had promised to Maggie, intending to get it into the mail before my daily walk with Freddy. Which would be followed by time on the porch with Henry. It was so warm outside, the idea of our daily cold cure made no sense, and yet, out we went, every day. I supposed fresh air and sweeping views of the Adirondacks were better for healing than the cough-infested infirmary. Getting to stare at Henry was healing my soul, that was for sure.

I couldn't make eye contact with Jimmy while wheeling up to my bed. He knew my dirty secret. So did Joan, of course, but for whatever reason, it didn't bother me to tell her. I got the feeling she had talked about much worse than that. There was something about her world that both intrigued and scared me. Being the only woman in a five-person band meant night after night surrounded by men. She assured me that her bandmates were like brothers to her, and that the one named Sam, who played the bass, was her most trusted confidante, but still. She spoke of puny, shared dressing rooms and long nights spent sleeping in their car, after more than a couple shots of vodka, compliments of the venue owner. It just all sounded so risqué. Not that I was condemning it. I wished it were me.

Back under my covers, with pencil and stationery in hand, I scribbled every last detail I could remember about my encounter with Henry in the dark. Just for a moment, I considered what might happen if my letter fell into the wrong hands, say Dr. Whitlaw or Nurse Doris or Mildred VanHoosen. My relationship with Henry would not only be officially over, I felt sure we would never be allowed to see each other again. That thought left a lump in my throat, and as I attempted to swallow it down, I signed my name, closed the envelope with extra spit to ensure it was sealed, and handed it off to Betty when she came by to give me my medication and put salve on my arms.

My whole like suddenly felt like one giant risk.

Freddy bounded over to my bed empty handed. "No walk today?" I questioned, trying to mask my hope with no walking frame in sight.

"Negative!" He cried, with all the enthusiasm of a head cheerleader.

"You're not going to make me play Twenty Questions, are you, Freddy?"

He shook his head at me, his smile never dimming. "You know I love that fire in your belly, Marilyn. You keep me on my toes!" He pulled back my covers and held out a hand to me. "Today, young lady, you get to walk on your own."

A rush of joy flooded my body. It's incredible how revitalizing it is to know you are getting better. I wanted so much to be better. To figure out my family. To help nurse Henry back to good health. To start the rest of my life, and to do it without Mildred VanHoosen.

I cordially placed my hand in Freddy's and he pulled me playfully to my feet. That boy liked me, there was no doubt about it. Hopefully, he liked me well enough to furnish me with some gossip about Betty. It was one thing to get to finally say what I knew out loud to Joan. But Freddy might be able to share something substantial. Something that would actually explain why Betty was being so crazy with a married man so dull.

Having both hands free while walking was something of a novelty. As Freddie and I small talked our way through the dim infirmary and out into the blinding sunlight, I made sure to include hand gestures every time I spoke, even to agree to something Freddie said or say, "Thank you," as Freddie held open the door for me.

We strolled along the paths past the Nurses' Cottage and Baker Chapel. The humidity of summer was taking hold, causing me to stop gesturing long enough to wipe away the telltale beads of sweat forming above my upper lip with the back of my hand. Freddie was chirping away about his plan to enroll in graduate school in the fall to become a doctor. He was practically electric as he spouted about it. The only time I felt anything close to that was when Henry and I were alone, and this awful fear I had about Henry not getting better made me wonder if I would ever feel that way again.

About anything.

"I don't know, Marilyn, but I think I'd make a pretty good doctor," he said, with a humble tone.

That was my cue. "Sure, you would, Freddie." There was a bench just ahead under an outstretched Elm tree. "Do you mind if we rest a bit?"

"Of course not." He let me get settled on the bench first before taking a seat close enough to sit on part of my robe. Freddie knew Henry and I were together, and yet, it felt like he would never give up his semi-subtle effort to be more to me than just a friend.

"Speaking of doctors, I'm pretty horrified about Dr. Whitlaw and Nurse Betty." I was planning to be a little less direct, but then, I figured, why bother? I wanted the truth, and beating around the bush wasn't going to get me closer to it.

Freddie's head whipped in my direction. "Dr. Whitlaw and Nurse Betty? What do you mean, Marilyn?"

I scrunched my shoulders and grinned sheepishly, pretending to be embarrassed to share what I know. "Oh, you know, they're having an affair."

"No, they're not!" Freddie shouted at me.

"Jeez, Freddie, why are you going ape over it? What, do you like Nurse Betty or something?"

"As a matter of fact, I do." He put his face close enough to mine that I could feel the heat coming off of him. "She is my friend, and I know without a doubt that they are not having an affair. Where did you get such ridiculous information?"

Angry Freddie was quite terrifying. He was downright irate with me, but he wasn't that good of a friend if he didn't know what was really happening in Betty's life. "It's my information. It's everything she's told me and everything I've seen her do."

"Like what?"

I exhaled heavily, as if exasperated that I would have to recount every little piece of evidence in order to be believed. "She cut her hair."

"So?"

"I'm not done," I scolded. "Do you want to know or what?"

"Yes, I want to know."

"Okay, so she cut her hair, and then she started wearing red lipstick."

"That means nothing."

"And she wouldn't say why she did those things. In fact, she would seem embarrassed or flustered when I would ask. And then she would change the subject or walk away."

"So, she's embarrassed to talk about her appearance. There's no correlation."

I crossed my arms. "There's more. She took a mysterious overnight trip to Brooklyn. She brought me back a treat from a bakery there, and when I questioned her about why she was there, especially for such a short amount of time, she got really angry with me."

Freddie popped to his feet and stood facing me, his hands on his hips. "Maybe she was cross because she brought you back a present and your reaction was to be accusatory."

I stood, too. "She was cross because I realized how early in the day she had come back to Trudeau on her day off. How early she would have had to get up to get on the first train out. And she knew she couldn't tell me the truth, so instead she got mad."

"And what, exactly, was the truth, do you think?" His foot was tapping repeatedly on the grass.

"That she met up with Dr. Whitlaw for a night of adulterated sex."

Freddie threw his head back and laughed, which stunned me into silence. "Marilyn, sometimes I forget you're a teenager, but let me tell you, you just reminded me how naïve you are!"

The insult made my heart race. "Just because you can't handle what your friend is up to doesn't mean you have the right to insult me, Freddie." I huffed away, trying to get back to the infirmary as quickly as my sturdier legs would carry me.

It only took steps for Freddie to reach me. He grabbed my arm and swung me around. "Marilyn, I can handle it, but nothing is happening! You have given me absolutely no proof!"

I tried to wrestle my arm from his firm grasp, but he wasn't letting go. "Fine, you want proof? I'll give you proof. After all that, I saw her sneaking out of Dr. Whitlaw's house in the middle of the day. And let me tell you, Freddie, she was sneaking. Running all the way back to the Nurses' Cottage like she was desperate not to get caught. She's having an affair with Dr. Whitlaw."

Freddie sighed and let me go. "No, you idiot. She's helping Dr. Whitlaw."

"Oh, I'm sure she is," I hissed.

"You have it all so wrong, Marilyn. She's been helping Dr. Whitlaw with his daughter."

"What?"

"His daughter, Irene, the middle one. She got pregnant. With a boy she met at a party. She was scared, devastated. She went to her father, hoping that a man of medicine would be more levelheaded than her very devout Catholic mother. And he was. Dr. Whitlaw didn't want his daughter to have a baby so young and ruin her opportunities. He wanted her to go to college and make a good life for herself. Irene wanted the same things. They agreed she would get an abortion. He trusted Betty, so he enlisted her to help them. That's why she was in Brooklyn. She was with Irene, getting the procedure done."

"Oh."

"And that's why Betty could never tell you anything. And as far as the hair and lipstick goes, I told her to do that."

"You? Why?"

"Because she's lovely and needed to gussy up a bit, put herself out there. She's at Trudeau all the time, surrounded by sick people – no offense – and never doing anything social outside of having a beer with me on a Saturday night. I want her to find love. She's a great girl. She deserves it."

"Aren't you interested in her?"

"Oh, sure I was, but unfortunately, it wasn't mutual. She thought I was too young for her. So, I did what any guy who couldn't get the girl who still wants to be around the girl does: I became her friend. Not the exact situation I wanted, but I got used to it."

"But wait, what was Betty doing the day we were out walking and I saw her run from Dr. Whitlaw's house?"

"Irene wasn't feeling well, and Dr. Whitlaw was busy with patients, so Betty snuck in to check on her while Mrs. Whitlaw was out shopping."

My shoulders dropped. Freddie was right. I was an idiot. "I actually got mad at her for doing something she didn't do," I confessed.

Freddie slung an arm around my shoulder. "You're only human.

And sometimes the truth is stranger than anything we could drum up in our heads."

We walked in silence the rest of the way to the infirmary, Freddie's arm glued in place on me. It was terribly comforting. I wanted so badly to be able to tell Betty how awful I felt: for imagining such horrible things about her, for gossiping about her, for getting angry with her when all she ever did was love and care for me. She was the best family I had and I treated her terribly.

Freddie opened the door to a disturbance in the hallway. Just in front of us was a tall man in a dark suit and matching hat, his hand clutching Betty's upper arm. In Betty's other hand was a suitcase. Her forehead was lined with anxiety.

"Betty!" I cried. "What's happening?"

Her eyes locked on me, and I swear the pain I saw behind them told me without a doubt that my betrayal set this moment in motion.

"Would Joan have said something?" I whispered to Freddie, my breath coming in short, quick gasps.

"Marilyn, you told Joan?"

Just then, Nurse Doris came into view, positioning herself just to the left of the man in the suit. Their heads where together and as she whispered to him, he nodded in understanding. Once her message was conveyed, she left the scene, never acknowledging Betty, but making sure to cast a cold glance at me, which was accompanied by an even colder smirk.

"Oh God, it was Nurse Doris. She must have overheard Joan and I talking." I replayed the scene in my head, trying to remember every moment, how I was positioned in the wheelchair with my back to the door. How the door was left open during our visit. "No, wait!"

I roared, but Freddie grabbed me, and turned me right back out the door. "Freddie, what in the hell are you doing? We have to stop them! She didn't do anything wrong!"

Freddie grabbed my shoulders. "Marilyn, we can't do anything. We can't tell them the truth. Betty made a choice to help Dr. Whitlaw. Right now, only Betty is in trouble. Yes, it's for the wrong wrongdoing, but at least this is Trudeau-only information. The Board of Directors won't take it to Mrs. Whitlaw. But if we were to tell the truth, Betty, Dr. Whitlaw, and Irene would be in way worse trouble."

I started to cry, my shoulders shaking uncontrollably while long, heaving sobs lurched from deep in my belly.

Freddie held me tight, his face buried in my neck. "I'm sorry, Marilyn. I'm really sorry. I'm going to miss her, too."

He waited a good half hour for me to settle down, Freddie quietly sitting beside me in an empty hallway just off the back entrance to the kitchen, his hand pressed lightly against my back while my fingernails dug into the bottom of the wooden chair.

"I have to get you out to the porch," he said, finally breaking the fragile silence. "We can't let anyone think that something isn't right."

I smirked, reminded of Mildred VanHoosen. "No, we couldn't have that, could we." I wiped my eyes and nose with the sleeve of my robe, got to my feet, and shuffled in the direction of the back porch, Freddie staying a few steps behind me.

The porch was mostly full. I spotted Henry in our usual corner, but there were no open chairs. Betty would have saved me one. "I want to sit next to Henry," I said boldly.

Freddie peered around. "Don't see anything available, and...I thought you weren't sup..."

"Betty always let me."

Freddie tried to take my hand but I yanked it away. "Marilyn, Betty isn't here anymore. The special treatment you got from her may be hard to come by from the other nurses." I know he didn't say it to be mean, but it pierced my heart like a poisonous arrow.

"Make no mistake, Freddie," I hissed, "if you don't get me next to Henry right now, I'm going to start screaming, and I won't stop until they lock me up in this godforsaken place."

He took a step back, startled. "Fine. Give me a minute." I watched with arms folded while Freddie located an empty lounge chair, hoisted it over his head, and carried it over to Henry, using his foot to push away the chair of a little old lady wrapped in a large floral scarf to make room for my presence.

It was my only victory of the day, and it was a small one, but I clung to it, desperate for anything to go right after all my wrongdoings. Even though my insides felt broken beyond repair, I still mustered a smile for Henry as I climbed into my seat. I needed to do something, anything, good for somebody I loved.

"Looks like Freddie's officially working for me now," I said, hoping my forced nonchalance came off as me having not a care in the world. The last thing I wanted to do was lose it and tell Henry what I had done to Betty. "Did you see what he had to do to get me next to you? Henry?"

He was positively limp. His eyes were cast straight ahead, but focused on nothing.

"Henry, can you hear me?"

I clutched his hand. He didn't return the pressure.

"Henry?"

It had been less than twenty-four hours since our almost encounter in the dark bedroom, and somehow, everything I had with Henry felt more precious than ever. Not because of Betty, or because he was scaring me in that moment. The intimacy pooled with our fear and vulnerability over Henry's condition made it feel like we knew each other in a way we hadn't before. Maybe it's that knowledge of another person – the good, the bad, the exposed – that creates a bond so fierce, even death would be unable to break it.

I didn't want to be thinking such depressing thoughts, but the truth was Henry looked terrible. For how spirited he was at the start of my birthday, he was positively drained now. I could have described him as lifeless, but I refused. Maybe he really did use up all his energy on me. Little did he know how my celebration had plummeted after we had parted ways. I needed to tell him. I had to tell him everything. Even about Betty. All I had left was my truth.

"It appears my father is a homosexual." Was there really any other way to begin?

Henry coughed lightly then, the first sound he had made since I sat down, but I don't know if it was in response to my news or his health.

I told him every last detail. My new bedmate, Jimmy, his knowledge of the Navy, and how San Francisco fit in; Joan's strong opinions based on her travels and relationships; and how it all added up with what I knew of my father. By the time I spewed out that much information, I was breathless.

Henry gave my hand a weak squeeze, startling me.

"Henry? Can you hear me? Are you okay?"

"Do you still love him?" he whispered.

That threw me. I twirled a lock of hair while I considered Henry's query. "Yes, of course. Why do you ask me that?"

He struggled to turn his head. I wanted to tell him to stop and conserve his energy, but I also was terrified of him in this state, and didn't know what to do. "Because isn't that all that really matters?" he labored. "He's your father. You love him." He had to stop talking for a moment to catch his breath. "So what if he isn't exactly what you thought?"

"I guess you're right." He lowered his gaze to his lap. He looked sad even though in his weakest state he still managed to be optimistic. "Is something on your mind, Henry?"

"It's making me think about my dad," he wheezed. "You know, he wasn't always blind."

"I didn't know that. What happened to him?"

"The doctors weren't sure. He had a few severe illnesses – he was never healthy to begin with – but no specific reason to cause him to lose his eyesight." He paused for a few shallow breaths. "It didn't happen all at once. It was a gradual process. His world getting darker all the time. All he can see now is shadows. He had to learn to live a completely different way." His breaths kept getting shorter and shorter, like he was running out of oxygen.

"That sounds terrifying."

"It was scary." His chest heaved. "But that's not why I'm telling you this."

"Oh. Then why?" I looked out at the grand landscape in front of us so as not to look directly at Henry. It was getting too upsetting. The tiniest bit of snow still clung to the top of the mountains, refusing to believe it was June, while the wood that climbed the terrain had grown thick with foliage. If I kept focus on the base of the range, I would eventually be rewarded with a glimpse of a creature, be it a rabbit or an opossum or a fawn. I tried to imagine what it would feel like not to be able to see it all. Wondered if I would forget how striking the world could be.

"In one way, my father became a different person," he continued, his breath now so heavy it was audible. "So much had to change in regards to how he lived his life, so it would work for him. It was difficult at first, but he got used to it. We got used to it. The unfamiliar became familiar."

I rolled my eyes at the mountains. "You're saying if I give my dad a chance, I'll realize he's the same person and none of it will make a difference."

"Such...a good student."

We sat in silence, my hand still clasping his, until Henry's breathing slowed. I was glad he had fallen asleep, because all I wanted to do was stare at him without having to explain. I needed to study his face. To memorize every angle, every mole, the exact shape of his full lips, the arch of his eyebrows, the curl of his eyelashes. It would be unthinkable to forget one inch of him. I wished I had a photograph of him, of us, but a camera was hard to come by at Trudeau.

That's when I realized his breathing hadn't slowed. It had stopped. Just as I jolted upright, my lounge chair was jarred so hard from behind I almost fell off. Grasping for the armrest, I glowered at what turned out to be an unnerved Maude bumping me hard with a wheelchair.

"Marilyn, quick, get in," she pleaded.

"No. Henry needs help."

"Marilyn, your mother is here and she's heading this way."

"I don't care," I pleaded, "something's wrong with Henry and I'm not leaving him."

"If you don't get in this chair, you will never see Henry Winters again." She pushed the chair, making it bump me again. "Now!"

I leaped into the chair, trying as hard as I could to slow my racing pulse, as Maude beelined me to the other end of the porch, my neck craning to see Henry. Maude yelled for a passing nurse to attend to Henry, who nodded and picked up her pace in his direction. Maude dumped me into the first open lounge chair like a fisherman throws an unwanted catch overboard. "Sorry," she whispered, zooming back to Henry. I dropped into what I hoped looked like a slouchy-resting position, eyes closed for full effect, when I heard that familiar sound of clicking heels.

She was here. Mildred VanHoosen had heeded my warning, and literally got her ass to Trudeau. Now, when Henry needed me the most.

It was torture not to see what was going on with Henry, although I could hear the commotion forming around him, but I held my position while the clicking stopped then started. Stopped then started. Clearly, she was looking for me. And then, found! The click-click-clicking was heading straight for me. The squeaky dragging of a lounge chair signaled she was willing to communicate with me in public, which was shocking. Would she hiss at me the way she did during her last visit when we were behind closed doors, or would she be on her best behavior so the other patients would only see the delightfully charming Mildred VanHoosen?

"Hello, my dearest Marilyn," she oozed, covering my hand with her own. It was all I could do not to recoil from her touch. She was going for concerned mother.

I blinked my eyes a few times to ensure she had, indeed, woken me from a peaceful sleep. "Mom?" I said, groggily. I could put on an act as well as she could, which was kind of depressing, as I hated to be reminded of our similarities. "What are you doing here?"

"Just checking on my daughter, of course."

How in the hell long was this act going to go on when Henry might very well be dying a porch-length away? And she didn't seem to notice that a patient was in distress, while everyone else on the porch was now focused on nothing but Henry.

"What a nice surprise." I pulled myself up and retied my robe. "Would you like to go to the dining room and get something cold to drink?" Sure, I could keep the charade going, but I didn't have the patience for it. We had too much to get to. "I sure am thirsty."

"Of course, Marilyn. Let me get you a wheelchair."

She clicked away for a bit, and I used the time to ask the feeble old guy next to me if he knew what was going on with the patient in the corner of the porch. He didn't.

I couldn't believe this was my chance to get real answers, and I would have been happier to go the rest of my life without knowing than have to leave Henry in this moment.

Dr. Whitlaw shot down the hallway with two nurses in tow, struggling to keep up with him. "Prepare the room," he commanded over his shoulder, as he passed us on our way to the dining room, his eyes darting from me to Mildred VanHoosen for a split second.

"This surgery is happening *now*."

She parked me in the farthest back corner of the dining room, well out of earshot from the few patients and workers occupying tables. Fetching us both hot teas with milk, she placed mine gingerly in front of me, as if doing something – anything – for me was an awkward endeavor. I wasn't much of a tea person, especially when it was warm outside, but Mildred VanHoosen neither knew nor cared about that fact. The basic off-white cup rattled on the matching saucer as I stirred in the milk, and shook even worse as I tried to bring the cup to my mouth to drink.

When I looked up, she was staring at me intently. "Let's skip the pleasantries. What in the hell do you think you know about your father?"

"Why don't you tell me?" On a different day, I would have been the picture of defensiveness, but my heart felt like it was being torn from my body, and I couldn't muster an attitude beyond forlorn. "He's your husband, not mine."

Her upper lip curled as her eyes went dark. "Always so smug, aren't you?"

"What are you so afraid to say?"

She sipped at her tea, holding her cup near her mouth as she glared at me. "I'm hardly afraid of you."

"I'm not suggesting you're afraid of me. I'm suggesting you're afraid of the truth."

Slamming her cup down, the tea sloshed up, clearly burning her hand. "Oh!" she cried out, as she grabbed for the napkin in her lap, and pressed the cloth around her first two knuckles. She swiftly regained her composure, but it was clear she was in pain. Welcome to my world. "Marilyn, you wouldn't know the truth if it hit you on the head."

"Something must be wrong with your head to marry my father."

She narrowed her eyes, still clutching the napkin fast to her hand. "You don't know the first thing about us."

I tilted my head back at her. All my emotion, first from Betty and then Henry had been churning in the pit of my stomach and was ripening into a thick concoction of anger and resentment. "That's where you're wrong."

"You keep hinting about all this mysterious information you have about your father, and yet, you haven't actually said anything. That's called a bluff, and I'm calling yours."

I pushed my tea away. "I know what I know, Mildred. I was hoping you would do the right thing for once and be honest with me."

She threw her napkin on the table, the burn obviously forgotten. "Don't you dare call me by my first name ever again," she said loud enough to be overheard by pretty much everybody.

"You got it, Mrs. VanHoosen." I felt sure she would volunteer no information. It was up to me to say the words. The thought of saying it out loud to her sent trembles down my body. Why was this so hard with her when I was able to talk freely about it with Henry and Joan and even Jimmy?

The heavy tread of Nurse Doris headed our way. I had become highly skilled in detecting people at Trudeau by their footsteps. It was all I could do not to get up and punch her in the face.

"You have a phone call, Marilyn. I explained you had a visitor and was not available," she said sweetly, knowing full well that I knew she ratted out Betty. She grinned in Mildred VanHoosen's direction as if they were old chums, "but the girl insisted she had to relay an urgent message."

Mildred VanHoosen's eyes met mine. I had my wheelchair backed up and turned around before she could rise from her chair. Pushing my wheels forward as briskly as my semi-frail body would allow, my heart raced faster than my pace. I made it out of the dining room and was rounding the corner, when I caught the chair's front wheel on the baseboard, halting me just long enough to back up a few measly inches to clear the intersection, losing precious seconds. Behind me, Mildred VanHoosen's heels clicked louder and louder. I turned my head and gasped. She was gaining on me, her face set with determination. Huffing and puffing, I launched the wheelchair forward, the telephone just ahead. I saw her shapely leg first, then her pert backside as she overpowered me, her right hand reaching out to grasp the receiver.

"Hello?" she sputtered, in a weird voice that sounded too much like me.

I froze, watching Mildred VanHoosen's body instantly relax, leaning casually against the telephone nook as she listened to the person on the other end of the line. The horizontal creases that had been marking her forehead faded away as a wicked smile played across her lips. "Well, thank you so much for the news, Maggie," she taunted, using her own voice now. "We're all well aware that Marilyn's father is a homosexual." My jaw dropped at her aloof use of the word, like it was no big deal that she was married to a man that was not attracted to women. Who was not attracted to her. Her heavy eyelashes fluttered up as she looked past me. "Isn't that right, Pierre?"

I whipped my head around to see my father and another man standing behind me.

"Don't do it, Mildred," my father begged. "Please."

The phone was still at Mildred VanHoosen's ear. She smiled slyly. "The critical piece of information you're missing is that none of this should matter to Marilyn because he's not her father."

PART 2

CHAPTER 21
CAST AN EYEBALL

The hilly landscape flew by at such an alarmingly fast rate of speed I had to stop staring out the window for fear of getting carsick. But keeping my gaze toward the window meant not having to look anywhere near Mildred VanHoosen, who was aggressively driving us home in a new Studebaker I had never seen before, my suitcase bouncing around in the backseat. So I closed my eyes and replayed my last moments at Trudeau, wishing it had all been an Isoniazid dream, and that at any moment, I would wake up and be back with an alert Henry.

My father grabbed the handles of my wheelchair and turned me around, swiftly heading toward the front doors, but Mildred VanHoosen screamed for security and they came running. Two hefty men in matching white uniforms blocked the exit, their arms folded as if daring us to try to get past them.

We came to a sudden halt, my body nearly catapulting from the wheelchair. Thankfully I had quick reflexes and grabbed the armrests in time to hold me in place.

"Step away from her, Pierre." I could hear Mildred VanHoosen's heels clicking toward us. "You have no rights to her."

I looked up at my father for confirmation. "What is she talking about?"

"I'll explain everything later," my father replied, his hands now firm on my shoulders.

"No, you will not," Mildred VanHoosen said behind us. "Now, move away from Marilyn or I will have you physically removed."

Nurse Doris arrived with my suitcase in tow. I assumed it was already packed. She handed it off to one of the security guys, threw a snide look in my direction, and squeaked her way down the long hallway. I was certain that would be the last time I'd ever see her. Which was something, I guessed.

Without allowing me to change into my own clothes, Mildred VanHoosen took the handles of the wheelchair and pushed me out the front doors, which were now politely being held open by the two big oafs. As soon as we were through, they followed close behind, clearly ensuring my father would not be allowed to intervene again.

I didn't get to say goodbye to Henry.

I didn't know if Henry was alive or dead.

Anguish washed over me. My stomach was in one giant knot. The air from my open window was warm and yet I was chilled to the bone. I had a few hours ahead of me in close quarters with Mildred VanHoosen. I could have asked her anything. Demanded answers about my father and their marriage and the war. But I had no fight left in me. I wouldn't have trusted her explanations anyways. The only thing I really wanted to know was if Henry was okay. And that was the one thing she didn't know. I learned into the hard door panel, pulled my robe tight, and pleaded with my head to let me sleep the rest of the way home.

It was way past dinnertime when we pulled into the driveway. I had successfully conked out for the majority of the drive, and while my stomach was growling – again because I can eat no matter the enormity of the tragedy – I did not want to interact with Mildred VanHoosen, so I went straight to my room, not bothering to turn on the lamp, and crawled into my soft, oh-so-comfortable bed.

"Your days of being waited on are over," she barked from my doorway, startling me. "Starting tomorrow, you will have chores to do, and by next week, I'll expect you to have a job."

I bit my lower lip until I could taste blood. It was better to painfully force myself to stay silent than interact with that woman.

Get a job? I was still undergoing treatment for tuberculosis, for Pete's sake. That is, before Mildred VanHoosen ripped me out of Trudeau, without getting approval from Dr. Whitlaw, mind you. Walking on my own was doable, but I don't know if I could make it to the bus station without help. How was I going to work even a few hours a day?

And another thing: why did I need to work? I didn't know what the hell that woman was talking about. She assured me there was no money since there was no insurance. Yet we have a new dinette set, she has new clothes, and that *car*. A brand-new convertible Studebaker. There was money. Clearly. But if there was no insurance – and based on what I now know for sure about my father there most likely wasn't – how was she paying for everything?

I fake slept until eleven the next morning (yes, I was still doing that), when Mildred VanHoosen rapped on my door and announced she was going out. One would think after all the dramatic events of the past twenty four hours that I would have slept like a baby, but instead I tossed and turned all night. Even with my plush mattress cradling me. I couldn't stop thinking about Henry. Thank God she was leaving. I needed to call Maggie.

As soon as she heard my voice, Maggie shrieked, "I'll be right there!" and hung up the phone. I knew she'd be quick so I hurried into the bathroom to brush my teeth and splash some cold water on my face. I finally changed out of that God-forsaken nightgown and robe, too, into a more me outfit of pedal pushers and crisp white blouse. Maggie was at the door in less than ten minutes.

She flung her arms around me, still careful to be gentle with me. "Mari-boo, where do we start?"

We sat at the new dinette, which I had to admit was as stylish as Maggie had promised, and I recounted everything that had happened once the scene with Mildred VanHoosen and my father had moved far enough away from the phone for Maggie to no longer be able to hear. Turns out no one had bothered to hang up the phone and Maggie had yelled into it for a good few minutes in hopes that someone passing by would hear and tell her what was going on.

When I finished, Maggie asked, "How do you feel about your dad, knowing what you know?"

Giving myself a hug to ward off the chill that wouldn't seem to leave my body, I considered Maggie's question, but only for a split second. "He's my father and I love him."

"Even if he isn't your father?"

"I don't know if that is true, or how it could be true, but he's the only father I know and he's never been cruel to me."

"Even when he stayed away from you after the war?"

I shifted in my seat. "Maggie, why are you pushing this? It isn't

214

like you."

She pressed her lips together and reached for her tan purse, pulling out a fat envelope.

"What is that?"

"It's from your father. He came by early this morning. Said he had been up all night writing this for you, and asked me to give it to you and make sure your mother didn't see." She gingerly slid the envelope across the table to me. "I had to make sure you wanted to hear from him in the first place before I shared whatever is in that envelope."

Taking the envelope into my hands, I considered the heft of it. He must have had a lot to say. Could all my answers be inside?

Maggie patted my hand. "I'm going to give you some privacy. Talk tomorrow?"

I nodded as she stood to leave. "Maggie?"

"Yes, Mari-boo?"

"Could we do something normal tomorrow? Like get a malt, or maybe you could introduce me to Ben?"

She smiled wide. "Of course. In fact, we can do both. How about that?"

"Yes, both would be swell." I grabbed her wrist. "But after that, Maggie, all efforts go toward Henry. I have to know what happened to that boy."

My Dearest Daughter,

I have so much to tell you. But first, I want to say I'm sorry. I'm sorry for the lies, I'm sorry for all the time I was away, and I'm sorry for what I must now tell you. It's true: I'm not your real father. But you have been my daughter from the moment you were born. I love you as my own, and while I realize you may not want to have a relationship with me once you learn the whole truth, know that to me, you will always be my little girl.

The following is my story. I won't be able to write it in one sitting, but I'll do my best to get it all down on paper as quickly as I can. I'm going to ask Maggie to get this letter to you. If she is successful, I'll send her the next one as well.

There is a quote, from the Bible, I think: "The truth will set you free." Marilyn, I am living proof that this sentiment is spot on. My greatest hope is that you will find freedom in it as well.

I first knew I liked boys when Eddie Franz walked into my fourth-grade class and was assigned the seat in front of me. We were already halfway through the school year, but his father was more concerned about finding a job than disrupting Eddie's education, so he moved the family from a coal town in northeastern Pennsylvania to Philadelphia in hopes of a better life.

He smelled like Lava soap, and on that first day, just before taking his seat, he flashed me a nervous smile that made the fair hair on my arms stand on end. Of course, I had no idea what it meant, only that I wanted to be around him all the time. So, I made him my best friend. Thankfully we had plenty in common, especially cards, dominoes, and baseball.

After chores on Saturdays, we often organized baseball games with some of the neighborhood kids over at the field at the end of my street. I could run fast so I was always one of the first kids picked for teams. Eddie was smaller and had terrible control of his body, leaving him one of the last kids standing around, kicking at the dirt like he really didn't care about not being wanted. But I wanted him, so I did my best to convince my team that Eddie had some unique skill, like being able to throw straight as an arrow, which of course he couldn't. I learned quickly how believable I could be, and as a result, Eddie always ended up on my team.

It was a skill that would come in handy throughout my life.

On my sixteenth birthday I touched Eddie in a way he didn't like, and he beat me up pretty bad. I limped away doubled over with two black eyes and a mouth so bloody from direct hits I couldn't eat for two days. My mother fawned over me as I recounted my believable but false story of an unknown pack of boys who bestowed me the beating of my life because I had nothing else to give them. But my father just stood there with his hands in his trouser pockets, considering me with an expression that made me feel exposed.

Boys liking boys was not an area that I knew much about, other than, if you were one who did, you didn't advertise it. While only a decade before being a "fairy" or "pansy" – as it was often referred – had some level of acceptance, in the 1930s you could be arrested for it.

While Eddie hurt me really bad the day I made my feelings known to him, nothing cut me more than him denouncing me a "fruitcake" as he spit at my swollen face.

I made it through my final year of school by keeping to myself, steering clear of Eddie, baseball, and friendships in general. It was a lonely year, but I couldn't imagine getting close to anyone. Instead I spent time with my dad, throwing myself into learning everything there was to know about fixing and maintaining the car he used to drive around his rich boss, William Baker.

He was a reluctant teacher, never quite seeming to believe my intentions. For how natural an actor I was in the eyes of everyone else who crossed my path, my father wasn't buying what I was selling. "Don't you have somewhere else to be?" he said each Saturday morning when I showed up to the garage where the car, a jaw-dropping 1936 Cord 810 Westchester Sedan, featuring a long, low hood and front-wheel drive, was kept.

"Nope," I responded, shrugging nonchalantly, while shoving a rag in my pocket to wipe my hands on later when they became greasy. "What are we doing today?"

My father was called Harold Sledge, which I thought was a very masculine name. His dominoes buddies called him Hal, and my mother never said his name at all, adoringly addressing him as "Dear," even when she lost patience with him, which was rarely.

Everybody liked my dad. But I didn't feel he liked me much at all. At most meals he spoke to my mother, the usual married chitchat about bills and grocery lists and which neighbor was believed to have a wandering eye. I can't remember him ever asking me about school or girls. I wasn't sure if it was because he didn't care or he cared too much to know.

Even when we worked on the car, it was a wordless togetherness, the silence only broken by a request to fetch him a screwdriver or make my layers of wax thinner. I spent every Saturday that year helping my father keep that Cord in pristine condition, and never grew closer to him.

Once I finished school, I found work at a garage in town, my year of Saturdays giving me the know-how to beat out two dozen guys my age vying for the job. I'm sure my father could have gotten Mr. Baker to hire me to do the same type of work, but the truth was I sorely missed talking to people. I needed more.

It was hard work, but I liked it. Over the months, my body got leaner and my muscles swelled. I began looking less like a boy and feeling more like a man. At least physically. I was attracted to a couple of the guys who worked alongside me, but I wouldn't dare do anything about it. Getting beaten by Eddie was one thing. Getting beaten by a crew of men with wrenches was something else entirely.

I even made a few friends – not with the handsome ones, that would have been too difficult – but there were two brothers, Johnny and George, who shared the same gorilla type of face, and another guy named Felix, who was a few years older than me and had no hair to speak of, even eyebrows and eyelashes. I assumed there wasn't any hair in the places I couldn't see, either. My ragtag group of friends suited me just fine. We didn't get involved in each other's lives, but enjoyed inhaling our lunches while talking about what we had read in the newspaper, and of course, girls.

I learned a lot about girls from those three. What they liked (flowers and declarations of love), what they despised (being stood up and having their guy overtly check out another girl), and what they smelled like (Shalimar for the rare ones with money, rosewater for everyone else). I learned that all three of them had crushes on girls who lived in the neighborhood, and not one of them had the nerve to make a move. I didn't tease them about it because I knew exactly how they felt.

A year-and-a-half had passed since I had started at the garage, and I had become a fairly happy person, one of the lucky ones to have a steady job and not be affected by the Great Depression. There were a few times I felt bad, seeing family men walking up and down the streets in their suits and ties, wearing signs that begged for any type of employment. They had known better times. I knew that technically I could be living off my father, and any of those men could have taken my job. I mentioned this to Felix once, and he responded, "How do you know they know anything about fixin' cars?" Felix always made good points. Maybe this was exactly where I was supposed to be.

I used my walks to and from the garage to think about my future, because it was the only time I was really alone, and I didn't have to worry what my expression looked like while I tried to imagine what lay ahead. It was a difficult task. Most people can't define the future without the aspect of love, but I couldn't see how love was possible for me. I was a grown man and still had no idea what it meant to be who I am. It wasn't like I had a manual to give me the answers. And it wasn't a topic that was going to come up over lunch or a game of darts. Even with friends, it was an isolated existence. It was dispiriting not to be seen.

It seemed my future would have a narrow path: I would work hard, save my money, buy a small but comfortable house in close proximity to the garage so I could keep up my walks, and maybe get a dog. I would try out a host of hobbies so my evenings and weekends would be full. And I would tell myself what I had was enough.

The only thing I hadn't settled on was how to explain my long-term bachelorhood. I was a pretty good-looking guy with a steady job. It wasn't a stretch to assume girls would want to go steady with me. Which means nosy aunts and well-intended wives of buddies would inquire, "Who's your girl these days, Paulie?" And when I would shake my head and say, "No girl, right now, no girl," they would of course respond with, "What do you mean, no girl? Paulie's got no girl? That settles it. You have to meet my sister/niece/cousin (insert name here). You're going to love her."

I couldn't deal with that for the rest of my life.

No, I would need a backstory. A great love who died, or better yet, dumped me just as I was getting ready to propose. She would be a flaxen beauty with eyes like jade and the grace of a ballerina. (She would have been professionally trained, of course.) The devastation was so tremendous, I never fully recovered, and pledged to live my days without accepting the love of another.

Everyone loves a tragedy.

One day I showed up to work and something was different. I gave a whistle to Johnny and George, like I always did, but they kept drinking coffee from their thermoses and looking in the opposite direction like I wasn't there. A couple other guys were looking right at me, and what I saw on their faces was contempt. I walked past the office and could see my boss, Mr. Forino, notice my presence, and nod to the owner of the garage, Mr. Weathersford, who was almost never around.

They knew. I didn't know how, but I knew without a doubt my secret was no longer a secret. The fear consumed me, and my body trembled. I kept walking, as if I was unaware of what was happening around me, and made it out the back door before anyone had the chance to openly accuse me of anything. Or everything. I made a beeline to my house, assured my nervous mother it was just a stomachache, and got into bed, pulling the covers over my head and leaving them there until morning.

I got up the next day to use the toilet and splash some water on my face and went back to bed. My mother arrived shortly thereafter with a tray of warm breakfast foods, but I insisted I couldn't possibly with my bad stomach, which only made her more uneasy, and she insisted I see a doctor. I refused and swore it was nothing, because it was nothing. It was

Just my life.

Two nights later, upon my father returning home from work, I could hear my mother pleading with him to go to me and find out what was wrong. I could hear my father making excuses on my behalf, for which I was grateful. He and I both knew to let sleeping dogs lie. But she wouldn't relent, and his heavy footsteps headed in my direction, giving me just enough time to smooth both sheets and my hair, and try to appear more like someone with an illness as opposed to someone no longer interested in participating in humanity.

He opened the door timidly. "Uh, you awake?"

I faked grogginess. "Yeah, yeah. Let me get the light." I reached for the lamp on my bedside table and pulled the cord. The dim light was blinding to these eyes that had gotten used to the dark.

He pulled the wooden chair away from my old roll-top desk and took a seat, placing his ankle over his opposite knee. "Your mom says you haven't been well."

"Yeah," I rolled onto my belly, placing a pillow underneath for maximum effect. "Stomach trouble. It's been rough."

"Hmm."

I hated the way he did that – completely disregarding my words with one half-hearted syllable. I groaned in hopes of shutting him up.

He switched his legs, ran his hands over his face, and exhaled deeply. "I ran into Tony at the hardware store yesterday."

"Tony?"

"Tony Forino."

"Oh."

"He said you were fired."

I bolted upright. "That's not true! I left! I quit!"

He cocked his head. "Why in Heaven's name would you quit a perfectly good job? Do you have any idea how difficult it is for a man to find work in this town?" His voice sounded more sad than angry.

"I had to go."

It was quiet for I don't know how long, but it was quiet. It was early September and the birds were still plentiful and warbling from the high trees beyond the alley. I closed my eyes and concentrated on their melodies, wishing I could be one of them. Wishing I could fly away from it all.

"I have a proposition for you," he finally said, the birds chaotically dispersing from my mind. I remained silent. "Mr. Baker has asked for my help. And, well, you could be instrumental in making that happen."

The pillow was starting to make my stomach hurt for real, or maybe it was the anticipation of what my father was about to ask from me. I placed it back at my head and rolled on my side away from him. He wouldn't get the satisfaction of watching my reaction.

"It seems his daughter, Mildred, has gone and gotten herself in trouble with an older gentleman. He was pretty hard on her, I was told, forced himself on her and then gave her a black eye and broke some bones. Maybe it was her arm or wrist, but she couldn't exactly hide her beaten state from her parents. When she started getting sick daily, the doc confirmed she was with child."

"How awful."

"Yes, it is. Understandably, Mr. Baker and his wife can't have the public knowing what happened. They've kept Mildred in the house for the past few months, but they know the situation must change. People are already Inquiring on her whereabouts. For now, they've said she's gone to stay with an aunt for the summer before starting Vassar in the fall. In the meantime, they want to present her with a new option. A new...opportunity." He stopped to clear his throat, and I could hear him change his position on the chair. "That's where you come in."

I realized I was holding my breath. As if letting it go would unleash a series of events that would forever change my life. On the one hand, I didn't want anyone telling me how I should live or who I should love, not my father, not the guys at the garage, not even Eddie Franz. But, on the other hand, I was so tired. I was so damn tired.

I exhaled.

"I'll marry her."

My father patted me on the back. "Attaboy."

More soon.

Affectionately,

Your father

CHAPTER 22
ODD BALL

By the next day, I had read my father's letter at least a dozen times. At my age, he had suffered so much more than I ever had. Sure, there had been plenty of low points for me – PLENTY – but at least I got to experience love without persecution. To know Henry intimately. To express my feelings without anyone trying to stop me. Anyone except Mildred VanHoosen, that is.

And her.

I didn't know what to think about her.

My father wasn't my father. My real father is some old guy who took advantage of a woman and then, what? Did he dump her because she was pregnant? Did he know she was pregnant with me? Or was I another undisclosed piece of information locked away in Mildred VanHoosen's arsenal of secrets?

The most depressing part was with Pierre not being my father, it was impossible for any of his good traits to have passed on to me. I came from bad and bad. That explained a lot.

For my afternoon with Maggie, and hopefully Ben, I put on my navy plaid skirt and light blue blouse, and strung my pearls – the only nice jewelry I had, given to me by my grandparents for my sixteenth birthday – around my neck. I was still swimming in my clothes, and planned to drink two malts to help fix that issue.

It would be my first time around kids I knew in six months. I was a little nervous.

Mildred VanHoosen kept her distance all morning, for which I was grateful. I knew things about her that, of course, I shouldn't, and truthfully, I feared I wouldn't know how to talk about, or that I would look at her differently, and she would know. Did I still detest her? You bet. But did I also feel a twinge of sympathy? Maybe the absolute tiniest bit.

I watched from my bedroom window as she met the mailman on the sidewalk, thumbed through the day's delivery, and tucked the envelopes into her bag, before taking off in the Studebaker.

Within the hour, Maggie pulled up in her father's Buick, with Ben – I assumed it was Ben as I had never laid eyes on him before – in the passenger seat. That made me chuckle. Maggie was the only girl I knew who would drive her boyfriend around town. For his part, Ben looked perfectly content with Maggie behind the wheel, animatedly talking about something that must have been pretty funny the way Maggie was laughing. I liked Ben already.

I stepped outside and offered a cheerful wave to them both, and made my way to the car, attempting to produce a walk that did not mimic my Trudeau shuffle. Ben slid into the back seat even though I fussed and insisted I could sit in back, but I was happy to be riding up front next to my best friend.

On any normal day, this would be my idea of a perfect afternoon.

226

Driving around with Maggie, a handsome older boy in tow, off to Don's Drive-In where the jukebox would have the kids bopping, and the aroma of the best burgers in Pennsylvania would steer carloads of customers in the direction of the waiting carhops.

But for how free I felt, my mind was chained to incessant thoughts of Henry.

My job was to enjoy my outing with Maggie and Ben while also working on a plan to get information from Trudeau. Hopefully they wouldn't be cross with me when I turned our friendly chatter into full-fledged scheming. They both had already taken on more underhanded endeavors on my behalf than most people would be subjected to in a lifetime. Maybe they would rather put their devious days behind them.

We slid into a booth near the entrance and bellowed for double-stacked burgers, with two malts for me and a vanilla shake for Maggie and Ben to share (adorable). Don's was packed, with teenagers bounding from table to table, and the jukebox blaring Nat King Cole. It was loud and chaotic. A perfect spot to hatch a plan.

"I want to thank you both for how you helped me while I was at Trudeau," I began.

"It was our pleasure," Ben said, sliding an arm around Maggie, who nuzzled into his chest in response. "I hope you found what you were looking for."

"Yes and no," I admitted. "I think there's a lot more to come." I looked out at a handful of couples dancing in the middle of the room, ponytails bouncing and jackets flapping in time to the music, and wondered if I'd ever have enough energy to join in. "There is also one teeny-tiny other thing I absolutely have to find out, and I'm not going to be able to do it on my own."

Maggie and Ben exchanged knowing glances while I held my breath.

"Would this happen to have something to do with Henry Winters?" Maggie asked?

I nodded, certain my face was turning purple.

Maggie giggled. "Mari-boo, how could we say no to you?"

Once we were properly stuffed, we drove back to Maggie's house, where it was decided that Ben would be the one to place the call to Trudeau. He would pose as Henry's uncle, inquiring about his nephew's health.

I crossed my fingers, toes, arms, and legs as we waiting for someone in the office to answer. Ben introduced himself as George Winters, mentioned he was calling from Illinois regarding his nephew Henry, and asked to speak to the nurse in charge.

Maggie patted Ben on the back, smiling her encouragement. She knew as I did that Ben sounded authentic.

"Hello?" he said, clearing his throat. "What's that, then?" He looked puzzled, then downright gloomy. "I see. Yes, okay then, thank you very much for the information. Goodbye."

My breath hitched. "Is he?"

"I couldn't tell you, Marilyn. They have strict instructions not to share any information about Henry Winters with anyone but his parents."

"Mildred VanHoosen strikes again," Maggie piped in.

Ben turned in her direction. "Do you really think..."

"Absolutely," I cut in. "She would most certainly make sure there was no way I could contact Henry again."

"But why?" Clearly Ben hadn't formed a strong enough opinion about Mildred VanHoosen. Yet.

"For spite, Ben," Maggie said, plopping down beside me and wrapping her arms around me. "It's why she does everything."

A few days later, Maggie picked me up and drove me to a park on the other side of town where she deposited me on a bench perched at the edge of a serene pond complete with a family of ducks darting away from my presence. She placed another thick envelope in my hands, and announced she would be reading in the car and to come back when I was finished.

I turned the envelope around and around. Was I ready to know more? I guessed there was only one way to find out.

My Dearest Daughter,

Writing my story to you has been consuming my days and nights. Hopefully you have read my first letter by now, and hopefully you are ready to continue the story. I worry you will learn everything there is to know about me and, at the end, decide you never want to know me again.

I married Mildred Baker at two o'clock in the afternoon on October 1, 1934 at the appropriately unromantic city hall in Darby, Pennsylvania, a town about six miles southwest of downtown Philadelphia, known for being the birthplace of W.C. Fields. I didn't answer right away when the judge performing the ceremony asked me the part about taking this woman in lawful matrimony. It wasn't because I was hesitating. I didn't recognize my own name.

Mr. Baker insisted I legally change my name prior to the nuptials to ensure no one would connect the dots and figure out that his lily-white daughter had, in fact, not left her family estate to make her parents proud at Vassar, but instead got knocked up against her will by a piece of shit, who wanted nothing to do with her or the baby, and had to enter into a loveless marriage with the town loser to save face.

The idea of a name change horrified my mother, who, to her credit, spoke up on the subject, but quickly relented when my father told her firmly, yet lovingly, that the matter had been settled. I was fine with it. How often do you get the chance to become a whole new person? To escape your secrets, and get a hefty allowance to boot? I got to pick the name, which I appreciated, and I thought long and hard about it before settling on Pierre VanHoosen. I sounded educated, worldly, and rich. It was a fine name that made me believe the future could actually be bright. When Mr. Baker's lawyer brought the paperwork to my parent's home on a rainy evening one week before the wedding, it was nothing for me to sign away my identity and say goodbye forever to Paul Sledge.

The only witnesses were our parents. While they were on opposite ends of the spectrum when it came to entitlement and lifestyle, on that day, they couldn't have been more similar beings. The two fathers stood on either side of us in their dark suits erect, solemn, resigned. They were there to complete a transaction and appear, in front of the judge, at least, that we had their blessing in the joining of our lives. The mothers – oh, the mothers. They couldn't hide a thing. I could only hope that the tears that were flowing from both of them read as tears of joy and not what they really were: utter despair. Each kept a hanky at the ready to pat the tears and blow out the snot. It wasn't their intention, but they made quite the clatter. On more than one occasion, the judge had to repeat himself so Mildred or I could hear well enough to respond properly.

When he proclaimed us man and wife, something in my head went gray, as if the place where daydreams lived was snuffed out. I shook it off and held out an arm to escort my new bride to our new life.

We celebrated with our first family supper around the corner from city hall at a fine Italian restaurant with dark walls, dim chandeliers and few patrons, considering it was still early for dinner. We spent our time getting acquainted. All of us. In the time my father worked for Mr. Baker, he had only been around Mrs. Baker a handful of times and had never met Mildred, and it was no surprise Mr. Baker had not met my mom or me. The parents did most of the talking – the fathers, really. The mothers nodded along, agreeing or exclaiming pleasantly, while nibbling on breadsticks, their hankies thankfully tucked away in their sleeves.

Mildred and I mostly snuck looks at each other. She was an attractive girl. Not that I was attracted to her, but you couldn't dispute, based on the symmetry of her face, big dark eyes, and slender frame, the likelihood was high that guys on the streets of Philly turned their heads as she walked by. It felt awkward to try to get to know her right in front of our parents, so I stayed silent, except to ask her to pass the salt. We would have the rest of our lives to learn about each other. The stories, the memories, the funny moments worth sharing could wait at least until morning.

That was the first time I thought about having to share a bed with her.

We would be living just a few blocks away. Mr. Baker had selected a small but well-appointed house for us. The furniture had only arrived the morning before, and I was clueless as to the upholstery colors or the wood of the tables. Apparently, Mrs. Baker had taken care of all that. One might think I would be perturbed not to have a say in my own home, but I decided since my own wife was a mystery to me, it was fine if my house was, too.

Outside the restaurant, I kissed my mother and shook hands with everyone else, while Mildred stood beside me, making no move to dispense a single hug, even to her mother. I thought it best not to bestow any husbandly advice just yet, and instead clasped her hand, turning her in the direction of our home.

We walked the three blocks in silence. It wasn't uncomfortable. I don't think either of us knew what to say. I was carrying a little piece of paper with the address wrapped around the key. Mildred spotted it first.

It was a beige two-story with a flat front and five shuttered windows surrounding the door, which boasted a small overhang to keep the rain off.

"Oh. It's kind of small." She sounded hurt by the realization.

"I'm sure it feels more spacious inside," I offered.

"Of course."

It wasn't more spacious inside to her, but it was a much nicer and larger house than the one I grew up in, so I wasn't about to complain. She let the white wrap she was wearing over her matching white silk long-sleeve dress fall from her shoulders, which she then caught and draped over a low railing that separated the entryway from the sitting room, and wandered away to explore. I walked straight through, until I found the back door, and exited to the yard, already in need of fresh air.

It was quiet, save for the distant shrieks of children playing a game of tag several houses away. The yard was basic, with a thick coating of grass and an oak tree with clotheslines tied to it that was large enough to shade half of our yard and half of the yard next door. I sat on the stoop, pulled out a cigarette, and lit it with the Zippo lighter Mr. Baker gave to me as a wedding present. I wondered if a part of him wished I would use it to burn down the house with the both of us in it, and end the scandal of our marriage and that unborn being of another man's that Mildred was carrying inside her.

By the time you were born, we had been accepted into the neighborhood like any other married couple with their future wide open and a few bucks in their pockets. We were invited to parties most Saturday nights, and even threw one of our own, complete with spiked punch and crystal cups that Mildred had picked up on one of her many shopping expeditions.

Oddly enough, we got along quite well, better than some other married couples I had crossed paths with, even though we had never so much as shared an impassioned kiss. I was grateful the topic of sex never came up. At the end of every night, we put down our books, turned off the lamps, and said goodnight as we got situated on our sides of the bed. A handful of times I had woken in the morning to discover our feet touching or her hand resting on my shoulder, but it didn't mean anything. It's human nature to want to touch and be touched. It didn't have to accompany feelings.

You entering the picture did change our lives somewhat. Before you, we spent our time at home lost in thought or functioning as solitary people occupying a house together. Now we had to operate as a team. We had to rely on each other. It got us talking more, that's for sure. Although sometimes it was only to charge the other with an immediate task, such as "Fetch me a warm towel to clean this mess," or "Walk with her a bit so I can rest." I know some men took no part in caring for their children, but I didn't mind helping out. It didn't matter that you weren't mine. You were all I had.

In the mornings, I would take my toast and coffee beside you at the table while you sat in your highchair, smashing bananas with your pudgy hands. You had a great laugh, and that laugh stayed with me as I drove in to the city each day to my job at Mr. Baker's Starbright Hotel. I was an assistant manager, and I was pretty good at it. The day manager, Mr. Penrod, said I had a way of getting my point across without making the front desk girls cry. I owned four suits, which I mixed with five different shirts, seven ties, and two pairs of shoes in black and brown. I had come a long way from the garage, and never let my eyes linger on a man.

On your third birthday, I was doing my daily rounds and thinking about the little party Mildred and I were throwing for you that evening, with a guest list that included both sets of parents – the first time any of them had been back to Darby since the wedding. It also included Mildred's new friend Dotty Sollars, who recently moved in next door with her traveling-salesman husband Tom. Mildred had baked a layer cake and decorated the dining room with streamers and candles. I had picked up a bright-red tricycle for you, and was eager to teach you how to ride it. I was so lost in thought that I bumped right into a gentleman coming out of the elevator, causing me to drop the papers I was carrying. We both stooped down to collect them, both of us uttering our apologies, and then I noticed his hands had stopped moving. I looked up and saw familiar eyes filled with hate.

"Well, if it isn't the fairy."

"Eddie." I snapped up the last paper and stood so quickly I became lightheaded. With my eyes cast at my feet, I turned to hurry away, but his voice held me fast.

"I heard you got married. To a woman. That's some kind of a sham,

234

don't ya think, Paul?"

I glanced around to make sure no one was in earshot and spotted one of the maids staring at us, her feather duster frozen in position like the Statue of Liberty.

I wanted to say so much to him, but nothing would come out. How do you defend a lie when it's dismantled right in front of your face?

He looked me up and down with disgust. "That girl must be either stupid or ugly to settle for a half-man like you."

My feet remained frozen in place, and I sighed with relief when he finally left me. The maid, however, was still there, and it was the clear understanding in her expression of pity that told me my time at this job was over.

I'm weary from reliving my own life, so I must stop for now.

Affectionately,
Your father

I folded the letter and stuffed it back in the envelope, pondering my father's life while I ambled back to the car.

"You haven't asked me about the letters," I said to Maggie as I slid into the front seat.

"I figured you would tell me when you were ready," she said, closing her copy of From Here To Eternity and setting it between us.

I grasped her hand and forced a brave smile. "I'm ready now."

CHAPTER 23
FLOOR IT

My father may be right. The truth may truly set me free. It was liberating to come clean with Maggie about my parents' life, or at least as much as I knew at this point. She was already aware of so much from all her sleuthing, she may as well get the whole picture.

She was sympathetic to both of them, while my sensitivities were mainly contained to my father.

One night, after Maggie's shift at Macy's, we were holed up in her room going over the details from my father's letters, when she caught me off guard by asking me why I didn't feel bad for Mildred VanHoosen.

"Why should I?" I demanded. "She was foolish, carrying on with an older man. I wouldn't be surprised to find out he was married, too." My thoughts darted to Betty getting physically escorted out of Trudeau, thanks to my empty accusations, and I shuddered.

"Maybe she was in love, Marilyn. Maybe she thought he loved her, too. I can think of somebody else who felt like that and wanted to go all the way with a boy."

I sneered. "Please tell me you aren't comparing me to that woman." I got up from the floor and walked over to the window, pushing the sheer curtain panel aside to gaze at the neighborhood activity below. Dads in rolled up shirtsleeves mowed lawns while moms chatted together in driveways with babies jostling in their arms or toddlers tugging at their skirts. A pack of boys shot marbles on the sidewalk across the street, and farther down the block two young girls with pale hair took turns throwing their pebbles and jumping along the hopscotch board.

They all looked so normal.

Maggie joined me at the window. "How many people do you think believe life is going to go a certain way and it ends up looking nothing like they thought?"

"I don't know." I sighed, everything feeling heavy. "Everyone?"

She playfully elbowed my side, but with my scrawny frame, it kind of hurt. "You're probably right."

It had been a week since I had come home from Trudeau. I still knew nothing about Henry, and Mildred VanHoosen had said about twelve words to me. We kept to ourselves in the house, and had yet to sit down to a meal together. I wished I could have a real conversation with her, but I can't recall ever having anything resembling a heart-to-heart with her. For as far back as my memories would allow, I can't remember feeling tenderness from her. That always came from my father. With her, well, she was there, sure, but I guess I could describe it now as going through the motions. She made me dinner and she bought me clothes and she made sure I did my homework every night, but I don't remember cuddling or compliments or...I think intimacy is what it was that was missing. The older I got, the general day-to-day stuff was delivered through tight lips, her demeanor simmering like a pot of spaghetti sauce. As the heat rose, the lid rattled, and if you weren't careful when you pulled away that lid, a bubble of burning sauce would burst and get you good.

The only things I did have after a week at home was two letters from my father, which led to more questions than answers. (Although I did have some pretty big answers now.) My irritation was palpable.

I wanted to know about the money. Why were there new things – very nice new things – when so much money was going to pay for my treatment? That still didn't make sense. And with my grandparents' wealth, why didn't they help their daughter? They wouldn't let her struggle. They never let her struggle. This was an important piece of the puzzle, that much I knew, but I wasn't sure how to get answers. Especially answers I could trust.

I must have been mostly healed from the tuberculosis, because I really did feel decent, even without my medication. The real plus was that my rash was disappearing! That was a relief because it was too muggy to wear long sleeve blouses. It seemed all that was left was to get my strength back, and I was the only one who was going to see to that, so I pulled the load of whites sitting in the washing machine, dumped the contents into a waiting basket, and lugged it out back to start hanging the clothes on the line. Thank goodness it was a small load, because that basket felt like it was weighed down with an anvil. I may have felt better, but I was easily reminded I wasn't one hundred percent. In addition to getting stronger, I hoped that if Mildred VanHoosen saw that I was doing chores, she'd lay off me getting a job for a while. It was going to be a few months before

I would be up to that level of activity.

Doing laundry was the most laborious task I had tackled since January, and boy, could I feel it. And yet it felt good to do something so ordinary. Without help. Without Freddy. Without Betty.

And then it hit me: Betty.

If I could reach her, she might be willing to help. The truth was, I didn't know if she was aware that the Dr. Whitlaw gossip had come from me. Nurse Doris could have pointed her stubby finger at me as the one she overheard talking about the affair. Not knowing twisted my stomach until it felt like it was housing a tree trunk.

I squeezed the bed sheet I had been holding and rammed it against my head in an effort to make me think. What was Betty's last name? Without a last name, there was no way I was going to be able to track her down. Had she ever told me? I doubted it. Betty had told me nothing personal, even her damn name. No one at Trudeau referred to her by anything other than Nurse Betty. Damn, damn, damn! Freddy would know. He and Betty were friends. I'm pretty sure he would tell me if I asked him. Wait, Freddy would know about Henry, too! Then I wouldn't have to talk to Betty at all. That would be even better. Freddy. Freddy. Flores. Freddy Flores! Oh my God, I knew his name!

I rang up Maggie, but she was at work, and Ben was picking her up at the end of her shift for a date, so I wasn't going to reach Freddy tonight. There was no way I was going to place a long-distance call from my house, and while I thought about going next door to the Sollars' to see if they would let me use their phone, I couldn't risk it. Mildred VanHoosen could have no suspicions.

She couldn't sense my ediginess, either. Fortunately, all the pacing around the house I had been doing had worn me out, or maybe it was the half-hung laundry I had attempted, and I was asleep on yellow sofa when she returned home. It took a minute of getting past the grogginess to realize she wasn't alone.

I knew him as soon as I saw him, and yet I didn't. He was familiar to me, but a stranger. He must have noticed the way I was staring at him because he cocked his head and flashed me a boyish smile in response. "Good to have you back home, Marilyn." His cadence was smooth yet measured.

A response would have been appropriate but I didn't know what to say. Clearly, he knew me. Did I know him?

He put a hand on Mildred VanHoosen's back and guided her into the kitchen, and I had to clasp a hand over my mouth not to cry out. "Mom?" I called out, causing them both to halt. It was foreign for me to address her this way, but I had to see him again. They turned back to me like a single unit, the man's hand still attached to Mildred VanHoosen's back.

"What is it, Marilyn?" She had the ability to fake her voice, too. I studied the man, his high cheekbones, the brilliant blue eyes.

"Never mind, I'm fine."

She clicked her tongue and they disappeared into the kitchen. The sound of ice cubes being dispensed into glasses and the heavy pour most likely from the vodka bottle told me I'd be on my own for the rest of the night.

Thank God. I needed to think. I had found the man from my dream.

. ❖

Maggie was off work the next day so we made plans to take a drive to Little Darby Creek to lift our skirts and walk barefoot in the water. We needed to do something to pass the time until Freddy was done for the day at Trudeau – I knew he worked Monday through Friday – and I needed privacy to work through the identity of the dream man.

It was a perfect summer day for a drive: low humidity, strong sun, and the gentlest of breezes. The sky was a vivid blue, with only a solitary cloud resembling stretched-out cotton candy willing to show itself. We rolled the windows down and hollered to each other over the noise.

It was lucky that Maggie's father took the train into the city for work, leaving his car at our disposal. Maggie was so lucky to have good parents. Parents who appeared to enjoy spending time together, laughed more than frowned, and always offered food to their guests, namely me, who always accepted.

Little Darby Creek is plentiful with trout, and you can always count on a mix of boys and old men along the water's edge, casting their fishing poles while chewing through sandwiches wrapped in wax paper. We bypassed the boys and climbed up to the arched bridge, our favorite spot, flanked on either side by high-climbing vines. We sat in silence beside each other with our legs dangling over the bridge, listening to the continuous burble of the water that was periodically pierced by the squawking of birds high up in the thick trees. Outside of any place that Henry was, this was my favorite spot in the world.

"Do you remember me telling you about the strange man from my dreams?"

Maggie lifted her chin, her eyes darting about. "Yes, I think so. Handsome in one dream and frightening in the other, right?"

"Right." I picked up a tiny twig that had fallen onto my dungarees and twirled it between my fingers. "I'm pretty sure Mildred VanHoosen is dating him."

I filled her in on the previous evening's excitement: the visitor's familiarity, how he most definitely knew me, and of course the chiseled cheekbones and the icy-blue eyes that could chill me to the bone.

"Honestly, he seemed pleasant enough," I admitted, "But when he said it was nice to have me home again, you would have thought he lived with us or something."

Maggie shook her head. "I can tell you I never saw a trace of him on the occasions that I snuck in while you were away."

"I suppose that's good." I flicked the twig into the water and tucked a leg under me. "It was so strange. She didn't introduce us, and they didn't spend more than a few seconds in my presence. She wasn't hiding him, but she also wasn't eager to have us together."

"Maybe she didn't want to answer any questions in front of him."
"That could be."
"I wonder how long they've been together?"
I huffed. "Wouldn't that be something to know?"

At precisely six-thirty that evening, I placed a call to Information, requesting the number of a Fredrick Flores in Saranac Lake, New

York. We were leaning against the kitchen wall with the phone between us, Maggie's head pressed against mine, struggling to hear. Maggie's brother Frankie was playing a Johnnie Ray record in the living room, and Maggie scurried out there more than once to make him turn it down.

With pencil and paper ready, I scrawled jagged numbers with my shaking hand and hung up the phone. I couldn't believe I was going to talk to Freddy.

We picked this time strategically, thinking it was late enough that Freddy would be home from work, but early enough that he wouldn't be out with his buddies yet, assuming he had buddies.

Why I was shaking, I didn't know. It was Freddy, after all. I could talk to him. He knew bad things about me and was still kind to me. He wouldn't be mad to hear from me. I just didn't know what he'd be willing to tell me. Two deep breaths later, I picked up the receiver, dialed the number, and waited while it rung. And rung. And rung.

"Hello?" The voice was winded.

"Freddy?" I practically whispered.

"Speaking." He sounded more like himself. "Who's calling?"

"It's Marilyn."

"Whoa." The line was silent.

"Freddy? Are you still there?"

"I am. I'm just surprised to hear from you."

"I know." I turned my back to Maggie, suddenly feeling exposed. "I'm sorry to call you out of the blue like this, but I really need a favor, Freddy."

"What sort of favor?"

"I need to know if Henry made it through surgery. Or if he even made it *to* surgery. Mildred...uh, my mother took me out of there so fast...I don't know anything, Freddy."

"Ah." He sniffed. Paused. The silence was interminable. "To be honest, I don't know. The only patients I pay attention to are the ones I'm working with."

"But you could find out, couldn't you?"

"Yes, Marilyn, I could find out."

The joy of his words flooded my body with warmth. "Oh, thank you, Freddy! I can't thank you enough!"

"On one condition," he commanded.

I stiffened. "What is it?"

"There's someone else you need to reach out to."

I gulped. "Betty."

"Yep."

Freddy took down Maggie's number, so he could relay news of Henry through her, and I reluctantly recorded Betty's phone number and address. All there was to do now was wait.

And figure out what to say to Betty.

Three days later, there was still no word from Freddy, but another letter from my father arrived via my best friend. I walked the four blocks to Maggie's house, feeling rather pleased with my endurance, and snatched the letter from her waiting hands, taking it to the backyard to read it in private under the shade of a towering weeping willow.

My Dearest Daughter,

It's been painful to record my life in this manner, reliving details I had put out of my mind for such a long time, but you remember what I said about the truth, and this is my truth, so it's important to face it.

It wasn't an everyday thing to just up and leave a cushy job at your father-in-law's company. At least not without getting fired for being a dope. If I was going to quit, it had to be for a hell of a reason.

Which is why I joined the Navy.

A love of country and desire to serve were the noblest of reasons to quit a job. Mildred might not be happy about it – after all, compared to being a manager rising up through the ranks at a first-class hotel, being a low-level serviceman made me common all over again – but at least in public, she wouldn't dare scourge my choice.

Leave it to Mr. Baker to ensure his son-in-law steered clear of commoner status. Thanks to high-level contacts in the government, he got me a nomination to the Naval Academy in Annapolis, Maryland, and it was no surprise to anyone (except me), that I was accepted.

It was a surprisingly joyous time. Going to college hadn't entered my thoughts. Ever. Working with my hands had come naturally to me, and I liked it well enough to do it the rest of my life and not feel like I had missed out on some grand opportunity to elevate my position.

Working as an assistant manager proved I had a knack for overseeing people, and could keep an operation running smoothly, even when a high-society wedding was taking place under the hotel's roof, and the hyper newspaper photographers were jostling for position outside the front doors to capture so much as a strip of netted veil for their curious readers.

Interestingly, it was both my mechanical expertise and my management capabilities that made me the ideal recruit, and in September 1936, I left behind Mildred and you to become an officer-in-training, known as a midshipman, at the Academy.

I joined the rowing team, studied hard, trained even harder, and got pretty good marks. I missed you like crazy – and if I were being honest, I would admit I missed Mildred a little, too. She had become a sort of sister to me. I wasn't a dummy; I knew she didn't like her life. She showed it daily with temper tantrums over anything and everything. Her life was a fraud. Mine was too, but the difference was I had made peace with it. Mildred never did. She wanted what every girl of her position did: love, romance, glamour, presents, and travel. I provided her with none of it. She did her best to make herself glamorous, getting the latest hairstyles and lipsticks, trying out every new beauty product she read about in her magazines, and learning how to fix a very dry martini, and then gulping it down in a single swallow. Her greatest problem was being accustomed to getting everything she wanted, and having that way of life vanish by getting pregnant. Or in her eyes, by getting married to me.

While I liked Mildred fine enough, she refused to like me. It would have been like admitting defeat. Put up with me was the best she could do.

I couldn't help but assume that my time away at the Academy would make her happy; give her the freedom she had longed for. Sure, she would be alone with you, but if she whined to Daddy long enough, Mr. Baker would supply her with a nanny for at least a few afternoons a week.

At least with our current circumstances she could exist in her own house and not have to fake a thing.

Missing you wasn't a surprise, but just how much I missed you was. Having been with you since before you was born, it was natural to think of you as my own. Funny enough, passersby assumed you were my daughter because we had the same color eyes – a hazel that veered from yellow to green, depending on the light, while Mildred's were so dark. Until the Academy, you were the only thing to put a smile on my face. Like Mildred, I, too, wanted love. But if I couldn't have romantic love, unconditional love from cute little you would be enough.

I did make trips home via train, but within twenty-four hours under that roof I would find myself restless and feeling trapped, no matter how good it was to toss you in the air and make you laugh. If the weather was fair, I spent as much time as I could in the backyard, still desperate for the fresh air as I was my first evening there. You and I could stay out there for hours, picking up sticks and fashioning them into little houses and hitching posts for imaginary families and their horses.

When Tom Sollars was around, we would fix drinks and drag chairs to the farthest reaches of the lawn so we could smoke and talk over the girls' giggling as they danced to The Ink Spots records. If anyone were to come upon all of us back there living it up, we would have appeared to be the most normal, happy-go-lucky folks around.

Nights were the hardest though. I had gotten use to sleeping alone again at the Academy, even though I shared a cramped room with three guys who seemed to be competing for most turbulent snore. Sharing a bed with Mildred, especially when she'd rest her foot on my leg then snap it away once she had stirred enough to recognize it was me, made me feel lonelier than ever.

When World War II broke out in 1939, the world changed overnight, and yet I remained at the Academy, training to be an Ensign, until 1941 when the Navy entered the war. That May, I was commissioned to the Atlantic Fleet to serve as an Ensign in the engineering division on the USS Mississippi, a battleship big enough to hold more than a thousand men and more than enough armament. Our duty was to protect American shipping as part of the Neutrality Patrols during the Battle of the Atlantic. It sounded more interesting that it was. For the most part, we were escorting British ships. It had nothing to do with my job. I predominantly worked in the engine room, keeping the turbines, boilers, and pretty much everything else, for that matter, running smoothly. It was better than manning a gun turret on deck. We were called "Snipes", me and the guys I oversaw, or the "Black Gang", because we were constantly covered in soot. It was hot as hell down there, so hot, in fact, we took salt tablets to make up for what we were losing in sweat. I was covered in grease, and my clothes were sweat drenched and foul smelling, and yet, I never felt that overwhelming need to rush up to the deck for fresh air. I was as home as I was ever going to be.

The Snipes went about our days as if there were no war, as we had jobs to do no matter what, whether we were in a perilous situation or cruising a peaceful sea. When we weren't working, we took our bland meals in an unbelievably cramped mess hall, and played cards, smoked cigarettes, or wrote letters home. I joined the boxing squad partly to pass the time, but mainly to learn how to protect myself. It was worth the jabs to the face to figure out how to throw a mean right hook. The worst thing that happened to us during that time was a storm so monstrous, we lost boats, equipment, and finally our main catapult from the quarterdeck. That was the only time I thought we might not make it.

In December, immediately following the Japanese attack on Pearl Harbor, Mississippi returned to its original Pacific Fleet, and I went with it, departing Iceland bound for San Francisco.

To say it was difficult to be on a crowded ship, with a plethora of rough seas and a minimal number of toilets for an extended period of time was an understatement. We never stopped sweating and were lucky to manage a shower once a week. It took me a month to get used to rocking below deck.

But one thing made that ship better than anyplace else I had lived: Matthew. Matthew Petry was a fellow Ensign – his focus was in administration – a year younger than me, with the toothiest grin I ever did see, and a strong jawline that forced my glance to follow their lines upward to land upon almost gray eyes that would have come off cold if it weren't for that grin to balance the glare.

He was so handsome, I had trouble forming coherent sentences in his presence, which he later confessed he had found charming.

I still had no experience with boys, and was clueless in deciphering who might be like me. A secret signal would have been appreciated. The only thing I had to go on with Matthew was his long looks in my direction. Guys did not do that. Not to other guys, anyway. The butterflies went nuts anytime I returned the stare. I felt so out my element and yet so unbelievably happy.

We had been exchanging looks for a few weeks, but had not yet had a real conversation – or anything else real, for that matter – when he was reassigned to my room. The bunk over mine, to be specific. When he walked into the crowded room with his arms encircling all his possessions, his wide smile said everything I needed to know.

It was common on ships for guys to create some semblance of privacy by stringing up curtains across the long side of their bunks. Much better for taking care of your needs in the dark of night. It also made it easy for Matthew to reach his hand down the side of the bunk against the wall on that first night in my room. I laid there on my back, my eyes open long enough to have already adjusted to the darkness, and fixed on that hand, while trying to keep my heart from bouncing off the bottom of his bunk. It felt like hours, but only a minute or so had passed before I got the nerve to reach my hand up to his, and lightly stroke his fingers with the tips of my nails. The electricity between us was so palpable, I couldn't help but check to make sure the other guys weren't perched on the edge of their bunks, preparing to beat us senseless. Hearing their synchronized snores allowed me to relax a little, and I returned my focus to Matthew and his soft, yet strong hand. We touched each other as far as the wrist until I was bleary-eyed, and I succumbed to sleep, pulling my arm under my cheek so I could drift off smelling his scent.

Anytime we were lucky enough to be alone in our room, we used the time to learn every detail about each other. He was from Fresno, had four older sisters, and his mother had died shortly after giving birth to him. His parents were determined to have a boy, and his father was sure his wife's death was a curse for not being happy with what they had.

"Imagine how cursed he'd feel if he knew that I'd never carry on the family name," Matthew confessed to me, his face drawn. I wanted to squeeze his hand or give him a comforting hug, but I wouldn't dare take that chance.

Like me, Matthew joined the Navy to escape his life, and like me, the decision was made better by our meeting.

He wasn't fazed by my marriage to Mildred. In fact, he understood. He knew our options were limited. He had enjoyed one short relationship with a schoolmate, but the other boy's parents got wind of what was going on and they moved away without warning.

I shared countless stories about you, and read out loud to him the rare letters I received from Mildred. The longer I was away, the more infrequent the letters became. For the bulk of the guys, the opposite was true. I could only assume Mildred was enjoying her husband-free life more and more. Maybe she had met someone. I wouldn't blame her if she did. I had, and was well aware of the positive impact it was having on my life. She deserved the same happiness. But I would have appreciated regular updates on you.

Days before Christmas, while still on course for San Francisco, I got the most miraculous present. Food poisoning was sweeping the ship. No one could pinpoint the cause, and guys were dropping like flies. Our bunkmate Neal was on duty that evening, and our other mate Gene had succumbed to the illness pretty bad, and was in Sick Bay for the night. Everyone was preoccupied with either being sick, helping the sick, or steering clear of the sick, which meant Matthew and I could close our door and really be alone.

We were terrified. On a normal night, our door would be open and guys would pop in and out like it was Grand Central Terminal. Even with a host of guys losing their stomachs all over the ship, we knew anything could happen. We had to be careful.

He pulled me just on the other side of the door, so in case someone barged in, we could break away in time. His kiss shattered me. It was like getting the answers to everything I never understood about life. We didn't have sex, we were too afraid to try something that bold, but I didn't care. To kiss him, hold him, stroke his face, and burrow into his neck – it was everything. I said "I love you" first, and stood there in his embrace, my breath hitched and every part of my body tense, bracing myself for him not to say it back.

"I love you, too."

We feel asleep to the sounds of vomiting in the toilet stalls down the hall. I had never been so happy.

We reached San Francisco in late January 1942. It was good to be back on land. Being in San Francisco was like being surrounded by the war. Virtually everywhere you looked around the bay, work was going on to further the war effort, especially shipbuilding. And so many women worked as shipfitters! They were even welding! It was exciting to witness such a shift from the norm of women tending to the house and children. And if truth be told, those women looked happy, too. You walked by any shipyard and you could see women working diligently alongside the men, and when they weren't working, walking arm-in-arm, full of life and smiles and possibilities. It was exactly how I was feeling.

There was a plethora of things to love about San Francisco, from the agreeable climate to the breathtaking beaches and the majestic mountains. But there was one other thing that made me love this city, that made me believe in possibilities: I wasn't alone here. It wasn't blatant, but there were other homosexual men here. I told Matthew about it and we went walking together one afternoon along the waterfront, passing by the far-stretching piers, trying to guess who was and who wasn't. Who knew that could be a joyous game?

For seven months we went between land and the Pacific, escorting convoys and doing training exercises. I had never been so content as during those months. I loved the west coast. I loved Matthew. I loved my strength and my abilities and my contribution to my country. It was funny, I had joined the Navy to escape my life, but it turned out that was right where I had found it.

I'll get the last of it down as quickly as possible.

Affectionately,
Your father

I was halfway through my second read of the letter when Maggie began screaming to me from the kitchen window, waving the telephone hysterically. Scooping up the pages and envelope and stuffing them under my arm, I bolted inside where Freddy was waiting on the other end of the phone.

CHAPTER 24

GO APE

"He's still here."

It was the most wonderful thing I had ever heard in my life.

Mrs. Ryder was in the kitchen preparing dinner, and while I'm sure she had some idea of what was going on, because Maggie told her *everything*, it was uncomfortable to take a personal call in front of not one, but two people. I was hoping like hell that Frankie and Ben wouldn't waltz through the door next.

"What else did you find out, Freddy?"

"Just the basics. He had the surgery, it was touch and go, but he made it through. Maude said he'll always deal with some health problems, but he'll live. Maude also said to tell you hi."

"Hi back." I crumbled to the floor, and Maggie stepped away from the counter to curl up next to me. She took the phone from my lap as I sobbed into my hands.

"It's Maggie. Thank you so much for your help, Freddy. I can't tell you how much we appreciate it."

She petted my head as she listened to Freddy.

"Okay, Freddy, I'll be sure to tell her. Bye now." She handed the phone off to her mom, who hung it up with one hand while beating eggs with the other.

"Good news, dear?" Mrs. Ryder asked, her hips sashaying in time with the beater.

I nodded and dabbed my eyes with my skirt. "The best news ever."

Maggie patted me on the shoulder and got up to assist Mrs. Ryder, running a chunk of yellow cheese across a grater, the confetti-like shards falling cheerfully into a large bowl. Mrs. Ryder melted butter into a saucepan, then whisked in flour.

"What are you making?" I couldn't imagine spending an afternoon in the kitchen with Mildred VanHoosen, splitting up a recipe and working as a team.

"It's a cheese soufflé," Mrs. Ryder said. "And I expect you to stay for dinner and try it for yourself."

I grinned. "I'd love to."

"Marilyn has some work to do first," Maggie said, not taking her eyes off the sharp grater as her fingers came closer and closer as the cheese chunk got smaller and smaller.

My head cocked in response. "What kind of work?"

"Freddy said you know what to do."

I pulled myself off the floor and plopped down at the kitchen table, taking a deep breath. "Got any stationery handy?"

At least fifteen minutes had passed before I finally put pencil to paper. I had to tell her the truth. Whether she knew or not, I couldn't go on wondering. It was too much to bear. But how do you apologize for having done something so terrible, you altered another person's life? It was difficult not to think of Mildred VanHoosen and my father. Their parents altered the courses of their lives by making them get married. Mildred VanHoosen altered the course of my life by not getting me the tuberculosis vaccine. My father altered the course of my life, too, by not being around to ensure I was being cared for. I didn't mean to alter Betty's life. I loved her. I was just being stupid. Maybe they all loved the person they were being stupid to as well.

My brain was drained by the time I finished writing the letter – two pages of apologetic scribble. Asking her to forgive me wasn't the hardest part. Telling her how much I loved her and appreciated her and thought of her as a mother was. The truth hurt. Even if she didn't reply, even if I never heard from her again, I hoped my words would free Betty from any sadness I had caused.

It was getting dark as I left Maggie's house, my stomach filled with yummy soufflé. I promised to help with the cooking next time, which was rich, because I've never cooked anything in my life. But it would be better to learn, even if I sliced my fingertips on that grater, than to write another gut-wrenching letter.

The crickets serenaded me as I meandered my way back home. As I approached, I saw that man help Mildred VanHoosen out of his car and hold her close. Their kiss goodbye was passionate, and for some reason, that made me sad. I stayed back in the shadows until she was in the house and the man had pulled away.

Closing the door quietly behind me, I walked around the main rooms, looking for her. I found her in the backyard, smoking a cigarette on the glider. With a deep breath, I took the seat beside her without asking for permission. Her eyes were suspicious but she didn't say anything.

"Your boyfriend is handsome," I began. "What's his name?"

She ashed on the ground and stared straight ahead. "Walter."

"That's a nice name."

"He's not my boyfriend. He's my fiancé."

I almost roared but I kept my composure. She was engaged?

"You're getting married?"

"Eventually. Once the divorce is finalized."

"You'll be a divorcée." I didn't mean to say it the way it sounded, but it just came out that way.

"Oh, Marilyn, I've been worse things than that. A divorce isn't going to kill anybody."

I wanted to tell her that I knew. That my father had revealed everything, or almost everything: what the older man had done to her, what her parents had done to her, but I wasn't sure she could take it. I also didn't want to screw up the first real conversation I had ever had with my mother.

"Did you used to smoke?"

She considered the cigarette butt between her fingers then flicked it into the grass. "Ah, it's a silly little habit. Picked it up from Walter. He likes us to come out here after dinner and share a cigarette and talk about the future." I swear she was blushing. "You could call him a romantic."

"Are you happy?"

She turned toward me. "Not yet. But I'm getting there."

"I want you to be happy, Mom, I really do." Without thinking, I threw my arms around her and pulled her toward me. She tensed up, but then relaxed in my hug. And then she hugged me back.

"There aren't many people who have wanted that for me." She pulled back and held onto my arms. Her eyes were watery, and she blinked back what I can only imagine was a lifetime of imprisonment.

I remembered what it felt like to be a prisoner.

My Dearest Daughter,

My story ends with this letter. At least my story to this point. I'd like my story to continue with you in it. What do you think about moving to Florida?

We spent that next year in combat, going from Hawaii to the Aleutian Islands to the Gilbert Islands. On November 20, 1943, there was an explosion in the number two turret. Forty-three men died. Among the dead was Ensign Matthew Petry, who was there receiving training from Petty Officer Robert James, who also perished.

I was in the mess hall eating lunch when word broke out. Dropping my utensils, I ran up to the deck to help, not yet fully briefed on the injuries or casualties. Guys were already there, pulling the dead from the debris and laying them out in a line on the deck. When I saw him, I lost my mind. The guttural screams wouldn't stop. I threw myself on his charred body, the heat permeating me, and I wrapped myself around him, my tears streaming onto his disfigured face. I didn't think. I didn't care. The devastation was too consuming to consider the consequences. They all saw me. They knew. My secret was out. My happiness was gone. I was alone again. And there would be trouble,

During the trip back to San Francisco, I stayed in my bunk, alone. We had lost enough men that was it easy for my bunkmates to move into other rooms. I only left to get meals, of which I could barely eat, and use the toilet. My grief swallowed me. I couldn't have concentrated on my duties if they had let me come back to work, which they didn't.

My duffel bag was packed and ready when we docked. I was informed I was leaving the ship and the Navy. It was never officially discussed, but I had received a Blue Ticket discharge. It was better than being court-martialed, which is what would have happened to me had it not been wartime, but still, that blue paper would taint my life forever.

It was strange to be back in my own clothes, alone and wandering the streets of San Francisco, which had once been such a merry place. I had no money and refused to contact my parents or the Bakers or Mildred, so I lived on the streets, begged for food, and fitfully slept on park benches and under bridges.

I lived like that for the next three years. It was during those years that I also had sex for the first time. With a man, a stranger, and then another and another and another. I wasn't looking for love. Love had already found me and deserted me. But I wanted to feel. Sometimes the men were nice and would let me spend the night, even give me a hot cup of coffee in the morning. But some were cruel, unable to come to terms with themselves, and they treated me like I was nothing, a thing they could use and dispose of as it suited them. And I was fine with it. I felt like I deserved it.

It was also easy for them to treat me that way because I no longer looked the part of the sailor or the boxer or the rower. I had lost a good twenty pounds and my muscles that I was once so proud of had atrophied, and I more closely resembled runt than war veteran.

In 1946, I got influenza so bad I was hospitalized, and it was during my stay that a kind nurse with strong arms and soft eyes, who helped me fill out my paperwork, also took the liberty to write a letter to Mildred, pleaded for her to come to California and bring me home.

What was most surprising is that she did come, begrudgingly, but she came. And I was forced to come clean. She deserved to know my truth. What she chose to do with it was up to her. She stayed for two weeks at a nearby hotel until I was well enough to travel. Mr. Baker had sprung for tickets on American Airlines, thinking he was welcoming home a war hero.

There were a few good things about coming home. You, now twelve and lovely, were the best part, although you had been without me for so long with our communication over the years nothing short of intermittent, that you barely knew me and had become shy in my presence. Hot baths and nourishment were tied for second, and I crammed in as much food as my reduced belly could hold. It was also quite nice to have money again, as everything I had earned while in the Navy had gone directly home to Mildred.

But I was terribly unhappy. This wasn't my life. This wasn't my wife. I didn't try to share a bed with Mildred, and she wouldn't have wanted me to, anyway. I stayed in the guest room, and spent most nights wrestling with insomnia and desolation.

I focused the next five years on you. You were the only bright point in my life and I decided to be grateful for you rather than wallow in all I had lost. We grew close again, sharing hot fudge sundaes at your favorite restaurant in Darby with the paper placemats that we turned into funny hats, going for bike rides on Sunday mornings, and talking about your schoolwork and friends and crushes on warm evenings in the backyard. I remember that fashion show I took you to where Maggie worked. I had to admit it was quite fun to witness all the pomp and circumstance of the society ladies clucking about, and the models gliding up and down the makeshift runway.

I was complacent, definitely not content, and told myself daily it would have to be enough.

You had grown close to Mildred's parents, who, I learned, spent some time at our house while I was away, especially Mrs. Baker, who did have a genuine kindness to her. I was happy you had other figures to care for you than only Mildred. I didn't want your views on the world to be too distorted.

Things got bad all over again in 1951. Mildred had quietly fallen in love with a banker named Walter and wanted a divorce. You were at the crux of your high school years, and were exhibiting all the self-absorbed traits of a teenage girl, including never being around. Our special together time in the backyard vanished, and I was back to feeling lonely. Mildred made it clear I would have to leave the house so she could be free to marry the banker, and I was guessing the kindness Mr. Baker had shown me in rehiring me at his hotel would be stripped away once he got wind that our marriage was over. I assumed he wouldn't be too kind to Mildred, either.

I needed to get away for a while to clear my head and plot my next move. I convinced Mr. Baker to send me to Florida to see about opening a Starbright on Miami Beach. It was a relief when he quickly agreed. I went home to pack a bag and relay the news to you and Mildred. You were sick and asleep. I felt guilty leaving you without saying goodbye, but Mildred insisted I leave you be. Needless to say, Mildred was thrilled with my "opportunity" to work in Florida, and literally helped me pack my bag.

I sat with you for a few minutes while you slept, and before leaving the house I kissed your hair, the heat of your fever radiating from your head. As I closed the front door behind me, a solitary suitcase in the other hand, I experienced a powerful awareness that I wouldn't be back again.

Miami Beach turned out to be a great choice for the next Starbright Hotel, and it was likewise a great choice for me. Sexuality was more open here, and I had emotionally healed enough to no longer welcome abuse, and instead accept that I deserved to love and be loved.

I met Thomas at the end of my first month in Florida. I hired his firm to handle the architecture, which Mr. Baker and I agreed would be different from its sister hotels. While the other Starbrights were very traditional in décor, this one would be modern, with rounded corners and neon and the largest pool in Miami Beach.

Thomas and I became fast friends, and as we sought out each other's stories, and found we were both alone with no girls to discuss, he straight out asked me if I preferred men and I said yes with no concern that my answer might get my bell rung.

Turned out Thomas had tried the married route, too, but unlike Mildred and me, he and his ex-wife Darlene had twin daughters together. I asked him how he had gotten through the sex, and he replied, "Very carefully." Thomas was funny that way.

In only two weeks, I checked out of my hotel and moved into his home, and his girls, Tina and Molly, came to stay with us every other weekend.

The girls were ten and not aware enough to question our living arrangement. We kept separate bedrooms, but only used them when the twins were on the premises.

We broke ground on the newest Starbright Hotel in June 1952, just before your eighteenth birthday. I considered calling you, or sending you a card, but I didn't. I had made peace with that part of my life being over. You may hate me for that, but you weren't really mine, and I didn't think I had a right to you. I also didn't think Mildred would allow me any rights to you. My usefulness for her family had run its course, and the truth was I didn't believe you would suffer any adverse effects from my absence. I figured you were used to not having a father around. I focused instead on the notion that I finally had a future that felt like me. And I wanted so much to enjoy every minute.

Construction was expected to be completed by Christmas, Thomas and I were in love, and his girls were delightful. On the weekends when Tina and Molly were at their mother's, we would travel around Florida, and even visited the Bahamas. Everything was going my way. And then, just days after breaking ground, I received a letter from a young man named Henry Winters.

Henry had located me through Dotty Sollars, who gave him the name of the hotel where I had been staying. The hotel forwarded the letter on to Thomas' house. Once I finished reading the letter, I sat down on the kitchen floor and cried. Mildred hadn't told me you had tuberculosis, or that you had been living in a sanitorium for months.

I called Dotty, and she filled me in on life in Darby after I left. She said that shortly after placing you in the sanitorium, Mildred announced to her parents that she wanted a divorce. Their initial response was to bribe

264

her. They gifted her with clothes and furniture and even cash. Still, she remained headstrong about the divorce. I was proud of your mother when I heard that. She had never stood up to them before. Never. The money, not to mention their judgment, had kept her in check all those years. Dotty said she almost fell over when their last-ditch effort showed up out of the blue: a brand-new car. Mildred took it all, then asked them to also gift her a lawyer. Dotty said that didn't go over too well. They cut her off from their money. Completely.

Marilyn, I want you to know that if I had known, I would have done something. I wouldn't have left you like that. Dottie said you were diagnosed just a couple of days after I left. I didn't know you were that sick. Were you even aware I was gone? Had your mother told you? It eats me up to think of my little girl having to go to a sanitorium all alone. You must have been scared. Or, knowing you, you were probably angry.

I wish I had known about your mother's financial strain, too. She wasn't my enemy, you know. The years made her colder. Once you resign yourself to the fact that life isn't going to be as you pictured, you lose your fire. We got stuck in a crummy situation together. And neither of us handled it well.

I kept picturing you in that place, surrounded by sick people, and I retreated to my room to start packing. When Thomas came in from the garden and saw me stuffing clothes into a suitcase, he panicked, thinking I was leaving him. I handed him the letter, which he scanned, before setting it down on the bed and walking out of the room without a word. I stood there not knowing what to do: Do I take the time to reassure Thomas or do I hail a cab and get to the airport so I could be with my daughter? I didn't have to decide. Thomas was back in mere moments with his own suitcase in hand.

"I was already packed for my business trip to Jacksonville. I'll take it as a sign."

It took three flights to get to the Saranac Lake Regional Airport. It was June 18, one day after your birthday, and I was going to get you the hell out of that place.

The last time I was that far north, I was sailing to Iceland aboard the Mississippi. How things had changed. How we all had changed.

I'm enclosing my phone number. Now that you know everything, I hope you will use it. I love you, Marilyn.

Affectionately,

Your father

"Hello, Dad?"

TWO YEARS LATER

EPILOGUE

Eighty degrees in December still felt strange, but that's what you got living in Florida. But it wasn't going to stop me from trimming the most beautiful tree ever. We were expecting a full house and I wanted everything to be just right.

Maggie and Ben would be here for the whole week between Christmas and New Year's, and the goal was to plan the majority of their May wedding while we were together. I was, as promised, serving as maid of honor.

When I talked to my mom last week, I let her know Maggie was extending a wedding invitation to Walter and her. I swear, I could hear her beaming on the other end. They got married in April 1953, and I felt terrible not being able to come, but I was finishing up my senior year of high school, and couldn't get back to Pennsylvania. She was understanding, but I know what she really felt bad about was her parents' refusal to attend. Turned out I didn't like my grandparents as much as I thought. They were fake, fake, fake, and while the presents flipped my lid, if there was one thing we learned from my father's life, being authentic is the only way to live.

The funniest part about going back to school was passing Henry in the halls. He finally got out of Trudeau in November of '52. My father and Thomas flew to New York to get him and bring him back here. My mother called up to Trudeau a couple of weeks after we had that talk in the backyard and granted me permission to call and write to Henry. We spoke every other Sunday and wrote letters as furiously as our hands would move. It felt like there was never a day between July and November that a letter from Henry Winters didn't arrive in the mail.

Just after the New Year, I got a piece of mail I never thought would come: a reply from Betty. It had been forwarded from my mother, and it took me a whole day before I got up the nerve to open it. Imagine my surprise when I read about her whirlwind romance with a forestry professor at Paul Smith's College not far from Trudeau. They eloped to Niagara Falls just a month after meeting in a coffee shop, and she enclosed a photo of her with a baby in her belly! She never mentioned what happened, and I was relieved. All I ever wanted for Betty was her happiness, and based on the look on her face, she had found it.

In the summer of '53, my father and Thomas took one more big trip: To bring Henry's parents to our home in Miami Beach to stay. There were eight of us, including Thomas' girls Tina and Molly on the weekends, living under one cramped roof, but we were madly happy.

Henry enjoyed spending time with his parents Bert and Irene, feeding his father oatmeal with cinnamon and raisins every morning for breakfast before he left for Thomas' architecture firm, where he worked as a project assistant after officially graduating high school in June. And in the evenings when the radio was on, he never failed to pull his mother to her feet and dance her around the living room, always causing her to giggle like a young girl.

Bert's cerebral palsy had advanced to the point of being wheelchair bound and unable to take care of himself, but with the help of Henry and Irene, who got around her new surroundings rather effortlessly despite being blind, they did a great job taking care of him.

I got a job, too, at the Starbright Hotel, checking people in at the reception desk. It was pretty cool, and I loved how smart my uniform looked. The straight blue skirt and matching short jacket with gold buttons finally provided me that sophistication I had envied in Maggie. I even learned how to do my own hair. I hadn't told my father yet, but one day I planned to run that hotel. What's really funny is that my grandfather never made an issue out of my father working for him after the divorce. I guess making him money mattered even more than appearances.

Henry never got back his full strength or breathing capacity after the surgery, and he was still on the scrawny side. But he laughed every day and lived his life to the fullest, his optimistic attitude never failing.

Recently, while on one of our slow evening strolls (about the only chance we had to be alone), I asked him about it, that attitude of his. How, no matter how sick he got, or his parents' ailments, or being stuck in that infirmary – for way longer than me, mind you – he never lost his buoyant outlook, save for those steroid-induced mood swings, of course.

"Oh, believe me, I was in despair," he admitted, wrapping an arm around me as our feet fell into rhythm crossing the street toward the beach, the regal palm trees and salty air awaiting us. "But then I saw you looking at me from the bed across the way, and I knew everything was going to be alright."

How can you argue with that?

ACKNOWLEDGMENTS

Many thanks to my family and friends for their unwavering support, willingness to plot away with me, and dependable eagle eyes, especially Stacey DuFord, Johnny Malatesta and Frank Buscemi.

Karen Buscemi is the author of two fiction titles: The Makeover (Starryeyed Press) and Saturday Nights at the God Café (CreateSpace); and two nonfiction titles: Split In Two: Keeping It Together When Your Parents Live Apart (Orange Avenue Publishing/Zest Books); and I Do, Part 2: How to Survive Divorce, Co-Parent Your Kids, and Blend Your Families Without Losing Your Mind (Norlights Press). She has been published in Women's Health, Self, The Huffington Post, Figure, Successful Living and The Detroit News, and even gave a TEDx talk. Karen lives in Rochester Hills, Michigan with her husband, two boys, and their hairy cat, Wyatt.

Made in the USA
Monee, IL
05 January 2020

19921897R00166